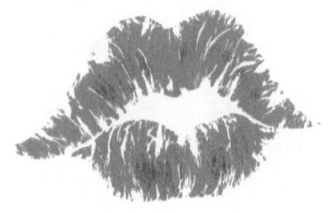

EVERNIGHT PUBLISHING ®

www.evernightpublishing.com

Copyright© 2019

Sam Crescent

Editor: Karyn White

Cover Art: Jay Aheer

ISBN: 978-0-3695-0107-3

BIKER BULLY

#

Sam Crescent

Copyright © 2019

❖

PART ONE
Chapter One

Chloe Decker sat on the park bench outside of school, waiting for her father to pick her up. She didn't know why she bothered waiting for him. It wasn't like he ever showed up on time. More often than not, he forgot, but that's what she got all the time from her dad. Her father, Kurt, was none other than a Satan's Crew MC lackey. They would never give him prospect status. Whenever she was near any of the MC club members, she always heard the lingering insults of "coward" thrown his way.

She tried hard to spend as little time as possible around the club. It helped that her mother didn't like it and would often avoid the family gatherings her father kept trying to pull them into.

"Look at it, if it's not fatty Chloe sitting on the bench. I bet the wood will bend and snap."

Chloe stared down at her book. She didn't need to look up to see it was Alfie Pace and his other MC brat goonies who were near her. They liked to take their time making her life a misery, and she had no doubt it was because of who her father was.

Ignoring them was easy. Most of the time they moved on, but not today.

Today she had a banana skin thrown at her, and she groaned, getting off the bench. She didn't need to wait for her dad. He was supposed to be taking her out to get new boots, but she'd rather walk home than have to put up with this kind of crap.

"What's the matter, fatty? Don't want to eat it? Shouldn't a fatty eat everything that's thrown at her?"

Forcing herself to look up, she stared into Alfie's sharp blue eyes. She hated this guy more than anything else in the world. For as long as she could remember, he'd been mean to her. He never had a nice thing to say to her, and part of her often wondered if he thought he was better than she was.

His father, Eagle, was the president of the Satan's Crew MC, and he was a merciless bastard. She'd seen him hit his son a few times. One of the first times she saw Alfie, he'd been thrown across his father's knee and spanked so hard. He'd screamed the clubhouse down until he finally apologized for whatever misdemeanor he'd done.

When she'd asked her father later that night what could have possibly earned such a harsh punishment, she'd been told "club stuff."

Which probably meant her father didn't have a clue what was going on either, but he liked to pretend he had a place.

She didn't say anything, but she'd have to pass them to make her way home. The last thing she wanted to do was get anywhere near those guys.

There was no way she was going to be able to avoid it.

Heart racing, she stepped on the path and began to walk toward them.

"Whoa, be careful, the ground is shaking," Ian said.

"Look at everything wobble while she moves. Be careful. She's going to eat you," Riley said.

There were only two other guys with Alfie, so she should really count herself lucky.

When she was only a couple of steps away from him, she stopped.

"Seriously? That's all you got? You're going to bully me on my weight or how about my looks next? You think I haven't heard this all before? You guys are pathetic," she said.

She spent way too much time trying to get along, pretending they weren't horrible people, but she was done being nice.

She was done being the girl that allowed them to get away with shit. Tonight was the last night she ever trusted her father to actually pick her up and take her to get boots. Once her mother heard what happened, there would be fucking hell to pay, but until then, Chloe was pissed off, angry, and just wanted someone to scream at.

Why go and throw herself on her bed and allow the pillow to take the blame when she had three men standing right in front of her? They weren't men.

Throwing her bag to the ground, she let her book fall on top of it and stared straight at the men. Her hands shook with rage, and she felt a sickness in the back of her throat as if she wanted to throw up, but she didn't back down.

"Go on. What else have you got to throw at me?

Or better yet, why not use me as a punching bag? I hear dickless assholes like to do that, so you must be all for punching a girl. How about it, Ian?"

"What the fuck?" Ian asked.

She had always taken their shit without causing any waves. Sure, they'd thrown her into her lockers, or shoved her over desks, or even tripped her.

All the bullying bullshit they liked to do, she'd taken.

She'd even had the tampons fall out of her locker, and it was all courtesy of a club whore spilling the details of Chloe's first period. Alfie had taken it upon himself to let the whole school know she was menstruating.

Never in all of her life had she been so embarrassed. She'd never trusted the club whore again, and in fact, unless it was with her own mother, she never spoke to anyone. At the earliest opportunity she wanted out of Satan's Croft, living far away from any small town or MC.

She had a life plan, and this place wasn't part of it. Her mother, who she loved more than anything, loved her and had told her to fly. To find her dream, and just go for it. To never look back and allow anyone to take her dreams from her.

"You're fucking crazy," Ian said.

"I am, or maybe I'm sick and tired of the same old shit. 'Chloe's fat. Look the earth is moving because she's so fucking fat it has to move'!" She yelled the last words, tired of the same old bullshit.

These boys, they were not men. To even call them men was an insult to the opposite sex.

She also wouldn't ever trust her dad again. Not ever. This was the last time he humiliated her.

She wouldn't put it past him to actually be having a drink with Eagle, or trying to work his way into the good graces of the club. That was the kind of man he was. He'd fucked up years ago, and rather than accept it, he did nothing but try to get back into the club by any means possible. The truth was, no one was ever going to accept him. They didn't want him back because he was a total fuck up.

The club lived by two values, trust and loyalty. She knew it extended out to other traits, but those were the two main words she always saw and heard with the guys. The women knew it as well, the old ladies and club whores. With her father running away years ago when times got tough, or something like that, he'd permanently cemented himself in the category of "hanger-on." She hated it.

The men treated him as lesser of a being, and she had to sit back and watch it tear him apart. Not to mention her mother.

"You're fucking crazy," Riley said.

"Am I? Come on. You're such big, tough men. Bring it. I'm tired of this bullshit. You want to throw stuff at me, fine. You want to push me against lockers, hurt me. Then do it right in front of my face. Let me see you be the big, tough men you claim to be." She stepped up to them and slammed her hands against Riley's chest. She didn't know which one had thrown the skin, and she really, *really* didn't care.

Pain filled her body, but it wasn't physical. This kind of pain was something she couldn't control. She could only stare in the faces of those around her.

She was tired of being second best to the club, but more than that, she was fed up of these guys getting to her. This was her last year of high school, and she wouldn't allow them to hurt her.

"Don't put your fucking hands on me." Riley shoved her hard, but she only went back a step.

Flicking her long blonde hair over her shoulder, she used her entire body, and rammed him hard in the abdomen, and Riley went tumbling. Hand clenched into a fist, she struck out at Ian, who looked positively shocked by her.

Next she turned to Alfie, who merely smirked at her.

"You think I'm not going to hit you because you're a girl."

"I'm counting on it," she said.

This guy was on her shit list, would always be on her shit list, and right now, she was sick of him. She hated him with every single fiber of her being.

She'd never considered herself a violent person until this very moment, and knowing it was because of him, it made her angry at herself.

She should just grab her stuff and leave, but they'd thrown a rotten banana skin at her. She deserved better.

Not once had she ever fucked with them, or taken her anger out on any of them. She didn't beg for their attention the way her father did.

There were plenty of girls already throwing themselves at them, and she wasn't going to be one of them.

"What's the matter, princess?" he asked.

"Leave me alone."

"You see, my two buddies are winded. Are you giving up? A coward like your father."

"I'm not a coward." She stepped up to Alfie, but unlike with Ian and Riley, she didn't know how to play this hand with him.

He'd hated her for a long time, far longer than she had him.

Taking a deep breath, she waited, one, two, three,

wondering what she should do. In the back of her mind she saw the boy screaming, begging for his father to stop as he got his ass smacked. It wasn't the first time she'd seen Eagle hit his son, and she had no doubt it wouldn't be the last, but right now, at this very moment, she didn't want anything to do with more violence.

Glancing away from Alfie, she saw what she'd done.

She'd actually attacked them. Feeling shame flood her body, she shook her head. No, no more.

"You know what? You're not worth it. None of you are." She reached out to grab her bag. "I'm not doing this."

She went to walk away, but suddenly her bag was yanked from her hands and she was thrown to the ground, and Alfie on top of her.

"You think you're better than us, is that it? You think you can throw your weight around, act all tough and when it suits you walk away? You touched two of my boys. Two of the club, and you will fucking pay."

"You're not even president yet. You're not patched in members. Not even prospects. I'm not touching the club. I'm touching their property. You're nothing more than property."

"And you think you're not? You think with your father sniffing around my father's ass all the time, you're not club property? You are. He can use you and discard you whenever he sees fit."

"Get off me."

"Or what? What are you going to do? I don't see any problems happening here. I'm just a guy putting you in your place. You think anyone's going to stop me? This town is full of cowards. The club, we're the ones that rule it, not you."

"Fuck you."

11

"No, but I get a feeling you really want to fuck me, Chloe. You want me to slide my dick in that fat cunt of yours. Show you what a man can do. I can make your dreams come true. Blow your freaking mind, but first, you've got to give me something that I want."

"Go to hell."

"Nah." He let go of one of her hands, but kept both of them locked above her head. The other, he stroked down her arm and got so dangerously close to her breast. This had never happened to her before.

The bullying had never extended to this scary realm of danger. The way he touched her, she didn't like it.

Nor did she like the smile on his face that told her he was loving just how uncomfortable he was making her.

"Get off me."

"Not a chance. You think you can go around putting your hands on the Satan's Crew MC. You've got another think coming, bitch. We own you. You think you're above the club, but your ass belongs to us. Every single inch of it." He pressed his pelvis against hers, and it scared her.

He was hard.

She'd never been with a guy before, but the threat was there and with no one around, it terrified her.

They'd never gone this far.

You've never lashed out.

"Let me go, please," she said.

He squeezed her breast, and she closed her eyes, wanting to be anywhere else but here. "You're going to learn the error of your ways, Chloe. You can't fuck with the club like you did today and not expect to get burned."

"Get your hands off my daughter."

They both looked up to see Lily, her mother, arms

folded, as she stood outside of her car. She wore a pair of jeans, a plain white shirt, and she looked deadly.

"Mrs. Decker," Alfie said, a smile to his lips.

"Drop the act. Get off my daughter now, or do you want me to report this to your father?" Lily asked. "I didn't think so. Get off."

Alfie gave her wrists a squeeze, letting her know without saying a word, this wasn't over. They were going to come to blows again, and probably soon. But for now, she was safe, or as safe as she could be.

Scrambling to her feet, she grabbed her bags, knowing she had fucked up tonight. She should have walked away without a backward glance, allowed them to push her, call her names, shove her. Do whatever they wanted but not attack.

By attacking, she'd given them the perfect ammunition to hurt her, to strike at her, and she wasn't going to let that happen again.

Rushing to her mother's car, she climbed in the passenger seat.

There were a few seconds more stare off between her mother and Alfie before she finally got in the car.

Chloe noticed her hands shaking and quickly sat on them. Lily, though, she looked calm and collected.

Chloe had been so lost in the moment with Alfie, she'd not even heard her mother drive up to them.

"Your father's not going to hear the end of this," Lily said. "I'm tired of his bullshit."

"You don't have to worry about it, Mom," she said. "Please, don't say anything."

Lily glanced over at her. "You don't want me to say anything about that club brat doing stuff to you?"

"No. It's fine. You know it'll only make it worse."

"I don't care. Alfie thinks because of who his

father is, he's above the law."

"Isn't he? If it was a cop driving past, they'd just keep on going."

She noticed her mother clenched her fingers around the steering wheel.

"It's the way it is in Satan's Croft. We can't do anything about it," Chloe said. "You know that."

"It doesn't make it right. Fuck!" Her mother slammed her fist against the steering wheel. "I'm so sorry, sweetheart."

"I'm fine. Really."

"Really? Your father didn't come and get you. You need new boots, and you're fine. No, you know what, I'm done with this bullshit." Right there in the middle of the street, her mother spun the car around.

"Mom, what are you doing?" Chloe asked.

"Something I should have done a long time ago." Lily pressed her foot on the gas, and Chloe's heart raced.

She felt sick to her stomach as she realized exactly where they were going. They drove past Alfie, Ian, and Riley, and she tried to avoid looking at them, but failed.

Her cheeks were on fire, and her breast felt scorched from Alfie's hand on it.

She had to put that memory away.

Nothing good could come from reporting him, and most likely, no one would believe her anyway. That was how this town worked. They made up their own rules to suit themselves, and everyone else, regardless of if it was right or not, had to fall in line.

"Mom, I know you're being a badass and all, but you're kind of scaring me."

"Good. I mean, no, it's not good that you're afraid. I don't want to scare you. Believe me, sweetie, I don't. But I'm sick and tired of all this bullshit with them all the time. It's time for me to stand up, and I'm going to. They don't own us, and we don't owe them anything. We're not going to allow them to come between us and our family." Lily nodded her head.

Again, Chloe looked at her mother's hands.

They weren't shaking at all.

Lily Decker was normally a calm, collected person. She was sweet, caring, nice, hardworking, and she put up with a great deal. The woman before her right now looked ready to chop men into little pieces and hide them in walls. Maybe a little exaggeration, but not by much.

The closer they got to the clubhouse, the more her nerves picked up speed. This wasn't what she wanted to do, or to happen. She was terrified of what this could mean. Her mother was a fierce woman, protective, loving. It was why Chloe tried so hard in school, to make her mother proud.

When it came to her father, she put in as much effort as he did into their relationship, the bare minimum. She knew her mother and father fought repeatedly about the same old stuff. There was never any break in their arguing, and it was always about one thing. Her father's need to be accepted by the club was a constant heartache to her mother.

It was driving a wedge between them all.

By the time Lily pulled up into the parking lot, Chloe felt sick to her stomach. Men and women were making out. Most of them had leather cuts on, and the women, well, she was lucky they at least wore underwear.

Her hands shook as she followed Lily into the main house. The scent of smoke and alcohol was heavy in the air.

People turned and watched Lily though.

Chloe noticed her mother was a beauty with her blonde hair. Most of the time she wasn't on a mission, and out of all of the club whores and wives, Lily got the most respect from the members.

Even Eagle respected Lily.

She had no idea why, but it was always there, especially as they walked up to his booth. Kurt was there, and there was a brunette straddling Eagle's lap, who he quickly pushed away when he saw Lily.

Did Eagle have a thing for her mother? She doubted it.

"Lily, baby, you made it," Kurt said, getting to his feet.

"I made it. Think really hard right now, Kurt. Where were you supposed to be?" Lily asked.

Silence fell in the club as they all took in the scene.

As far as Chloe was concerned, Lily had never caused a scene. She'd never overreacted to anyone. Again, her mother was known as a sweetheart.

"Baby? Why are you so angry?" Kurt tried to stroke Lily's arms, but she wasn't having any of it. She shoved him hard, much in the same way Chloe had Ian and Riley.

"You don't even remember?" Lily stepped to the side, grabbing Chloe's hand.

Her cheeks were on fire as people took them in. This wasn't what she wanted. This was bad news.

She hated it when people looked at her, and now, she wished she'd stayed in the car far, far away from this mess.

"Does our daughter ring any bells? You promised me you'd pick her up. That you'd take her for some new boots, and instead I got a call telling me that your son and his little boyfriends were bullying her, again!" Lily pointed at Eagle before returning her hands to her hips. "And yet, you're here. Again. Why am I not surprised? When are you going to realize they don't want you here, Kurt? They see you as nothing more than a coward, and you're still hanging around. Still hoping to be a patched in member. Instead of spending time with your family. With us, who love you no matter what, but you're here again, and not helping me." Her mother's voice croaked, and Chloe squeezed her hand, offering her some comfort. She adored her mother more than anything.

"Lily, I apologize on behalf of my son," Eagle said.

"No, I don't want to hear you apologize. I want you to keep that boy and his friends away from my daughter." She turned to Kurt. "We're done."

Chloe's mouth opened in shock.

They were done. Her parents were done.

Lily took the wedding band off. "I'm going to call my lawyer."

"Lil, babe, come on, you're overreacting."

"No, I'm not. I've been waiting for you to see your senses for the last eighteen years, and I'm tired of being second best. I deserve more. I deserve better, and it's not you. Don't come home. It's in my name anyway."

She handed the ring back, and taking Chloe with her, walked right out of the silent club.

Chloe couldn't believe what had just happened. Her mother had ended things very publicly with her father.

Climbing into the car, Lily pulled out of the clubhouse. Chloe glanced behind her to see Kurt running out, trying to chase them.

"Don't look back, honey."

"Mom, you don't have to do this."

"I do. I'm tired of being lied to. I'm tired of relying on a man who can never love me back as much as I love him. Sometimes in life, you've got to learn to just walk away. I'm walking away. The best thing Kurt gave me was you. I'll always treasure you, my darling daughter." Lily grabbed her hand, locking their fingers together. "We can always count on each other. Now, let's go and get you some boots."

She knew her mother was upset, and breaking apart inside.

Her parents had been sweethearts, and had gotten married at a young age, even before she got pregnant.

Resting her head on her mother's shoulder, she knew Lily would be crying tonight, alone.

She should have just walked home.

****

Arriving at the clubhouse, Alfie knew shit had hit the fan. There was a tension that he'd not seen for a long time. The Satan's Crew MC wasn't a well-liked club and they had a lot of enemies, but none of them had ever defeated the club.

His father, Eagle, was a force to be reckoned with.

"What's going on?" he asked, Betty, one of the club whores, or at least he thought that was her name.

"Kurt's wife just divorced his ass. She came in calling him on his shit. Putting the club first and well, you better get out of the way, Alfie. She told him about your bullying of her little girl. Eagle's not happy."

"Alfie, get in here," Eagle said.

Shit!

He'd been warned by his father several times not to touch Lily's daughter. It wasn't like he went out of his way to hurt Chloe, but she was always fucking there, and he was tired of it. Also, she wasn't even a club girl, or any relation to the club. Her father was a fucking loser, so why did he have to treat Chloe any better? The only reason Eagle and the club brothers put up with Kurt was because he'd become an easy target for all of them. No one liked him, but they liked to humiliate him. There was nothing Kurt wouldn't do. Be it clean the floors, or even lick a brother's boot.

Alfie had seen him in several compromising positions, all in the name of trying to earn back his reputation within the club.

Personally, he thought the guy should have given up, and he'd asked Eagle about it some time ago.

"Son, when it matters most, he'll run. Sure, he's good to lick shit off your boot and entertain you, but I don't need a man who can make me laugh. I need a man who'll take a bullet for me without batting an eye."

Since then, he'd never had respect for Kurt. By extension, he'd never liked Chloe either.

Standing in front of his father, he saw the anger simmering beneath the surface.

"Get in my office, now!"

Alfie walked past his father and stumbled as he was shoved hard. It wasn't the first time that had happened, and it wouldn't be the last.

Deep down, he knew his father loved him. One day he'd take over the Satan's Crew Mc, and to do that, he couldn't be soft.

Eagle had to show to the rest of the club he was a man. A man they could all trust, as otherwise, he'd be tossed out on his ass.

Ian and Riley didn't follow. They weren't allowed.

Alfie held himself perfectly still, arms by his sides, waiting for his father.

He'd not intended to hurt or bully Chloe tonight.

He'd seen her on the school bench, bag to one side, book in hand, but it had been Ian who threw the banana and Riley who called her names. He never disobeyed his father, and when given the order to stop bullying her, he had. Sure, he couldn't be held responsible for stopping his friends, or other guys. He watched them push her into doors, lockers, trip her up, throw stuff at her.

She was the school punching bag.

Seconds passed.

Then minutes.

He felt like he'd been waiting for hours before his father finally showed up.

"I can't believe I'm having this fucking conversation with you again." Eagle walked in and slapped him around the back of the head.

"Hey," Alfie said. "I didn't do nothing."

"Then why did I have to listen to Lily here less than two hours ago? You hurting her girl. Do I need to remind you what it means to disobey me?" Eagle asked.

"Why does it matter to you?" Alfie asked. "Chloe's a fat, fucking loser. No one likes her."

"She's a sweet girl. Regardless of her weight. I'm not asking you to fuck her. Am I?" Eagle glared at him.

"She's just a girl. Why does it matter to you?" he asked.

"Are you questioning me?" Eagle stepped right up in front of him.

Alfie wasn't afraid.

His father wouldn't kill him.

Sure, he'd have to take a beating, but it was being on the end of this man's fist that had made him the man he was.

"No, sir," he said.

"You stay away from Chloe Decker. I don't want no trouble coming to Lily. You hear me?"

"Yes, sir."

"Good. Now get out. Tell that to your two boyfriends as well. I don't want to hear a single complaint from that girl."

"Did Chloe tattle on us?" Alfie asked.

"No. Her mother caught you, and don't even think of lying. Lily's got no reason to lie."

"Is she going to be your new club whore or something?"

He should have expected the slap across the face. It was hard, and the metallic taste of blood filled his mouth.

"You're going to learn to have some respect, boy. I taught you better than that. No disrespect. Get the fuck out before I take my belt to you."

Leaving his father's office, he didn't even have to nod for Ian and Riley to follow.

They made their way out of the clubhouse, around the back, and down to the creek. There was a small lake about a mile off the clubhouse.

He opened the gate, closing it behind him.

One of the club brothers had ended up drowning in the lake, so his father had no choice but to put a metal fence around a couple of feet before the lake.

"You okay?" Ian asked.

"Peachy."

"You don't look it. Sorry, you don't," Riley said.

"You've got to stay away from Chloe. All of us do. It's an order from Eagle."

"Wow, is Lily already banging his ass?" Ian asked.

"I wouldn't go around asking those kinds of questions. He's likely to whoop your ass as well," Alfie said.

"So, we just let her go? I figured being the

daughter of a coward, and after tonight, I'm not letting her get away with her shit. She thinks she's better than us, so I think it's only fair we bring her down a peg or ten," Ian said.

"Not going to happen." Alfie wasn't interested in getting a beat down from his dad in any way, shape, or form.

He was done with all the bullshit it entailed, and just wanted to get through the last year of high school so he could start prospecting for real, and earning his place within the club.

"You know, we don't *have* to bully her," Riley said.

"Can't you guys just let it quit already? We're not going to win this, and I don't want to be on the wrong side of my dad, okay?" He looked at Ian and Riley.

They didn't look convinced.

"You two fuckers are really not going to let this go, are you?" he asked.

"Why should we?" Ian asked. "I've got the perfect way to make that little slut pay, and believe me, you're going to want in on the action."

Chapter Two

Two days later Chloe woke up to drawers slamming closed. Climbing out of her bed, she walked across the small corridor to her parents' room. The door was already wide open, and Lily stood, suitcase ready, as she threw in clothes.

All of them Kurt's.

"Hey, Mom," she said.

"Hey, sweetie. I'm sorry. I didn't mean to wake you. I'm making such a racket." Lily shook her head, tucking her long blonde hair behind her ears. She'd inherited her mother's blonde hair, only hers didn't have that sheen that her mother's did.

"It's okay. Do you want some help?"

Lily laughed. "Moving your father out of the house? No, this is something I need to do myself." She stepped over the mess and pulled her into a hug. "I love you so much."

"I love you too, Mom. Do you think you're making the right decision?"

"I can't help but think I'm screwing up something." Lily sniffled. "I've been with him nearly twenty years. I've loved that man for what felt like a lifetime."

"Then don't kick him out."

"The thing is, baby girl, he loves that club more than he ever loved me. When they needed him, he ran away. He came home and curled up in my lap, telling me how sorry he was with how pathetic he was." Her mother's tears broke Chloe's heart. "I never wanted to divorce him. I didn't fall in love with him because of a leather cut. I loved him long before he thought he wanted to be a biker."

"But you still love him."

"And I'm tired of the love not being returned. There's only so much empty I can take." Her mother tucked Chloe's hair behind her ear. "You're so beautiful."

"I'm not."

Lily sighed. "I hate the way you feel about yourself."

"I'm fat. You don't have to pretend I'm not."

"You're a beautiful woman deep where it counts. So you have a few extra pounds, but that doesn't make you who you are. Anyone who only sees the weight, they don't know the real you." Her mother held her close. "Don't ever let a man think you're any less than who you are. You're perfect just the way you are."

She held her mother a little tighter. "I love you, Mom."

"I love you too."

"I'll go and make you a hot chocolate."

"I'd love that."

Chloe stepped out of the room and looked back to watch her mother sit on the edge of the bed, one of her wedding photos in her hand.

This wasn't supposed to happen, but she knew things hadn't been going well between her parents for a long time.

The club was always getting in the way.

Giving her mother some privacy, she took a few steps, hearing the painful cry as Lily released it. She stopped in her footsteps and turned to go back, but paused. If her mother wanted to have someone to hold her, she would have cried while she was still there.

Chloe hated walking downstairs, but she did it. Going to the stove, she grabbed the milk out of the fridge, pouring a mugful into the saucepan.

Putting it on the heat, she grabbed her mother's

favorite chocolate. She looked up and saw her reflection in the toaster.

Lifting her hair off her shoulders, she pouted her lips, turning left then right, before shaking her head.

When the water was hot, she added the chocolate, a splash of vanilla, and a spoonful of sugar. She stirred it all together, and the bruise on her wrist caught her eye. Putting the spoon down, she wrapped her fingers around the marks, covering them.

She hadn't thought Alfie was that strong, and yet, he'd left his mark.

If her mother hadn't turned up, what would he have done? She tried not to think of what ifs, but like now, she couldn't help but wonder.

Would he have touched her?

Shaking her head, she pushed those thoughts out of her mind, and served up the hot chocolate.

To garnish, because her mother loved it, she placed a single cinnamon stick in the hot chocolate and carried it upstairs.

When she returned, the suitcase was packed, and in the trash bin she saw the shattered glass of the wedding photo.

She couldn't help but think her mother was acting too hastily.

If she wasn't careful, she could live to regret what she'd done.

"That looks lovely," Lily said.

Handing the chocolate over, Chloe looked back at the trash bin. "Why did you throw your photo away?"

Lily loved to look at it, and had spent hours doing it in the past eighteen years.

"I don't need a reminder of my failure." Lily lowered herself down onto the edge of the bed, pushing some hair off her shoulder before cradling the cup. "I thought we were it, you know? He told me I was his life. Then you came into the world, and we were complete." She sniffled. "They're all lies."

"I think Dad still loves you."

"Oh, I have no doubt. Just not as much as he loves the club. I'm not going to do it anymore, sweetie. I'm not going to let him constantly let us down."

The doorbell went, and her mother sighed.

"Who's that?" Chloe asked.

"Your father, if he's not too much of a coward to come and collect his stuff." Lily handed her the hot chocolate.

Chloe followed behind, sitting on the edge of the stairs, seeing the doorway. Lily dragged the suitcase down the stairs.

Each slap as it landed on each stair, she knew this wasn't going to change. Kurt Decker wasn't coming back into their lives.

Her mother wouldn't have him back.

The boots, it was the last straw for her mother.

Tears filled Chloe's eyes as she watched Lily take a deep breath, gathering herself together, trying to look strong, before opening the door.

Kurt was on the doorstep, but Eagle stood beside her father as well.

"Eagle, what's going on?" Lily asked.

"I came to make sure this guy didn't give you any trouble. You want him out of your life, don't you?"

"Yes, but I can handle him. He's never going to hurt me or cause me any problems. Are you, Kurt?"

"I want us to give this another try, baby. Please, for you and for Chloe."

Chloe held the cup a little tighter. She did love her father, but this was one step too far.

"It's too late. How many times are we going to go

through this before one of us realizes this relationship is way too toxic? I've got to set a good example to my daughter, and waiting at home for a man who doesn't show up when he says he's going to, and is always fighting for something else, I can't go through with this, not anymore. It sucks. All of this sucks. You think I want this? You think I enjoy having you on my doorstep, your belongings packed, ready to send you away?"

"Then don't. Let me prove to you I can do this. You know I love you more than anything. You and Chloe."

"And what happens when you get a call from Eagle, or any other brother from the club? I've been through this so many times. I've believed you and you've gone running back to them. No more. I don't want to do this with you anymore. I've already booked an appointment with a divorce lawyer. I've got to do this. For myself and for Chloe." She pulled the suitcase across the threshold.

When Kurt went to touch Lily, Eagle held him back.

"What about Chloe?"

"You can see your daughter any time you want, Kurt. I'm not going to keep her away from you. I'm hoping we can be friends. This doesn't have to end badly. I just don't want to be in a relationship with you anymore."

"Come on, Kurt, grab your bag and let's go," Eagle said.

Lily didn't close the door straight away. Chloe stayed on the stairs waiting. Kurt actually argued with one of the men who grabbed him, helping him move along. She didn't see who it was, but it surprised her all the same. It was the first time she'd seen her father fight a member of the club.

"I'm so sorry, Lily," Eagle said.

"It's not your fault. Not really. You've got a better hold of my husband than I do. I should have known years ago I'd never be good enough. Especially not compared to the club."

"Kurt's an idiot."

"He just wants to earn his patch."

"You know it'll never happen. I've told him repeatedly he won't. The brothers don't trust him."

"And I've told him the same, but again, he's determined. At least he's got a focus in life. Thank you for being here." Lily held onto the door. "I really need to get back."

Eagle looked past Lily's shoulder to Chloe. She held her hand up in greeting.

"I've talked to my son. He's not going to hurt you anymore."

"You really didn't need to do that," she said. On the inside, she was cringing at what it could mean. If Eagle had hurt Alfie, would she see the bruises tomorrow at school?

"I did. My son will learn one way or the other to act like a gentleman."

"Thank you, Eagle. I do appreciate it."

"Don't be a stranger, Lily." Eagle nodded at her, smiling at Chloe and then leaving.

Her mother finally closed the door.

"I think Eagle's got a crush on you."

"No, he doesn't."

"I've seen the way he looks at you. Whenever you enter a room, he's watching you. He's not married either."

"Chloe, sweetheart, you're eighteen and full of romantic ideas. Eagle doesn't see me in any way. I'm Kurt's problem. Not his."

"He's not married though."

"I am."

"Not for long. What will you do if Eagle keeps coming around wanting to spend some quality time?" Chloe asked, holding out the now-cooled-down hot chocolate.

"If that ever happens, which it won't, I will deal with it."

"And if it does happen?"

"Honey, sweetheart, I've been married for a long time. I'm trying to keep it together right now to prove to you I can be strong, but the truth is, I'm falling apart inside. Seeing your father like that, I wanted to take him back. My love for him hasn't gone away. It never will. I love him so much. This isn't going to be easy for me. I'm not going to start dating. I intend to spend as little time around men as humanly possible." Lily sat down beside her on the stairs.

"You don't want to date?"

"No. I hated dating even when I was younger."

"I've never been on a date," she said.

"I know. When you do, and someone will ask you one day, it can be the most amazing experience of your life. When your father asked me out, I was on such a high from being around him. He had a way of making me believe I was his entire world."

"You don't feel that anymore?" Chloe asked.

"Only when he's trying. After we've had a fight. You're not supposed to feel those things when the other person feels guilty. It's the kind of feeling that lasts forever." She sighed and shrugged. "You'll get what I mean."

"I do." She rested her head on her mother's shoulder. "I love you, Mom."

"I love you too. This doesn't mean I'll be upset

with you for hanging out with your father. I want you to have a good relationship with him. It's important for the two of you."

"Okay." Chloe doubted her father would come around to spend time with her. She knew he'd gladly be around Lily, but that was a given.

He'd lost the one woman who loved him, and now he'd fight to get her back.

Did she want to help bring her parents back together, or would she only be hurting her mother more?

****

Monday at school wasn't any different from any other day. Chloe walked in to find someone had spray painted "fat ass" across her locker, again. It wasn't original.

When she saw it, there were plenty of people to bear witness. She did nothing more than go and grab the necessary supplies from the janitor's closet, and start to scrub off the mess.

The janitor got so tired of his morning coffee being interrupted that he told her where to find the supplies and where the spare key was.

Returning to the locker, she began to scrub. The cold, disinfected water slid down her arms, and it was a struggle for her to reach high above her head, but she tried to, and absolutely failed.

"Here, let me help."

She jerked back as someone put a hand on her back. She turned to see none other than Alfie himself, helping her.

"What are you doing?"

"I'm helping you."

"Didn't you do this?" she asked.

"Not this time. Besides, I have learned the error of my ways."

"The error of your ways? Your dad told you not to bully me anymore."

"And look at me, I'm listening to him. There must be something in the water." He winked at her.

She shook her head, a little dazed. "There's no other cloth."

"Then hand me yours, shorty."

"I can do this."

"And I'm saying you don't have to. Stop being such a dork. Let me help."

Chloe looked at him. "I don't need help."

"And you're going to be incredibly difficult about this, why?"

"Hello." She lifted up the cuff of her shirt. "You think I don't remember getting a banana thrown at me, and you pinning me down?"

Alfie looked at the bruise, and she saw his frown. "I didn't hold you that hard."

"Yeah, well, it hurt, and now look. I don't want to get into this argument with you. Just leave it alone, okay? I can scrub the insults off my locker every single day of the week." It was one of the many reasons she came to school earlier than she needed to.

"Look, I'm sorry, okay? I didn't mean to hurt you, or leave marks. Did you show your mom?"

"No. Of course not. She doesn't need to know about them." It was a bad enough weekend without adding to it with her own problems.

"Can we start over here?"

"Alfie, I don't trust you. Let me clean up my mess and move along. Join the rest of them who enjoy watching this." She turned her back to him, expecting him to go and do whatever it was he did when she cleaned her locker.

Instead, he reached over her, pressing her against

the hard metal, and took the cloth right out of her hands.

"Hey."

He then pressed one hand in her face to keep her back from him.

"Stop it. I mean it. I can clean my own locker."

"And I can do this for you. Consider it a penance for all the bad shit I've done to you over the years."

"Alfie, stop it."

She grabbed his arm and tried to move it out of her way, but he wasn't having any of it. Alfie was by far stronger than she was.

He only let her go when he finished scrubbing the words off her locker. It sucked, and she hated he was able to do it without her.

"There, all done. It looks awesome."

"You didn't need to do that." Did she now owe him a favor or something? This was one of the reasons why she didn't want him near her stuff. "What do you want?"

"What do I want?"

"Yes. Don't for a second think I don't know you do a good deed, you want payment."

"I thought I said this was already payment for what I owed you. I'm sorry for what I did. The bullying and shit. It's going to end."

She stared at him, still lightheaded. This couldn't be happening to her.

"I've got to get to class." She opened her locker and prayed nothing was inside. She just wanted to have a dignified exit, if that was even possible.

"You don't have to run off. Maybe we can get to know each other."

There was nothing inside her locker, and she grabbed the couple of books she'd need.

"That's not going to happen. I'm not stupid. You

think I don't know what is happening here? I don't know what it is you guys have planned, but I want no part in it. I'm sorry if your dad did anything." She noticed how he tensed. "I begged my mom not to go to the clubhouse, not to talk to him. I know you hate me, and you get some sick, twisted pleasure from hurting me, but I didn't want to say anything. My mom, she's tired of all this. So, I'm sorry if you got hurt or if your dad said anything. If this is really true, you don't want to hurt me anymore, then just leave me alone. Please."

She turned her back on him and walked away, heading in the direction of her class.

This was why she tried to avoid being near any of the club when she was at school. For the most part, they owned the school. Teachers were afraid of them, and most of the other people were too.

What they said was law.

Standing outside her homeroom class, she wanted nothing more than the door to be open to allow herself inside, to sit in her chair by the window, and just to disappear.

She'd never been good at making friends. It was one of the reasons why she was on her own all the time.

Friendships didn't come naturally to her. There were a couple of times she thought she had connected with a couple of girls here, but it had all been part of a joke.

They would hang around with her, pretending to like her, studying with her, watching movies. Then there would be some gathering, and they'd want her to do some stupid initiation stuff to make her be like them.

She'd always walked home, head held high. The only person who really understood her was her mother. The door finally opened, and she slid inside.

Miss Hops smiled at her. "Did you have a good

weekend?"

"Yes." She liked Miss Hops, who also taught history as well. "Did you?"

"The best."

The conversation was cut short as other students started to arrive. Sitting by the window, she glanced outside, staring out across the field. It wouldn't be long before the football team was out practicing for the big game.

She jumped as the chair at her table was pulled back, the sound drawing everyone's attention to her.

Alfie was sitting down. He'd dropped his books onto the desk, and even seeing them was a surprise.

He went to this school, but didn't actually attend it. He often showed up to class with no books, no paper, and no pens.

"What are you doing?" she asked.

"What does it look like I'm doing? I'm taking a seat right here."

"You can't sit here."

"I can't? I don't see a problem. If my memory serves me right, I can sit wherever I want." He leaned back in his chair, his arm resting across the back of her chair.

"Yeah, you can, but why here?"

Her heart was racing. She didn't dare look anywhere else in the room.

Miss Hops approached her table. "I don't want any funny business happening in my class, Alfie."

"There's no funny business going to happen, Miss Hops. I'm sitting with my friend Chloe, here. Believe me, we're like BFFs, now."

Chloe gritted her teeth.

"Is this right, Chloe?" Miss Hops asked.

"Erm, yeah, sure. It's fine. We're both friends."

If she tried to get him moved, it would only end badly for her.

Turning to the front, she tried to ignore how close he was.

Miss Hops walked to the board at the front of the class. It was one of the old-style chalkboards. This was the only classroom in the school that hadn't had a marker board installed.

Chloe tensed as she felt her hair being played with. She normally wore it up in a ponytail to keep the long locks out of her way, but after waking up really late, she'd left it down, with a quick run through with a brush.

"What are you doing?" she asked.

"Your hair is soft."

"You think I don't see what is going on here?"

"What is going on here?" he asked.

"I don't know, so stop it. You're being nice again, and stop touching my hair."

"If you want you can touch mine."

"No. No, thank you."

She grabbed her hair, pulling it down over her shoulder so he couldn't touch it.

"Spoilsport."

Homeroom never lasted so long, and she kept glancing at the clock, hoping it would tell her she could move on and be out of this nightmare.

It was nice, Alfie being this way, but it wasn't real. She knew it wasn't. Tapping her fingers on the desk, Miss Hops took attendance, and then started to talk about personal space. Each homeroom class was the same with Miss Hops. She believed she was preparing them for the outside world, for what to expect when they got a job, and had to start paying bills and taxes.

"Do you think she even realizes people don't give a shit about all of this?" Alfie asked, leaning forward.

"I don't know, but she's trying, and the least we can do is pay attention."

"True, but come on, no one cares. I think they're all interested in why I'm sitting right beside you."

"Then they need to get a life, because this is nothing. This is you doing whatever it is you're doing to prove a point. I don't buy it either. No one else should."

"Come on, you're telling me you're not loving me sitting beside you? There's a hundred girls right now who'd love for me to be sitting in this very spot with them."

"Then go and find them. Sit with them. Hang out with them. I don't care. I don't want you to sit next to me." She wasn't stupid. Something was going on, and she'd figure it out soon.

Alfie sighed. "You know, you're a hard person to win over."

"I don't want to be won over." The bell rang, signaling the end of class.

She picked up her books, wanting to go, but Alfie threw his chair back, standing up. He stopped her from escaping.

"Will you cut this out?" she asked.

"No. You're going to have to learn to trust me."

"And you think stopping me from getting to my class is magically going to do that."

"It's going to do something."

"Alife, move please."

"What do I get out of it?"

"The pleasure of knowing you did an amazing deed with getting nothing in return?" she asked.

"Nah, you see, I don't do anything for nothing. You want me to move aside, you've got to do something for me. In fact, you've got to do two somethings for me."

"Why two?"

"I helped clean your locker."

"You didn't give me a choice. I didn't ask for help. That one doesn't count. Neither does this one. I don't have to pay or owe you anything. Being a gentleman and common courtesy, you should just move."

"Kiss me here," he said, pointing to his cheek.

"Not a chance."

"I'm not moving."

Miss Hops was still in the room.

"Miss Hops, Alfie won't move to let me pass." She knew it was a bitchy move, but there was no way she'd kiss him.

Not his cheek, or lips, or any part of him.

"Alife, do I need to escort you to the principal's office?"

"No, you don't. Well played, Decker," he said.

Chloe walked right on past him, and left the room. Just as she crossed the threshold, someone put their foot out. She didn't see it until the last possible moment, and she went flying. Her books were flung from her arms as she cried to catch herself.

The corridor erupted in laughter as she landed. She winced as pain shot through her hands. She'd landed a little funny, but nothing could ever save her from the embarrassment of Alfie witnessing it.

Scrambling to her feet, she grabbed her book and kept on walking.

Her face was on fire.

"She did a floor flop!" someone yelled.

Gritting her teeth, she rushed to the bathroom, and luckily no one was inside.

Putting her book behind the taps on the sink, she grabbed the edge of it and took several deep breaths.

"It's fine. It's fine. It's fine." She closed her eyes and tried to get a hold of her emotions. It didn't matter about the laughter. She was used to being the butt of everyone's jokes.

This time, it felt a little different.

She didn't see who had tripped her.

Whenever she went down like that, with a loud slap on the tile, it was always her mission to get the hell out of there. She hadn't been prepared for the fall. Sometimes she was and was able to catch herself. This time, she didn't.

She'd actually been enjoying Alfie's company.

Her first biggest mistake.

Running fingers through her hair, she looked up and finally stared at her reflection. "It doesn't matter. You're a good person. Hold your head high. The countdown to leaving is already happening." She took deep breaths. The tears didn't come, nor did the sadness.

She could get through this.

It wasn't the first fall she'd taken, and it wouldn't be the last.

Chapter Three

Alfie found Ian, Riley, and a couple of the other guys hanging out at the bleachers. The football team was doing some warmups, and as he approached, Ian stood up.

"Hey," Ian said, winking at him.

He got close to his friend, shook his hand, and then punched him in the face.

Ian went down onto the bleachers.

"What the fuck?" Riley asked.

"You tripped her, didn't you?"

"What?" Ian asked, covering his eye. "That fucking hurt, man."

"You tripped Chloe when we were leaving homeroom."

"Damn, is this what I get for helping out?" Ian asked. "A black eye? It's no different than what we normally do. You really think she's going to fall for a sudden change of heart? You want this plan to work, you're going to have to get in the game and become her knight."

The guys were sniggering, and he didn't like it.

Ever since they'd come up with this plan over the weekend, Alfie had been torn back and forth between going through with it and just leaving shit alone.

Right now, he wanted to walk away. Chloe was more trouble than she was worth, and if his dad ever found out what he was doing, well, it would probably go from the belt to a proper beating with a metal bat. He didn't know for sure how far his dad was willing to go with getting his son ready for the real world.

"You're not going to help." Alfie had seen how she'd gone down and knew she'd been hurt. He hadn't had a chance to help her up though.

"Look, I trip her, point at someone else, and you play the hero, helping her. It's not my fault she actually moved faster than your ass to help her up," Ian said. "You should be thanking me. So far, your show of being the nice guy is cringeworthy."

A couple of the other guys agreed.

"I don't know. I thought you were handling it well," Riley said. "I mean, first cleaning the shit off her locker."

"Who did that?" Alfie asked. "I know it wasn't us."

"I haven't written shit on her locker in years," Ian said. "It got boring really fast, and to be honest, she doesn't even react to that shit anymore. What's the point of doing something that's so boring? She just goes to the janitor's closet, gets her things, cleans it up, and goes to class."

"She does this often?" Alfie asked.

Riley chuckled. "You never noticed?"

"I'm starting to think one of you two should be acting my role seeing as you know so much about her," Alfie said, finally taking a seat. He should be in history class, but he had no interest in learning about the past.

Sure, he should be sitting next to Chloe, trying to bring down her defenses, but he needed a break.

Before the guys had come up with their plan, he'd bumped into her most days of the week, nearly every single hour. Today wasn't one of those days. He'd barely seen her after her fall.

He'd gone to help her up, but she'd grabbed her books and run away.

The laughter had followed her down the long corridor. He'd never lingered on the outside of the bullying before like this.

He either wasn't around, or part of it.

This had been different.

"So, why aren't you in class?" Riley asked.

"Same reason you guys aren't. I needed a break."

"In case you haven't seen it yet, Chloe's not going to be an easy target. I've seen her around you already, and she doesn't trust easily." Ian dropped his hand from his eye, and it was red and bloodshot. Alfie didn't feel any remorse in hitting his best friend.

"Yeah, and whose fault is that?"

"It's everyone's fault," Ian said. "But that means you're going to have to work hard."

"She's not going to fall for this. This is a stupid plan," Alfie said. "You two can't come hanging around with us either. You guys are everywhere with me."

"Which is why I think it would be good if some of us stayed hating her, helping with the hurt. Come on, what chick wouldn't fall for you picking your girl over your best friends."

"I don't like this," Alfie said.

"It's going to be fun. Believe me, when we're done with this at the end of the year, you're going to thank me."

The bell rang, and Alfie wanted to just leave. The lessons he had left this afternoon were all pointless ones anyway. It wasn't like he needed them. He was hungry though.

"Come on, Alfie, this is going to be fun," Riley said.

"Fine. Fine." He got to his feet. "We do it my way though."

"Of course, man," Ian said. "This is all on you. This was your plan to start with. If you remember, I just wanted to pay someone to do this shit. You were the one willing to make the ultimate sacrifice."

The plan was mostly his idea, but Ian and Riley

had helped to build it up to what he knew was going to happen, so long as Chloe played her part well.

"I'm starving," Ian said.

It was lunchtime.

They all headed into the cafeteria. Like most high schools, the cafeteria was where anyone could find out the groups of different people who attended the school.

The jocks with all the cheerleaders sat to one side.

The bikers tended to take the opposite end of the hall. It was their space, and their own bunch of groupies would surround them.

Then you had the nerds, and other groups of kids, waiting. Some of the beauty queens, and then the losers' table as well.

He didn't pay attention to any of them.

All of his crew pushed in line, grabbing a couple of sandwiches, pizzas, and fries, and they headed toward their table.

Ian nudged him, pointing to the corner, near the wall. Almost invisible, Chloe sat on her own, eating her lunch, staring at a book.

Why was she always fucking reading?

"Go, have some fun with this."

Alfie glared at Ian. He was going to have to kick his ass so the guy knew his place. No one was replacing him at the top of their group.

With his tray in hand, he walked over to Chloe.

She didn't look up for several seconds, and he got tired of waiting for her.

"Is this seat taken?" he asked.

Chloe looked up, her eyes going wide. "Why?"

"I was thinking we could hang out today. It'll be fun." He didn't wait for an invitation. "You're going to have to tell your friends to fuck off." He took a bite of his large pizza.

"I eat lunch alone. I don't have any friends."

He knew that. She never hung around anyone. Was always alone. It made sense.

Again, he hadn't paid particular attention to what she did or didn't do.

"So what are you reading?" he asked.

"A book." She slid it closed, and he watched as she took a bite of apple. "Why are you sitting here rather than with your friends?"

"I think a change is as good as the rest. How is your, erm, face?"

"My face?"

"You took a nasty fall."

Her face went bright red. "Oh, I'm fine."

"You okay? It wasn't me who tripped you."

"I know. Someone in front of me did."

"You didn't see who it was?"

"Nope. Have no clue. It's fine." She finished her apple, and he realized she wasn't looking at him.

"You know it's rude not to pay your dinner guest any attention."

She glanced up and quickly looked down. "I don't feel comfortable you being here."

He also noticed her leg was constantly moving, bouncing up and down.

His presence made her that nervous? Taking another bite of pizza, he tried to think what to say. What did he say to this girl? He wasn't used to trying to be nice.

Gritting his teeth, he looked for anything to talk about. "I'm sorry about your dad."

She looked up then, her blue eyes staring right at him. They were the color of the ocean, brighter than his own blue.

"You are?"

"Yeah, I heard what happened at the club. Your mom finally ending things with him."

She nodded.

"Will you see him again?" he asked.

"I don't know. I haven't seen him since she kicked him out. Your dad was there when she handed him a suitcase full of stuff."

Alfie had noticed when it came to Lily, his father liked to bend over backwards to help. It wasn't like Lily gave Eagle the time of day either. At one point, he thought they were having an affair, but it wasn't the case. Lily was truly oblivious to the attention coming her way from Eagle.

"Did he make it easier for her?"

"I don't know. I think he was there to stop my father doing anything stupid, you know?"

He was probably there to stop Lily from taking Kurt back, but Alfie didn't say anything. "How was history?"

"You care about history?"

"Yeah, I do. I mean, I suck at it."

"That why you don't turn up?" she asked.

"One of the many reasons I don't turn up. Besides, after this morning, I didn't want to see Miss Hops. Did she notice I wasn't there?"

"Yeah, she did."

"Damn."

Chloe chuckled.

Alfie stopped as he listened to it. The sound didn't last for long, and it wasn't fake either. It was a sweet, light sound.

He realized he'd never heard her laugh, chuckle, giggle, or make any kind of noises other than anger and frustration.

"It would have been hard for her not to notice you weren't there. A little advice in the future, cut class with a teacher who hasn't seen you before that lesson."

"You ever cut class?" Alfie asked.

"No. Never."

"That is lame."

"Yeah, well, I have a plan, and I've got to stick with it, to see it through."

"A plan?"

"Yep, a top secret one." She tapped her nose.

"You're not going to tell me."

"Nope."

Now his curiosity was getting the better of him. "I know what my plan is."

"Yeah, I think the entire school knows what your plan is. Take over when it's time for your dad to give up his cut, right?"

"How do you know that?"

"My dad, coward that he is in your eyes, he knows a thing or two about the club. A girl picks it up from time to time."

"So now you know all club business."

"Not at all. I have no desire to either."

"You always felt you were better than the club," he said. The words sounded sharp, angry.

"No, I don't. I've never thought that at all. Why would you think that?" She frowned at him.

"Because of the way you are. You're rarely around the club, and when you are, you're always on your own. You never mingle or try to join in. A miss goody-two-shoes who doesn't know a fucking thing about trust or loyalty."

Her mouth went open, and he'd clearly shocked her. "Wow, just wow."

"What's that?"

"You don't have a fucking clue, that's what. I can't believe you'd even think that. I can't process everything right now. I need to, like, have a break or something." She got to her feet, and he reached over, forcing her to sit down. He held her in the same place where her other bruises were, and he cursed as she hissed from the pain.

"Shit, I'm sorry."

"Why can't I leave?"

"You think what I said was wrong?"

"It *is* wrong."

"Please."

"Look around you, Alfie. I don't make friends. I don't mingle well. Half of the guys at the club want nothing to do with me because I'm Kurt's daughter. You think it's easy for the daughter of a coward? He spends so much time trying to impress you people that he doesn't see what it's doing to his family. My mother is sick of it. I don't think I'm better than you, or Ian and Riley, or anyone else. I'm just me. I've never been good at thrusting myself into these kinds of situations. I don't have friends. I'm done talking about this with you." She grabbed her bag and tray.

This time, he didn't force her to sit down.

He watched her leave, throwing her lunch into the trash before leaving the main hall.

No one followed after her. No one fucking cared.

Getting to his feet, he carried the rest of his food over to his buddies.

"Didn't go well? I thought you were the kind of guy women loved to get your dick wet with all of your smooth talking to the ladies."

"Clearly, I've got to work at this one," he said.

He finished his pizza and listened to the people at his table talking about bikes and pussy, but the truth was, he couldn't stop Chloe's words from ringing in his ears. Had she even tried? Had the club even tried? It made no sense for them to push her aside. Sure, the club treated Kurt like shit, but that didn't mean Lily or Chloe were treated that way. At least, from what he'd seen.

Chloe had no friends. She never had, not that he could remember.

Why did he have a feeling something that he was about to do was so damn wrong?

****

Kurt couldn't cook.

Chloe sat opposite her father at the local diner. He'd ordered himself a big steak, and well, she'd gone for a garden burger. It was the only thing she liked at the diner.

"So, how was school?" he asked, digging into his food.

"It was okay, I guess." She'd not had another encounter with Alfie after the confession she made at lunch. She was pleased about that.

She didn't like talking about her lack of social skills.

"What's your favorite class?"

"Dad, are you really going to talk to me about school? You've never cared before." She wasn't saying it to be harsh to him, but she knew there were other things he wanted to talk about that were more important to him than her school.

"You're right, kid. I'm sorry. I know I should be a better dad and want to know everything going on at school, but how's your mother?" he asked.

"She's doing okay, I think."

"Just okay?"

"Dad, she's hurting."

"Do you think she'll take me back? I mean, I

forgot you once?" He laughed. "It's not the end of the world."

Pressing her lips together, she wanted to not say anything, but he was clearly deluded. "Dad, it wasn't just one time. Every single time Mom asks you to do something, you either have club business or you forget. The club has been coming first a lot lately. You're never home. You don't pick up her milk. Do you even realize you missed your anniversary?"

"What?"

"Back in July. Mom planned a big meal for you guys. I was going to hang out with friends."

It was a big lie. She'd had every intention of staying home, just being in her room alone. She'd told her mom she'd leave as soon as Dad arrived. Only, he never did. The food had gone cold and her mother sobbed while watching a movie.

As far as Chloe knew, he'd never made up for it, if he even knew.

"Shit. Fuck. I can't. I'm so sorry."

"I'm fine with it, Dad, really. It was Mom. She was upset."

He sat back, running a hand across his face. "I fucked up so many times. I love her, Chloe. I love you too."

"I know that." He just had a funny way of showing it.

"I can't even think of all the bad shit I've done right now. I'm sorry. She's never going to forgive me."

Chloe pushed a fry into her mouth so she didn't have to confirm it. She'd spoken to her mother a couple of times, and she was determined to not take him back, or to listen to him.

"How about I take you for boots now?" he asked.

"Sure." Her mother hadn't gotten around to

taking her, not that it was a problem. She had sneakers, but she did love her boots. The last pair she'd kept for over three years before they'd fallen apart. She had tried to fix them, but glue wasn't going to repair them this time.

"Finish your food and we'll go."

She grabbed her burger and took a bite.

The door to the diner opened, the bell ringing as it alerted the staff and diners to another guest.

Chloe saw ten of the Satan's Crew MC enter the diner, and her heart sank.

This was going to end with her alone, she just knew it.

She took another bite of her burger as the club saw Kurt.

"Kurt, just the man I wanted to see." Several men sat down, and Chloe wanted to disappear. They were large men. The scents of cigarette smoke and leather were heavy in the air.

Her nerves picked up a notch as they were all smirking, clearly knowing that whatever they were going to ask her father, he'd do.

"Sweetheart, you know Stallion and the guys." She nodded. "Guys, this is my daughter."

They gave a nod.

"So, we heard what happened with you and Lily, and well, a couple of the brothers are heading over to titties to have some fun. You want to come?"

"I'm spending time with my daughter," he said.

"Oh, come on. Seriously, I know you'd love it, and besides, we need a driver and all the prospects are busy. Come on, you'll love it."

Sipping at her water, she watched her father, and she saw the bait and hook. Stallion had said it simple. The club needed him, and Kurt couldn't walk away from the chance of being needed.

"Can we take a raincheck, sweetie?" he said.

Chloe didn't say anything as the table hooted.

"Come on, we've got to go now. The good chicks are always on early."

Within a matter of minutes, the food was paid for and she was sitting alone.

The waitress came over. "Would you like me to call someone for you, honey?"

"Nah, it's okay." She stood up, grabbing her bag. "Thank you for the food."

"You didn't finish it. You can sit and enjoy."

"I've got to head home. Thank you."

She left the diner, wrapping her arms around herself and going straight home.

"Chloe, is that you? I thought you were spending the evening with your dad?" Lily came out of the sitting room. She was dressed in an old nightshirt, and she had a book in one hand, and a pair of glasses in the other.

"I decided to come home."

"Chloe Decker, tell me."

She removed her jacket, putting it up onto the hook near the door. "Why? You're only going to hate him."

"You're my daughter, and I trusted him again. Tell me, now."

"Fine. A bunch of men from the club came in and they gave him an offer he couldn't refuse."

Lily growled. "Yes, he could refuse. What is with him?"

"It's fine. Really."

"No, it's not. I'll deal with it."

"It's fine." She walked past her mother, kicked off her sneakers and curled up on the sofa.

Lily joined her, putting the book and glasses on

the coffee table. She pulled Chloe into her arms.

"We'll get you a pair of those boots tomorrow after school. I'll pick you up."

"We don't have to."

"Honey, you're a good girl, and you've been patient with all of this. You're getting new boots."

"Can we even afford it?"

"I'll get some money off your father tomorrow. Trust me. He can afford it."

"Will we have to sell the house?" she asked.

"No. The house is all paid for. I can support the two of us, Chloe."

"I love you, Mom."

"I love you too, sweetie. You will always come first." She closed her eyes as her mother stroked her hair. "I love how blonde your hair is. I bet girls are envious of these long locks."

Chloe giggled. "Sure."

"Would you like to get it styled? We could have a girly spa day this weekend."

"I'm good on the haircut. I like my hair long. The spa day sounds cool though."

"I'll arrange it. Another gift from your father, believe me. How was school?"

She thought about Alfie and it was on the tip of her tongue to tell her mother, but then she decided against it.

"It was okay. Same old, same old."

"It does get better. I promise you."

"Did you love high school?"

"I had your father, so I loved everything about it. Even though my parents hated him. He made me feel special. I always imagined growing old with him. I never for a second thought it would end like this."

Chloe opened her eyes. "It doesn't have to end.

He'd come back, you know that?"

"I know, but that's one of the reasons why I've got to end it. He's bad for both of us. When you find a guy in your life, you'll understand. You've got to learn to walk away when you spend more time hating your life together than loving it."

"Do you think you'll date again?"

"One day, maybe. I'm not looking to date anyone right now."

****

The following day Lily made her way into the clubhouse. She was going to get money for Chloe's boots but also for the spa day. Entering the main room, she wrinkled her nose at the stench. It was disgusting, and surrounded her.

Kurt had yet to find a place to stay, so this had to be where he was living for the time being. She wouldn't put it past the club to actually force him to live in the basement, and because he was chasing their approval, he'd do it.

Her man could do so much better, but he'd never believed her, never listened. All he wanted, his every waking moment, was consumed by this club, and how they saw him.

It sickened her.

Several of the club whores were naked, legs splayed with men all around them. They looked like they were in desperate need of a shower.

"Lily, what are you doing here?" Eagle asked, coming out of his office. He was the only one who didn't look like he'd partied last night. "Is it about my boy?"

"No. I'm here to see Kurt. Where is he?"

"In his room, second floor on the left."

"Thanks."

"I don't think you want to go up there," Eagle

said.

"Why not?"

"He had a lot to drink last night. A couple of girls from the strip club returned with him."

Pain shot through Lily. "Women? When he was supposed to be spending time with our daughter." She had to see this. No matter how painful it was. She turned on her heel and walked to the second floor. There was only one door on the left. She knew it was an old storage room.

She didn't give herself the chance to second-guess what she was doing. She gripped the handle and opened the door.

Tears filled her eyes as she saw what lay before her. Kurt was naked, the evidence of his betrayal even more so.

Used condoms were on the floor, and there were three naked women in the room.

He was starting to wake up as Lily took a step back.

"Lily," Eagle said.

Kurt opened his eyes and stared right at her. "Lily, baby, morning."

The tears fell down her cheeks, and he clearly remembered what he'd done, because he shoved the girls off him.

"This is not what it looks like."

"I shouldn't care, but this is what you did, rather than spend time with Chloe. You call me, leave endless messages on my answering machine how you're a changed man, and yet, *this* is what you'd rather be doing. Did you do this before? When you were with me?"

"What? No. Of course not. I wouldn't do this."

"I can see with my own eyes. I need to leave." She pushed past both men, rushing out of the clubhouse.

Before she left, she did hear Eagle and Kurt fighting, but she didn't know what about. Did it really matter anymore?

There was no way she was going to get over this kind of humiliation.

What if he'd been sleeping with other women before? She'd have to get herself tested. It had never entered her mind to ever doubt him, and now, her entire life felt like a giant, fucking farce.

She wanted to scream. This wasn't how she intended for her life to end, not like this.

"Lily. Lily. Lily. Don't go. You don't need to leave," Eagle said.

"I do. Has he always been like this? Has he cheated on me before? Do you know?"

"No. I don't think he's ever done this before. With the divorce, I guess he figured you guys were over."

"Are you kidding me right now? No, I'm not over. It's not ever going to be over. I can't even think of this right now. I thought ... I've yet to see a lawyer." She ran fingers through her hair. Had she hoped to finally wake Kurt up to see what he was losing out on? She didn't know anything anymore. "I only came to ask him for the money for Chloe's boots and a spa day." She sniffled. "I've got to go."

Eagle grabbed her before she climbed into the car and hugged her. It was the first time he'd done anything like this with her.

She didn't read anything else into it, and simply held onto him, holding him as tight as she could, hoping more than anything that the pain she was feeling would go away.

"Let me take care of you and Chloe, okay?" Eagle pulled out his wallet and began to count bills.

"No," she said, putting her hand over his wallet. "This is not your concern, and I won't take your money."

"I want to treat you girls. On behalf of my son and the club."

"Not going to happen. You're not responsible for us. Thank you for the thought though." She let him go and climbed into her car.

She would never take club money, or that of another man.

Chapter Four

Today on her locker was "fat-arsed slut," spelled exactly like that. Chloe tilted her head to the side. If she had magical powers, she could just swipe the nasty words away, but it looked like she was going back to the good old approach of a cloth again.

People were watching and sniggering.

She didn't look in their direction. Turning on her heel, she made her way to the janitor's closet. He wasn't around, as he loved his morning coffee, so she found the hiding place for the key, reached in, and grabbed the necessary tools.

As she spun around, she knocked into someone, making her drop the water, which didn't topple over, and landed hard on the floor on her ass.

"Shit, I'm sorry," Alfie said.

The guy she'd run into was none other than the guy she'd been hoping to avoid.

"No worries."

"Why do you have cleaning supplies?" Alfie helped her up as he asked the question.

"The usual. I've got some nice comments on my locker. I've got to clean them off and, seeing as the janitor likes his mornings, I do it. It's my locker."

"There's no way it's on there again."

"Come and see if you don't believe me." Not that she was inviting him to spend more time with her. That wouldn't be what she was trying to do, at all, was it?

Alfie walked with her to her locker, and sure enough, the words were still there.

"See, welcome to my world." She got started cleaning the mess and noticed no one was talking now.

Alfie moved her to one side.

"Alfie, seriously, you don't need to do this," she

said.

"I know, but I want to, and now that I'm doing this, maybe they'll think twice about writing on your locker."

Again, the whispering started up, but Alfie held her hand as he washed off the insults.

She couldn't believe he'd taken over and was doing this for her, when he really didn't need to.

Once he was done, he stepped back. "Grab your books. We'll take this back and go to homeroom."

"You can't be serious."

"Do you want to give me your locker combination or just tell me?"

"No, I'll do it." She stepped forward, making sure he didn't know it.

Today, her locker wasn't going to play nice.

She stepped back, and tissues fell out of her locker. She hoped none of them were used. They had done this to her when all the tissues were out of a trash can, and she didn't want to think about what was on them. She'd bought new books, and written all of her notes in brand new ones so she could burn the old ones.

"This is new," he said.

"Not today. I sometimes get one or the other, or both. This is a both day." She shrugged. There were some rubber gloves the janitor left her. She put them on and got to work on cleaning up the brand-new mess.

She wrinkled her nose, but so far, no smell.

Alfie didn't help her with this, but he did drag over the trash can.

She noticed a couple of people stood away from him, almost as if they were afraid of what he'd do.

Would it be too much for her to hope he'd defend her?

Putting all the tissues in the trash, she grabbed her

books, closed her locker, and made a quick new combination. She didn't know who kept figuring it out, but she was just going to have to keep changing it, maybe daily would help.

Alfie picked up the supplies to the janitor's closet and urged her to lead the way.

"You don't have to do that."

"I want to."

She didn't say anything as she didn't want an audience to her questions.

Following behind him, she waited as he put the supplies back.

Hands on her hips, she waited as he turned to face her.

"Wow, are you going to spank me or something?"

"What's going on?"

"What's going on?"

"Yeah, and don't pretend to be all coy like you don't have a clue what is going on. You know something, and now, I'm curious and when I get curious, I want to know."

Alfie smirked. "You look cute when you're nervous."

"I'm not stupid, Alfie. Tell me what is going on."

"Nothing. You ever thought I've learned my lessons?"

"Alfie, you've been bullying me for as long as I can remember. Now all of a sudden you want to be my friend. What gives?"

She wasn't blind or stupid. Nothing had changed between them.

"Look, my dad knows you and your mom are having a hard time. Okay. It's clearly rough at home for you, and well, I get it."

"That's it?" Chloe asked. She wasn't buying his

bullshit, but she'd figure it out.

"Yeah. You and I, we're kind of the same."

"How are we?"

"Our home life is not always perfect. We make the most of a bad situation, and it's tough. Really fucking tough, and I get it, I do."

Chloe pursed her lips, waiting, wondering. She didn't for a second believe him, but she wasn't going to tell him that, not right now. Not today.

"Okay, fine, I'm sorry."

"Now, can we get to class? I'd hate for you to ruin your perfect record and skip a class."

"Sure."

Alfie went to grab her arm, but she flinched away from him.

"I'm not going to hurt you."

"It doesn't matter. I can walk beside you." Pushing her hands into the pockets of her jeans, she walked side by side, keeping an eye on him out of the corner of hers.

She was nervous.

Whatever Alfie had planned for her, she had to figure it out before he hurt her.

It would all be a little too easy for her.

"So, erm, did you hear what happened last night?" she asked.

"What happened last night?"

"Between my dad and me?"

"He left you alone in the diner?"

"Yeah, he did," she said. "At least he paid for the food."

"Did you eat it?"

"Went home. Hung out with my mom. Relaxed." She wouldn't give too much away but would stay cautious with him. She kept expecting to have Ian, Riley, or one of his other cronies listening in.

No one was around, so she didn't know what to expect.

Arriving in homeroom, she went straight to her seat and Alfie joined her. This time Miss Hops didn't come and intervene, but Chloe wasn't happy with that.

She wanted Alfie away from her. She wasn't fooled.

Yes, it was nice to have someone to talk to, and to even have a buddy to clean up the mess others created, but still, she wasn't stupid.

Whatever Alfie had planned for her, she'd be ready.

****

By the end of the day, Alfie was exhausted. Ian and Riley were the only ones waiting for him.

They climbed off the bench, throwing their cigarettes to the ground as he approached.

"You fucked her yet?" Ian asked.

Alfie slammed his fist into Ian's face. "Got pretty yet?"

"Chloe makes you want to be violent, that's an interesting development," Riley said.

"Look, it's taking a lot longer than I planned, okay? She's not trusting." He ran fingers through his hair, irritated. She had pretended today to believe him when he tried to explain. He saw her complete lack of trust. She didn't buy his bullshit, but then, he'd not exactly spun it right either. There was only so much he could train for, and clearly, he'd fucked up one too many times with Chloe.

"No shit. We didn't say this was going to be easy," Ian said. "I don't think I'll have my eyesight by the end of this."

"Stop spouting shit I don't want to hear and I'll

stop hitting you."

"We don't have to do any of this. We could just leave it," Riley said.

"No. I started this, and now, I'm going to see it through." He wasn't going to back down. There was no way he'd look weak. If he looked weak this year, by the time he took over as club president, they'd never respect him.

"What do you think you need to do?" Ian asked.

"I've got to spend more time with her. It's the only way for her to be convinced I mean business."

"This is starting to sound like a lot of hard work."

"You're quitting on me?" Alfie asked.

"Hell no, I can't wait to see her face when we do the big reveal. It's going to be fucking incredible. She'll rue the day she thought she could take us on."

Alfie nodded. "Come on, let's head back to the clubhouse." It was the only place he'd be able to get some food.

His father was rarely home, and Alfie didn't fancy himself a cook.

"Did you see the tits on Melanie today?" Ian said, putting his hands in front of his body. "I'm going to be bending her over my bike and showing her what a real man can do." He grabbed his crotch. "She'll like a big stiff one."

"She was also hanging off the head of the football team," Riley said.

"That's what makes her so fucking juicy. It's the chance of some easy pickings. She won't dump his ass, but she'd love to ride mine, and I can have a taste of her whenever I want."

Alfie smirked. "Until you get the taste of football cock."

Riley burst out laughing.

"Damn, I didn't think of that," Ian said.

"Yeah, now who is the dumbass?" Riley said, laughing. "Besides, Melanie doesn't have the best tits. Sharon does, and she knows how to suck a cock as well."

"If we're talking about bitches that know how to handle you, go with any of the club whores," Alfie said. "They know a thing or two about taking care of the old wood."

"I can't wait until we're members. I'm going to make sure there's at least six whores to one guy at the club," Ian said.

They arrived at the clubhouse.

Alfie spotted several of the club women in a huddle, smoking. They looked cold, seeing as they barely had any clothes on and the temperature was dropping for that time of year.

"What do you think is going on?" Ian asked.

They had stopped laughing as soon as they entered the parking lot.

It wasn't just a couple of the club whores outside, but all of them, which was unusual.

Walking toward them, he asked for a smoke, and they all held one out. Ian and Riley took a smoke from them as well.

"What's going on?" he asked.

"Kurt's woman stopped by today. She caught him with a couple of the women from titties. It didn't exactly end well. Eagle's on a warpath with Kurt."

"Why don't they just get rid of him?" one of the women asked.

Alfie didn't know her name.

He rarely knew any of the club whores. More often than not, they were getting their asses kicked out because they felt they had a prior claim over a brother than someone else, which was never the case.

"They like him. Kurt's fun when he's not trying to win the brothers over."

Alfie had heard enough.

Throwing the half-finished cigarette to the floor, he ignored the woman's cry at him wasting valuable nicotine and walked in.

What he saw, well, Chloe shouldn't ever have to see anything like this.

Kurt, for Eagle's pleasure, was dressed in a maid's outfit while a naked woman, he didn't know who, spanked him, and kept on hitting him as he cleaned the floor with a toothbrush.

"Geez," Ian said, pulling out his cell phone.

"Are you fucking serious right now? Don't ever show club shit outside. You fucking asshole."

This was going to be forever burned on his retinas. He didn't need to see this.

As he entered the clubhouse, his father was sitting back in his own private booth, smoking. He took a long pull on his cigarette, tilted his head back, and blew out rings of smoke.

"Hey, Eagle," Alfie said, taking a seat. "What's going on?"

"I needed some entertainment, and Kurt, he was happy to provide it."

There was a sudden cry of pain, and Alfie looked to see another woman with a whip.

"Do all the guys get this for stepping out on their woman?" Alfie asked.

"Are you questioning me again, boy?" Eagle asked.

"No, but I think a couple of the guys will be wondering what all this is about." Alfie didn't know if he was speaking the truth or not. He knew he'd be wanting to know if this would be the punishment now for all.

"Well, it's up to them and their dick what they do. It's my job to do this and to serve justice."

"Is it because it's Lily?" Alfie asked.

Eagle glared at him. "Why are you in my club? You're not a prospect yet nor a patched in member. You're ruining my buzz."

"I came for food."

Eagle reached into his pocket. "Here, take some money. Get the fuck out, now."

There was at least three hundred dollars, and Alfie had every intention of keeping it all.

Leaving the clubhouse, he thought about his father's little obsession with Lily. It hadn't just started up but had been growing for some time. For all Alfie knew, it could have started years ago, before Kurt even joined the club.

"So, are we going to do some planning of what is to happen next?" Ian asked.

"He's already the talk of the high school. People are wanting to know what's going to happen. They don't for a second believe you've got the hots for Chloe."

"Of course I haven't. That would be fucking crazy. I've got plans, but no one, not even you guys, are going to hear about them. She doesn't believe me. I've got to break away from the short path," Alfie said.

They made their way to the diner, and while his buddies picked a seat, he ordered them a couple of pizzas and fries. Taking a seat, he saw Ian and Riley waiting.

"You've given this some thought?"

"Why not? I'm sick and tired of people believing she's this sweet little girl, and I don't care what she says. She thinks she's better than us. Well, let's see the little princess fall. You're going to have to follow my lead and not question my methods."

"As if we'd do that," Ian said.

"You do it all the time."

The pizza arrived. Alfie took a large slice and bit into it, moaning as the flavors exploded on his tongue. He was fucking starving.

"This may mean I won't be hanging out with you guys so much either."

"Suits me. I can't wait to see her face when she realizes. It's going to be fucking epic."

Chapter Five

"I'm sorry about the spa day," Lily said.

"Mom, this is just as awesome." Chloe slipped her finger across the spoon. It was covered in melted chocolate. Rather than have a spa day, as they couldn't afford it because her mother no longer wanted to rely on Kurt, her mother had taken her for new boots, and they'd decided to stay in and make cupcakes.

Lily rarely baked anymore, but when she did it was a treat.

"Stop stealing all the chocolate," Lily said. "There won't be enough for the frosting."

Chloe stepped away from the counter and held her hands up. "I need to stop eating it. It tastes so good."

"How is school? You haven't said anything recently."

For the past two weeks, Alfie had stayed by her side nonstop, at least when he could. They didn't share all the same classes. It was nice to have someone near, but at the same time, she knew something was up.

"It was okay, you know."

"I know that sound. What's bugging you, sweetie?" Lily asked.

She didn't want to get Alfie into trouble, but she couldn't help but wonder what was going on.

"Alfie."

"Do I need to go and kick his father's ass?" Lily asked.

"No. No." The memory of Alfie taking a spanking was all too much for her to bear. She didn't want to get anyone else into trouble and Alfie may not like her, but she had nothing against him. "It's fine. Really. For the most part I mean. It's just, he's being nice to me."

"And this is a problem?"

"Kind of. Don't you think it's a little strange that the guy who likes to bully me suddenly wants to be friends?" Chloe asked.

"You don't think he's just listened to his father this time?"

Chloe shrugged. "I don't know. What if it's not though? What if he's planning something horrible?"

"Have I turned you into this nervous person who believes the bad in everyone?" Lily said, approaching her. She pushed some hair off her shoulders.

"No. No. I know Alfie and his little clique, and I know me. I don't know. Maybe I'm obsessing a little too much, do you think?"

"I personally think it's good to obsess, but so long as that brat is not spoiling my daughter, I don't care." Lily hugged her as the doorbell rang. "You go and answer that while I finish up the cupcakes."

Lily ruffled her hair, and Chloe was smiling as she answered the door.

Alfie was standing there, arms folded, looking a little nervous.

"What are you doing here?" she asked.

He'd never been around her house.

"What does it look like? I decided to call on you."

"Now, I don't get this. It's kind of creepy. You don't just call around for someone you don't like," she said. The words were having absolutely no filter, and she was just blurting them out without a care in the world.

She did care. A lot.

Alfie gripped the edges of the doorway.

She could slam the door closed and poof, fingers gone. Regardless of what happened the other day, she didn't believe in violence.

"Who said I didn't like you?"

"Years and years of hatred."

"Ah, but in all those years did I ever say the words, 'I hate you, Chloe'?"

"You just did."

"Doesn't count."

"What do you want, Alfie?" she asked.

"How about we hang out? Spend some time together."

"Not going to happen," she said.

"Who is it?" Lily asked, coming up behind her. "Oh, Alfie, honey, you're here."

"Hello, Mrs. Decker. I'm sorry to just arrive like this, but I was hoping to take Chloe out for a little bit."

"I've told him no," Chloe said.

"Why would you do that?" Lily asked.

"I don't want to go, and no one can make me." She looked toward Alfie. "I already made plans."

"Well, how about he joins us?" Lily said.

"Mom!"

"I'd love that, Mrs. Decker."

"Come on in then, Alfie, wash your hands. We're in the kitchen."

Chloe's mouth dropped open. She was pissed off, angry. "What the hell?" she asked, closing the door.

"Keep your voice down," Lily said.

"I don't want him here, Mom."

"Look, you don't think he's changed and something is up. I trust my daughter, and this is my way of seeing if it's true and helping you. I don't like how you're pushing everyone away in your life."

"This is insane. You know that, right? He's Eagle's kid?"

"Eagle's a good man."

"Please." She hadn't told anyone about the beating Alfie had gotten.

"I'm going to be here the entire time, Chloe. Trust me, okay? I won't let anything happen to you. I love you." Lily leaned in close and kissed the corner of her mouth.

"Fine. Fine. If he irritates me once, he's gone."

"It's your home, honey. I'm just here to make sure you don't do anything naughty."

"Mom, that's not ever going to happen. Trust me."

"I do. Always."

They entered the kitchen, and Alfie was in fact standing at the sink, doing the dishes.

"Isn't that nice of him? Thank you, Alfie. We were going to go to the spa today, but we settled on baking anyway. We've been using up the last of my supplies." Lily went to the small pantry she had, opening it up.

"Smells good." He finished washing up a dish and dried his hands on a cloth.

"Why don't you try one? I rarely bake for anyone but Chloe."

Chloe grabbed a towel and began to dry the dishes.

Her gaze stayed on him because even if her mother trusted him, she didn't.

Eighteen years they'd known each other, since birth. According to her father, they'd once shared a crib, but that was it. She had no good memories with this guy.

Alfie bit into a cupcake and moaned. "Fuck."

"Language," Lily said.

"Sorry, Mrs. Decker. They're so good." He took another bite.

"Please, call me Lily. I don't like the whole Mrs. Decker thing. Not anymore. Excuse me."

Chloe watched as her mother left the kitchen, her

heart breaking for her mother.

"I'm sorry," Alfie said.

"It's fine."

"She's taking the breakup really hard?"

"Yeah."

"Didn't she instigate it?" Alfie asked.

"Doesn't mean she stopped loving him. She does, but it's hard for her now because there's no coming back from it." She sighed. "Why are you here?"

"I knew you didn't trust me."

"Alfie, it's going to take a lot more than classroom buddies, and scrubbing off insults from my locker for me to believe you're not up to something."

"And you think I'm the bad person."

"What do you want? You've never called here before, and yet here you are. What gives?"

"Nothing gives. I figured you didn't believe me, so I'm here to clear a few things up."

"Those things being?" she asked.

"I want us to be friends. I want us to start over. Clean slate. From the beginning. We weren't always enemies."

Again, she thought back to the time of his spanking.

They'd never talked about what they'd seen or what he'd been through.

She ran fingers through her hair, glancing around the kitchen. This was supposed to be a day with her and her mother.

"I think you should go."

"I won't upset her okay. I've got nowhere else to be."

Chloe frowned. "Don't you have an entire clubhouse full of people?"

"Yeah, and you think they want an eighteen-year-old kid hanging around?"

"Shouldn't you be jumping through all of their bullshit hoops for them?"

He chuckled. "I only get the pleasure of doing that when I graduate high school."

She wanted to kick him out, but if she did that, her mother would question her, and then she'd have to go through an entire explanation of why she'd done it.

"Fine. But don't hurt her again. Call her Lily."

"Will do." He put his fingers to his head and saluted her.

She rolled her eyes. "I'll be back in a minute."

She left Alfie alone with the cupcakes in the kitchen to find her mother in the bathroom.

"You okay?" Chloe asked.

Lily looked up, swiping away her tears. "Yes and no. I love him so much."

"Then go and fix this."

"No. It's completely over now."

"It can't be. Not with the way this is all making you feel." She knelt down on the floor, putting her hands on her mother's knees. "Talk to me, Mom."

"I don't want you to hate him. Your father and I, we're through. We're so through. I don't want to affect your relationship with him. I will be fine one day. I don't know if I'm getting all emotional because it's your father, or because I know I failed."

"You didn't fail."

"I did. I should have seen the moment he ran, the instant they branded him a coward, that it was never going to be the same." Her mother sniffled. "It hasn't been the same, you know. Something is missing. It will always be missing."

She moved up and hugged her. "You'll always have me."

"The best part about any friendship." Lily stroked her hair. "Now, you go downstairs and make sure that boy doesn't eat all the cupcakes. Ask him if he's staying for dinner."

Chloe groaned. "Do I have to?"

"Yes. It's only fair you do." Lily cupped her cheeks. "This is a chance for you to have a fresh start."

She wished she had her mother's kind of enthusiasm. She didn't.

Getting to her feet, she found Alfie eating another cupcake in the kitchen. Gathering her hair up into a bun, she secured it with a clip.

"You're liking the food?" she asked.

"They're the best."

"How many have you eaten?"

Alfie looked a little guilty, and it was the cutest sight she'd ever seen.

"Erm, I don't know. I lost count. Should I not have?"

"No, it's fine." Chloe opened the pantry door to find the flour had dropped off the top shelf and spilled to the floor. "Shoot."

"What is it?" Lily asked, entering the kitchen.

"We lost our last bag of flour."

"Here, go and get some more," Lily said, grabbing her purse.

"Mom, we were only supposed to be using up."

"I know, and we've got a couple of other things to use up before they go out of date. Please, head to the store. I'll clean up the mess, and finish those dishes. Alfie, will you go with her?"

"Of course."

Chloe wanted to curse a little more, but instead, forced a smile to her lips and grabbed her jacket. It was cold out.

Leaving her home with Alfie was weird. Stepping out onto the street, she could imagine all the curtains twitching and the topic of conversation being Alfie and her, alone together.

When she glanced toward him, he seemed calm. His hands were in his jeans, his jacket like a neon sign.

It wasn't a proper leather cut, but it was what most of the Satan's Crew MC kids wore. Anyone who saw it knew he belonged to the club, and if anyone messed with him, they messed with the whole club.

"So, crazy week at school, huh?"

"Every single day you had something else scribbled on your locker," he said.

"I know."

"Doesn't it bother you?" he asked.

"It used to. Words hurt a whole lot." She shrugged. "I guess I got used to the same old insults. Besides, it's not like I can change people's minds. They all needed a punching bag, and I guess I was the one that got the highest score."

"Some people would have left the school by now," he said.

"Was that your hope? Getting me to leave?" She stopped walking to turn to him. "You do realize all of what happens is because of you and your little club, right?"

"No, it's not."

"Yeah, it is. You, Ian, Riley, and a couple of the others were the very first to write on my locker. Things like fat ass, fatty, whale, slut, whore, coward. Everyone else, being the sheep they are, followed in your direction. They find it funny to trip me, push me, hurt me. It all started because of you. It's why I'm surprised you're even helping me right now." She held her hands up in surrender. "What is it you want?"

"To make amends. I had no idea I'd been the cause of all that."

She laughed. "You knew. You know that regardless if you play football or not, you and the biker brats' clique in the school is the most popular. People are led by your example." She shook her head. "I don't want to talk about this." She began to walk away.

"Wait, you can't just throw that kind of shit at me and walk away."

"I can. Years of being the butt of the joke gives me that right, Alfie. Look, I don't know what this is, but I'm not stupid. Whatever it is, leave me out of it. What did I ever do to you? Huh? What did I ever do to hurt you? I've been nice all the time to you guys. I've tried to stay out of your way, and yet, I'm your first enemy, and I've done nothing wrong."

"I know."

"Then tell me what the fuck is your problem?" she asked.

She had stopped once again, but she didn't want to just stand around talking. They needed to get to the store before it closed.

"Look, I was a dick, okay? I didn't like your place in the club. No one likes Kurt. They use and humiliate him at every single turn. I didn't get why you were there."

"I never got any special treatment, Alfie. I was the coward's kid. It's why I tried to leave as quickly as possible. To a young girl, some of the stuff they said, it was horrible. I didn't have to listen to it. I'm not a horrible person, and I would never run away like that." She pressed her lips together. "I think you should go."

"I go now, your mom is going to start asking you a whole lot of questions."

She growled. "Stop it. Okay. Just stop with the

whole bullshit that you care."

"I'm not going anywhere. You can keep shouting at me, but I'm sticking around. You're stuck with me, and I'm going to prove you wrong."

"To what end?"

"For you to know, people can change and it doesn't take some miracle to happen." He winked at her, grabbing her arm. "Now, let's go shopping. You're getting a brand-new bestie."

She groaned as he grabbed a cart. He refused to let her go though and kept her by his side as they walked into the supermarket.

The moment some of the customers saw him, she knew he made them nervous and he hadn't done anything.

"Does it bother you the way people react to you?"

"Used to. Doesn't bother me anymore. The entire club is treated that way, and it's a good thing."

"Really?"

"Yeah, it means people will think twice before messing with us."

"I don't know. It sounds kind of sad."

"It's not sad."

"No one trusts you though. Trust and loyalty are what rule your club."

"What rules the club is trust and loyalty with each other. We don't care what a bunch of civilians think. They can all suck my dick as far as I'm concerned. You should try it."

"Don't worry. I don't think they should all suck my dick. I failed to care a long time ago."

"See, you're learning."

"I was taught by the best." She pulled away, but Alfie caught her hand. "Seriously, this is kind of freaky. I need to grab some flour."

"I know, but we're not at the aisle yet and I'm trying this out."

"You know this is what couples do."

"Do you want to be my girlfriend?"

She laughed, drawing attention to them. "I'm so sorry. I didn't mean to laugh."

"Yeah, you did."

"No, I really didn't. I'm sorry. I shouldn't have laughed. Really. No, I don't want to be your girlfriend, Alfie."

"I'd make a good boyfriend."

"Have you ever been anyone's boyfriend?" she asked.

"No."

"Then you can't go around saying how good you'd be at it." She smiled. "I … this is all so new. I didn't mean to insult you."

"But you did it anyway."

"I'm sorry. Please, forgive me."

"Of course, so long as you kiss me."

"That's not going to happen." She glanced at his lips.

"I don't believe you."

"All because I won't kiss you?"

"A kiss is really, really important."

She frowned, folding her arms. "Okay, explain to me how this works with you? A kiss is that not important."

"It goes to show you know nothing."

"I know a whole lot of things," she said.

"A kiss shows you're starting to trust me."

"And by me not kissing you, it proves I don't."

"You're not even giving it a real shot. You should kiss me. Give me a real shot. I won't let you down."

Chloe nibbled her lip.

She wanted to trust, but she had this sick, twisted feeling in her gut that told her not to trust. Something bad was going to happen.

Rather than have him make a scene, she stepped up to him, placed her hand on his arm, and pressed a kiss to his lips. It was short, sweet, but it was a kiss.

"See, my first one, Alfie. I can start to trust."
****

Her first-ever kiss.

On Sunday, lying in his bed, Alfie stared up at the ceiling and played the events in the supermarket in his head. They'd gotten the necessary flour and returned home, but that kiss... It had meant something.

He'd been her first kiss. Was it crazy to actually be happy about that?

There was a knock on his door.

Turning his head, he asked who it was.

"Me," Eagle said.

Alfie sat up, and his father entered a few seconds later.

"Hey, son," Eagle said. "I was thinking of going over to Lily's place. I passed it a couple of days ago and saw the lawn was overgrown. I figured she could use some help."

"Do you want me to come as well? I know they were talking about doing some yard work today," he said.

"You did?"

"I went and hung out with Chloe."

"Why?"

"Making amends," he said. Eagle didn't need to know this was all part of a bigger plan to put her in her place.

"Good. Lily worries about her a lot. Yes, get dressed. You can help. No bullshit while we're there."

"Do club rules stand?"

"No. We're going as a family."

Club rules stated he was not to call him "Dad," or to question him. Going as a family would be different. He'd have to call him "Dad," and questions were allowed. This was going to be surreal. Ever since he became a teenager, his father had been training him for the role of taking over as club president. When it finally happened, he intended to take care and make sure no one doubted his position within the club.

Pulling on a pair of jeans and a shirt that had seen better days, he grabbed a cup of coffee and joined his father in his pickup truck.

"Dad, do you have a thing for Lily?" Alfie asked, climbing into the passenger truck.

"That's none of your concern, son."

It never failed to amaze him how quickly his father could turn on and off the president role.

"She's still hung up on Kurt."

"That asshole never deserved her."

"Did you know them, growing up?"

"Yes. Your grandfather, he was in charge of the club."

"You're also a couple of years older than them."

"I know."

Alfie looked at his dad. He knew his father never loved his mother. It was why after she spat him out, she went packing. No one had seen or heard from her since.

From what he'd discovered, Lily had taken care of him a lot of the time. There were tales of him sharing a crib with Chloe.

"One day you will understand, there are women who are meant to be taken care of. Who you're supposed to love from the very beginning and deserve for you to bend over backwards for. They're loyal, trusting, and they own your heart."

"Does Lily own your heart?"

"I don't want to talk about this now. You don't fucking say anything. You be good."

"I will."

He had his own agenda to work on.

Arriving at Lily's place, he saw Chloe as he'd never seen her before. Even though the weather was starting to turn cold, they had a freak heatwave over the weekend, which was why he knew they were planning on doing all the necessary yard work.

Chloe was dressed in a pair of shorts and a black crop top. Her long blonde locks were pulled up into a bun, and she had on some kind of head scarf.

She looked … sexy.

No. There's no way he was thinking in terms of sexy.

She wasn't sexy.

This was all in his head, and he was imagining it.

As he shook those thoughts from his mind, she looked up to see him and his father climbing out of the truck.

"Alfie, Eagle, what brings you here?"

"I saw the yard was in serious need of being mowed. I figured we'd come and help."

"Oh."

"Hey, sweetie, does that thing even work?" Lily asked. "Oh, Eagle, Alfie, hi." Lily gave them both a smile.

"Wanted to come and help."

"Really?"

"Mom, I can't get this thing to work."

"Your dad was supposed to fix it. He broke it the last time. Let me look."

Lily bent down, turning the mower onto its side.

Alfie watched as she gathered the rotting grass off the bottom. "I have no idea what I'm looking for," she said, laughing.

He smiled. Lily had always been nice to him. Everyone at the club adored her.

Glancing over at Chloe, he saw her nibbling on her lip, glancing over at Eagle. He had to remember that she wasn't stupid. It was why she didn't trust him. Not that he could blame her. He wasn't trustworthy.

"I'm going to go and weed the bushes," she said.

"Okay, sweetie."

"Here, let me have a look at this," Eagle said.

"I'll come and help you."

His father must have been waiting as patiently as he could for Kurt to fuck up. It was the only explanation for all of this.

"Hey," he said. "Do you feel like kissing me again?"

"Oh, please, why are you and your dad here?" Chloe asked, entering the back yard.

It was a small yard, and it had been left to overgrow.

Chloe bent down, picking up some gloves and a trowel. He couldn't help but notice the curve of her ass.

Why hadn't he ever noticed her curves as being sexy rather than being fat? He was tempted to cup them, to touch them and to make sure his eyes were actually seeing what was really there.

"Earth to Alfie," Chloe said.

"We wanted to help and do the neighborly thing."

"I can see your dad has the hots for my mom," she said.

"Has the hots?" Alfie couldn't help but smile. "It sounds so cute. I'm sorry."

"Seriously?"

"Look, I think he does have a little crush, but for the most part, it's harmless."

She folded her arms. "There's no way that can be harmless. My dad is still begging to be accepted by your club after all these years."

He liked how she called it his club. "It's not going to happen."

"Exactly. You don't see it."

"I see it, Chloe. I'm not stupid. For years your father begged to be part of the club, and rather than let him, my father broke him, piece by piece, until his wife left him. Now, he's looking to get into his place as man of the house. Not that he wants this house. He wants Lily. I get it."

"And you don't care. You know what it means if they get together, right?" She pointed at the two of them.

"We wouldn't actually be related."

"I know that, but I don't want to be your step-anything."

"You'd come between your mother's happiness."

"I wouldn't dream of doing that, and you know it."

Alfie held his hands up. "I'm not here to start a fight."

"Then what are you here for?"

"To help you clean up and to say, leave them alone. Let them figure this thing out. It's not up to us to make this right."

"I know it's not, but you saw how my mom reacted the other day when you called her Mrs. Decker. She's not ready to commit. She will always love my father, and Eagle will have to handle that."

"You're nervous," he said.

"Wouldn't you be? My mother is getting a divorce. She feels like a fucking failure because of it."

81

Alfie did something he never thought he would. He stepped up to Chloe, wrapped his arms around her, and held her.

"What are you doing?"

"I'm letting you know it's going to be okay."

"You're kind of creeping me out right now."

"I know, but every now and then, someone needs a hug."

She started to laugh. He held her a little tighter and detected the hint of vanilla coming from her.

She pulled away first, and he knew he'd have to make her more comfortable around him.

"I better get to weeding. Have you ever done yard work?" she asked.

"Nope."

"Then why did you come over here?"

"To see you."

"Really?"

"Yeah, like I've said before, I'm trying to make amends."

"You're going to need another pair of gloves. Those nettles like to sting."

She walked away, and he watched her go. Her ass swayed, and he again had to wonder why he hadn't noticed her curves before. He'd been with plenty of girls, and club whores, and he knew there were many different body shapes to love and to fuck.

In her own element, Chloe shone.

Grabbing a pair of gloves, he wondered if he should go and check on his dad but decided against it. His father didn't need a babysitter.

Getting down on his knees beside Chloe, Alfie helped her work through the flower beds, taking out the weeds.

Halfway through the job, she left to go and get

some drinks.

She was taking a little longer than he thought was right, so he joined her in the house. He found her in the dining room, looking out onto the front yard.

The grass hadn't been mowed yet, but it looked like his dad was giving Lily a lesson in mechanics.

"You worried?" he asked.

"I took them out their drinks and Eagle held the glass to my mom. She sipped from the straw."

"You're obsessing about this."

"What good could come from this?" she asked.

If their parents got together, it would give him more of an excuse to get close to her.

The plan.

Whatever happened, he was determined to see it through.

"Has anyone ever told you you worry too much?" he asked.

"All the time."

"Well, don't worry about the little things. Just worry about the things you can change. I'm parched. Where's my drink?"

Chloe giggled. "Come on. I'll show you."
****

"The motor looks good. Clearly, there was too much grass. It hadn't been cleaned properly," Eagle said.

"Of course. I mean, who would have thought it, huh?" Lily asked with a smile.

Being this close to her after all this time, knowing she was a free woman, or at least, would be really soon, was testing his restraint.

For years, he'd watched Kurt and Lily. She'd been one of the prettiest girls in school. Not the sexiest, and a couple of people had tried to bully her, but he'd put a stop to that shit. Anyone who hurt her had to come to him. He was five years older than she was, but to some, he could have been ten or fifty. Being the brat of the president of the MC, it meant there were rules in place, and one of them involved underage girls.

Lily had been younger than he was, so he had no choice but to wait around for her to be the right age, which fucking sucked, big time.

By the time she was of age, she was already with Kurt, marrying him, and having his baby.

In anger, he'd ended up knocking up a club whore, who'd given him Alfie, and then left just as quickly. Not that he had a problem with that. Kurt spent so much time around the club, Lily would take care of both Alfie and Chloe. Seeing his son in Lily's arms had been like fucking torture, but he'd known he couldn't have her. She wasn't the kind of woman to step out on her man. It was part of what made her so damn loveable as well as having many other traits.

With Kurt out of the picture, he didn't have to worry. He would finally get his chance, and he wasn't going to let her get away. Not again.

"If there's anything you need, just give me a holler, you know. I'll be happy to drop by and help out."

"You really don't have to do that."

"I know I don't have to. I want to." He smiled at her. She would always be the prettiest woman in the world to him. "I better get this yard mowed." He winked at her and got to his feet. Like so many times before, Lily merely smiled at him and offered to get him another drink.

Small steps.

Really small steps.

It was going to fucking kill him.

Chapter Six

Wednesday into the third week of school and Alfie being around her, there was yet another message on her locker. This one was spelled so badly that she couldn't make anything of it. She was about to turn to go and collect the cleaning stuff when Alfie's growl echoed down the hall.

He stood right behind her.

The entire corridor went silent, and even her heart started to pound. He looked livid.

"What the fuck?" he said.

"It doesn't matter."

"To you it doesn't matter. I'm tired of this shit. Who did this?" he asked, looking toward the groups of people. Several of them looked away. "Not so fucking tough now, huh? Who does this every single morning? I will find out, believe me. I've got no problems waiting, and I will find that person. Is it you, Reese?"

Reese was one of the football players.

Chloe recalled he'd tried to get into the biker brats' little club, but seeing as his father was some kind of lawyer, no one would have him.

"Nah, man, of course not."

"I want to know who did this. We're not cleaning this shit up again." Alfie slammed his fist against the metal. "And don't think of covering for them either. Whoever did this, you know about it, you come to me."

"Alfie, I've got to clean this up," she said, touching his arm. "I know you don't like it and you want to leave it. It's still my locker."

"You're not cleaning it. I forbid you to clean it."

"Are you a god now? I have to obey everything you say?"

"It would do you good to listen to me. I know

what I'm talking about."

She chuckled. "Fine. I won't clean it, but you're never going to find out who did this."

"Why are you so certain?" he asked.

"Because I've tried to find out, and for the past couple of years, you know what I've got? Nothing. I've got nothing. I've got graffiti on my locker nearly every single day. Believe me, I'd stop it if I could."

"So I have your permission to hurt whoever did this?"

"Sure. Why not?"

He wasn't going to find the person responsible. She didn't for a second believe it was possible.

"Grab your shit, we've got homeroom to get to."

She had stopped asking him why he escorted her to homeroom, or sat with her, spent lunch time with her.

If she kept asking the same questions, she'd only sound like a broken record, so she had decided to just enjoy his company.

She wasn't fooled by his sudden interest in her either. She would be forever on guard around him, but that didn't mean she couldn't enjoy his company as they did.

Neither of them spoke as she grabbed her stuff from her locker, and they walked side by side down the long corridor toward their classroom. She held her books protectively, being careful so as not to trip over any stray legs.

She wouldn't put it past all of them to try to trip her.

In fact, just as they turned a corner, someone was there, leg out, and she felt herself falling, only she was grabbed before she could.

Her book wasn't so lucky and ended up on the floor.

"You okay?" Alfie asked.

"Yeah, I'm fine. Perfectly fine." She felt a little sick.

It was the first time she hadn't gone down.

Glancing to her left, she saw Daniel, one of the football guys, standing there, looking a little shocked.

In the next second Alfie was on him.

"You fucking prick. You think it's funny to trip a lady?"

Her cheeks were on fire. Alfie raised his fist and hit him.

She gasped. Violence always disturbed her. It was why she had felt sick after attacking Riley, Ian, and Alfie on the day they'd thrown the banana at her.

This wasn't the way to make things right.

"Alfie, stop."

Daniel wasn't one to take the punch. He began to hit back, and she gasped as she was suddenly pushed back against the metal from their sparring.

"Dude, teachers are coming," Ian said, appearing out of nowhere.

Thinking without reacting, she jumped onto Alfie's back, wrapping her arms around him, and pulling him off Daniel, who looked a little dazed.

Now that she'd shocked him completely, she knew she had to do something that would stop Alfie from getting hurt.

The guys would cover with Daniel, but she couldn't think.

Her mind was a complete and total blank.

What should she do?

Grabbing Alfie, she spun him around, wrapped her arms around his neck, and kissed him. She forced him to kiss her.

It was so surprising that for several seconds,

neither of them actually did anything.

Alfie's hands were wide, not holding her, and they looked so out of place, or at least, she imagined they did.

Within seconds of hearing the teacher, Alfie seemed to get with the program, grip her ass, and really kiss her.

It started out as a way to distract him from hurting Daniel, and suddenly, she felt a stirring within her body as Alfie traced the edge of her lip.

Someone cleared their throat, and she had no choice but to pull away.

Her lips were tingling, and she knew her face was hot with embarrassment.

"This is not a place for you to make out. Get to class. Now. What is going on here?"

"Nothing, I walked into a locker," Daniel said, sniffling blood.

"Excellent. What's your excuse, Alfie?"

"I bumped heads with my girlfriend." He wrapped his arms around her, and there was a collective gasp.

She was able to keep hers locked inside.

"Daniel, go to the nurse. Alfie, fix your problem. If I hear there was fighting, I will deal with it, severely." The teacher offered them one last glare before leaving.

"This isn't over," Alfie said.

"Fuck you."

Alfie went to go for him again, but she was able to stop him, holding him back.

"I've got a first aid kit in my locker. Let me take care of your face," she said.

She held his hand and saw Ian and Alfie share a look before he followed her.

Neither of them spoke, and her hands were

shaking. Once she had the kit, she took him to the boys' locker room.

"What would you have done if this was full of guys?" he asked.

"Taken you into the girls' and let them deal with you. They'd have patched you up real good."

"I'm starting to think you're a little jealous," he said.

"Not jealous, just busy. Take a seat." She put her bag on the floor and opened up the first aid kit. "He got you a good one," she said looking at the kit on his lip and on his eye.

"Yeah, I wasn't focusing."

"You didn't need to fight him for me."

"I did. No one will trip you when I'm around, and there's no chance of anyone hurting you on my watch."

"You can't protect me all the time. The bullying's not going to end until I leave here."

"You're leaving?"

"Let's not talk now."

"Are you, like, running away?"

"Hell, no. I'm not running away." She didn't want to talk to him about her plans.

"You know, boyfriends and girlfriends share everything together."

"They do, do they? We're not dating."

"Now you're just being mean."

She chuckled. "We're not dating. We're … abiding each other's company."

"I'm wearing you down, and you know it. You're going to be my girlfriend soon, Chloe. You may as well get used to it."

"Not happening, Alfie." She opened up an alcohol wipe and pressed it against his cut. He winced. "You may have to go to the hospital and get some stitches."

"No, I won't."

"You don't have to be brave and tough for me."

"You think this is the first time I've gotten a cut eyebrow and lip? Please, this is child's play in the club."

"It looks bad."

"I don't care. Just put a bandage or some tape over it. It'll be good."

"You winced at an alcohol wipe."

"I said I don't need stitches. I didn't say anything about not behaving like a baby over it. Come on, I can handle it."

She smiled and cleaned him up.

"So that kiss, huh? Would it be natural of me to think that was your first one?"

"Yes."

"And I was the one to give it to you."

"Why do you have to make everything sound so dirty?"

"It is what it is," he said. "So I was? You know, your first?"

She rolled her eyes. "Yes, you were my first. I had to figure out a way of getting you to stop punching him. I didn't want you getting in trouble for me."

"Why not?"

"I just don't want you to get in trouble. I've dealt with more of this, and I'm fine with it. There's no reason you should be dragged down. I don't think your dad would be happy about coming down here to deal with you."

"He'd be happy to know I was doing it to defend you." He reached out and pushed some hair out of the way.

"Well, thank you, all the same," she said. "I do appreciate it."

"You're sure? I'm not feeling the appreciation here."

"I stopped you from getting suspended or your dad coming here. You got a kiss out of it as well, and I fixed your face."

"I wasn't able to enjoy the kiss."

"And everything else?"

"I thank you, but I think you should kiss me again."

She giggled. "You do, and why?"

"I'm your savior. I'm your personal knight in shining armor or whatever bullshit that is called," he said.

"You're really going to use that as a reason to get another kiss?"

"I'd rather use no reason and just have you kiss me, but I don't seem to be getting what I want."

"You want me to just kiss you?"

"It's what normal people in a relationship do."

"We're not in a relationship."

"You're hurting my feelings, Chloe." He put a hand over her heart, and as she put away the first aid kit, he took her hand. He pressed his lips to her knuckles and smiled at her. "I'm wearing you down. I can see you want to kiss me. You do."

"I do not."

"Why don't you try it and we'll see."

She laughed. "You think I don't know where you're going with this? I do. I can see right through you."

"That's scary."

He cupped her face, and before she knew what was happening, his lips were on hers. The kiss seared right to her soul, and any laughter died as he actually kissed her. It was slow at first, exploratory, and changed within seconds as he ravished her mouth.

After only a few seconds, but felt like longer, he pulled back. "That was the first kiss I should have given you."

****

"You want to take her on a date?" Lily asked.

She was walking around the supermarket, picking up some fresh produce.

Alfie had been on his way to the clubhouse when he saw her.

"Yeah. Me and her, doing something together."

Lily put the peppers into her trolley and frowned. She opened her mouth and closed it. "Why are you asking me?"

"You're her mother."

"Yes, and you're not going to be dating me. You're going to be dating my daughter. You see the problem here?"

"I know, but Chloe and me, we've not had a good start."

"Believe me I know, and I can't say that I blame her." Lily tilted her head to the side.

He didn't know why he thought this would be a good idea. Getting her mother to like him would only allow Chloe to trust him more, right?

"We haven't always been close."

"I know you bullied my daughter, Alfie, and I'm not going to give you permission to date my daughter. I don't trust you."

"I'm proving to you that I care. That I've changed."

"No one does that quick a turnaround. Believe me, I know about men and their behavior. You want to date my daughter, fine. You will come to dinner tonight. You and your father and I will see if you have the right personality for my girl."

"Seriously? You're going to do this right now? When I'm proving to you that I'm different. I help her at school. I'm stopping all the bullying."

"That I imagine you helped to start in the first place. I'm not blind to everything going on, Alfie. I've given you the conditions for you to date her. Take them or leave them. I will never be the one to encourage my daughter to go on a date with her bully. Not now, not ever."

Alfie watched her as she grabbed the shopping cart and moved on. This wasn't exactly what he had planned.

Fuck!

Shit!

Cock!

Balls!

Chasing after Lily, he stood beside her. "You're not going to budge on this?"

"Nope, I am not. Tell me, Alfie, will I be cooking for four or two?"

He gritted his teeth. "Four."

"You better check with your father first in case he won't make it."

"He'll make it." Alfie had no doubt he'd use any excuse to be with Lily, including his intended dinner date. Dialing his father, he waited for Eagle to pick up.

"What is it, son?"

"Dad, will you be available to have dinner tonight with Lily and Chloe, and myself?"

"Dinner?"

"Yes. She's offered to cook."

"Give me the phone," Lily said.

He didn't exactly get a chance to tell her no, so he watched her.

"Hey, Eagle, Lily here. So your son asked to date

my daughter, and well, I've got a bit of an issue. I know I should give him the benefit of the doubt, but I figured a nice dinner with all of us. I can judge myself. Seven o'clock sound good to you? Yes, excellent. I'll put your son back on."

He was given the phone. "Hey, Dad."

"You better not fuck this up. Do you understand me?"

"Yes, I hear you. Loud and fucking clear."

"Language," Lily said.

"You heard her. You better watch your language." Eagle hung up.

"Be a gem for me and go and grab me some maple syrup. I'm out."

Pulling up Ian's details he sent him a message.

Alfie: **Not tonight. Change of plans.**

Ian: **Dude, seriously? She turned you down.**

Alfie: **The mother did and she won't let me date her unless I prove to her I'm legit. I've got dinner with dad and her, and her mother.**

Riley: **You really think this is worth it?**

Alfie: **Where are you?**

Riley: **At Ian's. We were waiting for you to tell us what was going down.**

Ian: **Clearly nothing is.**

Riley: **If your dad is involved, this could end badly for all of us.**

Alfie: **I can't back down now and stop showing an interest. It would look fucking odd.**

Alfie had wondered if he should stop with the whole bullshit of trying to date Chloe and just stick it out being nice to her.

This was starting to become more exhausting than it needed to be, and now with his father knowing, it wasn't going to end well.

He had to stop this farce.

Ian: **Then I say we just stick to you being nice to her. Maybe we all are, and wait it out.**

Riley: **Are we really that scared of your dad?**

Ian: **Dude, he's the fucking prez of the Satan's Crew MC. He gets to decide if we're in or out. I'm not going to risk my patch for a chance to make some chick look like a slut.**

Alfie: **I've got to go. Talk later.**

He put his cell phone away, grabbing the maple syrup. He didn't know what to do anymore.

The plan had been to fuck Chloe and to show the entire school her naked and for all to see. It was a classic and of course to make the last part of her high school year a misery. She thought she was better than all of them. Well, he was going to prove to the entire town she wasn't.

She was just a regular chick with a pussy and needs.

His father could destroy him. He loved the club more than anything, and he wouldn't risk fucking it up in the name of revenge. Not anymore.

He would have to play this out, though, as turning back wasn't an option.

****

"You invited them for dinner?" Chloe asked.

Her mother threw more peppers into the pot and began to stir them around with more garlic and ginger. The stir-fry smelled amazing, and she'd already started to cook the coconut noodles with equal parts coconut milk and stock. This was one of her favorite dishes and her mother's specialty.

"Why not?"

"I don't know, because why invite them in the first place?

"You need to stop worrying. If you must know I invited them for you."

"Why? Is something going on between you and Eagle?"

Lily snorted. "No, of course not, silly. Why would you think of something like that?"

"Why did you invite them for me?"

"Well, if you must know, Alfie came to me and asked if he could date you. I know you're nervous about his intentions, and rather than throw you to the wolf, I figured in this kind of controlled environment, I'd get a good reading on the kid."

"The kid?"

"You know what I mean."

"I do, and I don't think this is a good idea. You should call him and cancel." Chloe hadn't told her mother about the kiss, or about anything at school. Not even the fight he got into with Daniel. It was pointless to do so.

"I'm not going to cancel. You're worrying unnecessarily. It's all going to work out. You will see." Lily patted her hand.

"I don't want to be here."

"Stop it. Now I mean it. This is not going to be bad. It's going to be awesome, and you're going to stop worrying about every little detail." Lily gave her hand a squeeze.

"Have you heard from Dad?" she asked.

"No, not yet. I have initiated the divorce papers. I don't imagine it will be long now."

Chloe nodded. She couldn't believe this was happening. It was the end of an era with her parents. Their divorce would be … it wouldn't be good. She'd not seen or heard from her father either. He hadn't been around town, and she hadn't asked Alfie about him either. Keeping Alfie at arm's length was the only logical way to go.

The doorbell rang. "I better go and deal with that, hadn't I?"

"Please, while I'm finishing up."

Chloe left the kitchen.

"Don't be rude. Remember I raised a lady, not a thug."

She rolled her eyes, put a smile to her lips, and opened the door. Sure enough, there stood Eagle and Alfie.

"Evening," she said.

Eagle had a small bundle of flowers.

"My mom is in the kitchen."

"It smells incredible." Eagle brushed past her, leaving her alone with Alfie.

"You tried to get a date with me by asking my mother?" she asked. She didn't let him in. She stood in the doorway, not giving him room to move.

"I can see you're upset by that?"

"Nah, this is my amused face."

"I don't get to see it all that much. Forgive me for not noticing it."

"Why?" Chloe asked.

"Why what?"

"Why ask my mother when you could have asked me?"

"Would you have agreed to go on a date with me?"

"No." The truth just kind of slipped out, and she gritted her teeth, hating herself for it.

"It's why I decided to ask her. She doesn't trust me either, so this is what we get. I have to watch my father drool all over your mother."

She gave a shudder. "You know my mother

doesn't have a clue."

"I know. She is completely clueless to my dad's obsession. This is going to be one interesting night." He took a step toward the door. "Are you going to let me in?"

"I'm thinking about it." She held her hand up.

"Hopefully this will win me some points. Flowers for you, pretty lady."

"You think flowers are going to butter me up?"

"They always do the ladies, and seeing as I was your first, I'm guessing I'm the first guy not related to you to give you flowers."

"Yes, you are."

"See, I've got a lot of firsts coming up here."

"Come in, Alfie. Make yourself not at home," she said. With his back to her, she smiled down at the flowers and breathed them in. They had a subtle, sweet scent, which she liked.

"You do like them?"

She looked over the edge of the flowers and nodded. "I do. I'll go and put them in a vase." She left Alfie, as her face heated up once again. He'd caught her sniffing his flowers and liking them.

In the kitchen she paused as she saw Eagle standing close to her mother, but she also saw the intense way he stared at her.

Chloe had always thought the man had a thing for Lily, and now since her father was out of the picture, he clearly wanted to be the only one she turned to.

"Sweetie, you got flowers too?" Lily asked.

"Yes, pretty flowers," she said, holding them up.

"Will you take Eagle to the table so we can start enjoying this food? It's nearly done," Lily said.

"Eagle, would you like to follow me?" She showed them to the dining room where her mother had already put everyone in place. They had a small table, so she and Alfie would be sitting opposite each other while Eagle and Lily did the same.

This was going to be *so* much fun. She kept her mouth shut though, so no one would be able to detect the sarcasm.

"How's school?" Eagle asked.

"You're talking to me?" she asked, pointing at her chest.

"Yes. Alfie tells me you and he are now friends."

"Oh, no—" She didn't get the chance to finish as he kicked her under the table. She pressed her lips together but so wanted to kick him back.

Instead, she forced a smile to her lips.

"We're really good friends," he said.

"Kicking a girl under the table doesn't make you very good friends, Alfie. I taught you better than that."

Chloe bit her lip, seeing the glare in the man's eyes.

"We are good friends," she said, quickly coming to Alfie's defense. "In fact, he wanted to ask me out on a date and my mom said no. It's why you got invited, so she can see we're bosom buddies and all that." *Shut up, Chloe.* "Without him you wouldn't be trying my mom's cooking, and believe me, you'd be missing out."

She really needed to stop talking. There was no time for Eagle or Alfie to say anything as her mother came out, carrying the large wok filled with her coconut stir-fry.

Chloe's hands were shaking, so she was more than happy to have her mother serve the food.

The conversation was rather dull, talking about school, work, something to do with the club. Chloe didn't pay attention. She was more interested in her food and not thinking about Alfie across from her.

Between kisses, proposed dates, and him standing up for her, she was all over the place. It was much easier when he hated her.

After dinner, her mother served cake, and to get away from all the awkward tension, Chloe offered to do the dishes, leaving her mother alone with Eagle. It wasn't the choice she wanted to make, but she had to make her escape.

At least she knew Eagle wouldn't hurt her mother, or she hoped not anyway.

"You're running away again," Alfie said, following her into the kitchen.

"I'm not running away. These dishes do not do themselves."

"Noted. We have a club fairy come and take care of them."

"Of course." She turned the tap on, heating up the water.

"Why did you save me in there?" he asked.

"I didn't."

"Yeah, you did. You saw the way my dad was reacting, and you told him about us dating, and how you wanted to. You gave the sense that you did, and I know I didn't win you over that easily."

Chloe averted her gaze, not wanting to look at him.

"Look, I saw all those years ago. I saw him hurt you. I don't know what you'd done, but I can imagine living with him isn't easy."

"I know you saw."

She turned to look at him. "I figured it was one of the reasons you hated me."

"It was, but what you don't know is I deserved it."

"No, there's no way a child could deserve that."

Alfie laughed. "I know my dad loves me. He's president of the Satan's Crew MC, and with that comes a whole load of responsibility. He has to make sure I'm a good man. The kind of man who can take over from him some day, and I will. That day I got that beating, Ian was locked in the old barn, and I was messing around with matches and I set fire to it. Nearly killed Ian. He got out, but he did suffer from smoke inhalation, died on the table for a minute before the doctors were able to bring him back. My dad, he got home and gave me a beating so I would know never to play with matches like that again. But you're right. I hated you for seeing that. I'm sorry."

He put a hand on her back, and she did no more than hold him close.

Chapter Seven

Chloe's life over the next month and a half was surreal. The graffiti on her locker stopped completely, which she wasn't going to complain about. People stopped trying to trip her in the hallway, and she stopped having things thrown at her, or put in her locker.

For the first time, she got to live a painless, happy time at high school.

Surreal as fuck.

Her parents' divorce, against all the odds, was also going smoothly. Kurt didn't contest it, and she hadn't seen her dad since that time at the diner, which did suck. She had hoped he'd stop by to say hey. Even though most of his time had been spent at the club, he was still her dad, and she did love him.

Day by day, her mother began to glow again.

The tears finally stopped, and she was able to live her life without thinking about Kurt. What Chloe didn't want to think about was Eagle.

He'd started to hang around a whole lot more, and she didn't know if she liked him being near her mother.

Like tonight.

It was a Friday night. Alfie had offered to spend the night with her, and in doing so, Lily had agreed to go out on a date with Eagle, not that she would agree it was a date. Far from it.

"You're sure you're going to be okay?" Lily asked.

"Yeah, Mom. I've got popcorn, and I think Alfie has ordered some pizza. We're good. Believe me. We can handle one night of you having fun."

"I can stay. This is so stupid. I haven't been out in a long time. I don't even know why I'm bothering with all this," Lily said. "The divorce is not final."

"But it has been signed, and everything is fine. You should go out tonight. In fact, you need to go out. I demand it," Chloe said.

"Why?" Lily asked. "I was eighteen once, and I remember why I wanted someone to go out."

Chloe rolled her eyes. "Not like that. I promise you. Never, not in a million years is it going to happen. We're really good friends. I promise you, I'll be good, in all things."

"I don't know."

"Trust me, Mom, really, trust me. I just want you to have some fun tonight."

"It has been so long since I dated."

"You'll know what to do. I have faith in you."

Lily laughed. "I'm the grownup here. I should be the one giving you advice."

Chloe hugged her mother tightly. "I know, and one day, you will." She closed her eyes, hoping her mother would have an amazing time tonight. "Go out. Have some fun and know I'm not going to do anything crazy."

"I know boys that age. They want something, Chloe."

"I'm not going to give in. Trust me."

"I know I can trust you." Lily hugged her again, but this time, the doorbell went. It would seem they'd forever be interrupted with the bell. "There's no backing out now."

They made their way toward the door, but her mother made a pitstop at the living room.

"No funny business in my house. I don't care what you guys are calling it nowadays. Not in my house, understood?"

Alfie saluted her. "You got it."

"Good."

Chloe wanted the world to open up and swallow her whole. It was the only way she'd be able to deal with this kind of embarrassment.

Opening the door, Eagle was there, without his leather cut, which was a surprise. He held a bouquet of flowers, and this huge smile on his face. He also looked nervous.

"Lily, you look beautiful."

"Thank you. Are those flowers for me?"

"Yes."

"They're pretty. Erm, I better put them in water."

Chloe took the flowers from her mother. "I can do that. Have fun."

"You're sure?"

"Yes, Mom, I'm sure."

Lily nodded, but her nerves were still there.

Finally, she made it out the door, and Chloe rested against it, wondering if she should have advised her mother to stay home.

"You okay?" Alfie asked.

"Yeah, I'm fine. Your dad won't hurt her, will he?"

"No. He won't."

"I have a hard time believing that."

"I know. The only time I've seen my dad look so happy is when he's around Lily."

"What happened to your mother?" She slapped a hand across her mouth. "Forget I asked. It was so rude of me." She stared down at the flowers. "I better put these in some kind of water before they die." Her mother would take it as an omen the date was bad.

Walking past Alfie, she went into the kitchen, putting the flowers in one of the few vases, and filling it with water.

"She left," Alfie said.

"Your mother?"

"Yeah. From what I know she was a club whore who got knocked up, not intentionally either. She didn't want to earn herself a patched member, or even a prospect. All she wanted was to have some fun. The idea of a kid terrified her. Once she had spat me out and gave me to my dad, she was gone. Promised to never return."

"Do you think she ever will?"

"Nah, it hasn't happened in the past eighteen years, and it never will."

"I'm so sorry."

"Why? It's not like I've got anything to compare it to. There's no memories for me to hate or to hang on to. It's all a blank for me. Unlike your dad. He's disappointed you all the time. You have those memories and your hatred of what he's done. At least I don't have that."

"I see your point. I don't like it, but I see it."

He chuckled. "Are you going to hug that vase forever?"

"I'm going to take it my mom's room. I think they'd make her happy to roll over and see them in the morning. I'll be back in a second."

Leaving Alfie in the kitchen, she walked up to her mother's room. There was nothing to resemble Kurt in the room anymore. Her mother had completely rid the space of anything that reminded her of him.

Putting the flowers on the side of the bed, Chloe ran her hand down the covers.

"Nice," Alfie said, making her jump.

"What are you doing up here?"

"You didn't say I couldn't see the upstairs of your house."

"I thought that was a given."

"You need to learn to communicate more."

She sighed.

"Show me your room," he said.

"Are you kidding me?"

"What? I promised your mom no funny business would happen tonight, and I mean it. I always keep my promises. Now, show me your room. I won't fuck you tonight."

Chloe's hands clenched to fists at her side. "You won't be having sex with me ever."

"Don't get all stuck up about this. I didn't mean it like that. I've yet to learn how to use tact."

"Or manners."

He wrapped his arms around her. "I'm sorry. Forgive me." One of his hands sank into her hair as the other moved down to her ass, squeezing the flesh.

"Enough, mister," she said. "I forgive you, but stop talking about sex."

"You know it's nothing to be afraid of."

"Says the guy who has done it a thousand times probably."

"Nine hundred and ninety-nine. Saving the one thousandth for you."

"How sweet," she said.

"I'm teasing. Yes, I've had sex before, which is why I know you shouldn't be afraid of it."

"I'm not afraid of it. I'm just not ready, and I don't want you to push this." She didn't see Alfie being her first.

Sex was something she did want to experience, but right now, no. Not with her doubts still about Alfie. Sure, he'd not given her a reason to doubt him, and there were times she'd find herself feeling sick to her stomach because she wanted to believe him so much.

"I'm not going to push this." He pressed a kiss to

her lips. "I'm happy for you to take your time, to get ready."

She stared at his chest and wondered if there would ever come a time when she did feel ready with Alfie.

"I would understand if you wanted to date someone else?"

"Why would I want to date anyone else?"

"I'm not giving you what you want," she said. "We're not committed together, you know. You don't have to go without."

Alfie chuckled. "Wow, you're giving me the go-ahead to sleep with other girls even though I've said it's me and you. We're together."

"We both know that's not true."

He slammed his lips down, holding her into place as he ravished her mouth. She gasped as he slid his tongue across her lips, and she opened up for him to deepen the kiss. It was so ... unexpected and magical.

They had kissed a couple of times but never like this.

By the time he released her, her lips tingled.

"I'm not going to be seeing any other girl. I'm not a sex-starved man, Chloe. You're going to learn to trust me."

****

Eagle held the door open for Lily and took her arm, escorting her into the bar and grill.

"I wanted to take you to some fancy restaurant, but I'm kind of banned from all of them."

Lily giggled. "It's no problem. I'm not the kind of girl who needs fancy. This is nice though. I like it."

He'd reserved a table, and he helped her into her seat before taking the one opposite her.

She was so nervous, and he wanted to calm her

down, or at least to make sure she knew there was no pressure tonight.

"Well, this is really amazing," she said. "You know it has been over twenty years since I went on a date with Kurt. Shit, I'm sorry. I shouldn't have said anything."

He reached across the table. "I know all about you and Kurt. You two were inseparable."

"True. You know he always wanted to be part of the club. Always. When he told me what he did, how he ran away rather than stay and fight, part of me was glad."

"Really?"

"Yeah. I mean, I was young, alone, with a baby. I was also taking care of Alfie at the time. Kurt was the only one earning as well. I didn't want to be alone. I don't know if he ran away out of fear or if he was doing it for me. I always thought he'd come to me because he loved me and didn't want me to be alone."

"I can see that."

"I don't know if that's the truth."

Eagle didn't believe for a second Kurt would have run away to just be with Lily. She deserved someone better.

Over the years, because of his love for Lily, he'd given Kurt so many chances. Chances even the club didn't know about, to see if he was truly a coward or just had better instincts.

Each time he failed.

A fight, he'd run.

Shots, he'd cower.

There was no real man to him.

He wanted to be part of a club, but not pay the true price through trust and loyalty. It's why he could never have Kurt as a full patched member. His father had once told him that no matter how much you liked the guy, you sometimes had to cut loose the weak ones to make room for the ones that will make you stronger, which was exactly what he did.

"Don't think about it," Eagle said.

"You're right. I'm here with you, on our first date, and I don't want to think about anything but having a good time. So, tell me, Eagle, what interests you?" she asked.

"You."

She smiled. "You're saying all the right words."

"No, Lily, I'm saying everything I mean. You're the only thing outside of the club, I have any interest in. Watching you and Kurt has been real fucking hard, and now, I can't pretend."

"Eagle, please, not tonight. Can we just … you like me?"

The surprise in her voice was so endearing. She didn't have a fucking clue about him loving her.

"I more than like you, Lily."

"Oh. I … I had no idea."

"I know." She didn't have a single mean bone in her body. "I don't want to talk about it tonight. I know you're not ready. I'm not going to rush you into anything. So, what do you feel like ordering?"

"Eagle?"

"No, I didn't come here to tell you all of this. I wanted us to have some fun, and that is exactly what we're going to have, fun."

Lily squeezed his hand, and then, right there at the bar and grill, she got up and walked to his side, cupping his face.

Her nerves were so clear to read as she leaned in and brushed her lips against his. Eagle knew if she'd been in his life from the beginning, he'd never have made so many fucked-up mistakes, especially when it came to his son.

He'd not been ready to take care of a kid, and over the years, he'd pushed him away to make him a man, but he'd done so with so much regret. His father had loved him in his own way, and he'd done exactly the same to his boy.

"Thank you," she said. "For being so patient with me."

Eagle had been waiting for this woman for so long. What was wrong with waiting a couple more days, months, or even years? For the right woman, he'd do whatever it took to win her.

He had nothing to do with Kurt's infidelity or abandonment. That was all on the man himself. But he wasn't going to step away now, for another man to take his place.

Lily would belong to him.

****

Thanksgiving came and went, and they moved toward Christmas. Eagle spent a great deal of time with Lily, especially after the divorce went final. The club hadn't heard from Kurt since the morning he'd woken up with the strippers.

Chloe had asked Alife about her dad, but she didn't want him to find the man for her.

For his father, he knew the relationship was going slow between Eagle and Lily, but it was happening.

Every weekend, they were both at her house, and if they stayed over too late, Alfie got the spare room while Eagle slept downstairs.

After putting up the Christmas decorations in Chloe's sitting room and drinking way too much hot chocolate, Alfie couldn't sleep.

The television was playing downstairs, and he didn't know how close their parents were getting yet.

Even if they did, he had no intention of treating Chloe like his little sister.

Any plan he'd originally thought to do was now out the window.

Ian, Riley, and he had all agreed, especially after they saw Eagle making out with Lily. It was only the one time and he'd watched Lily end it.

He and the guys had come to the conclusion they couldn't follow through. Any kind of trick they had planned for her, it would only fall back on them, and his father would go on a rampage, no doubt about it.

Lily would side with her daughter, and he'd risk his father's happiness by trying to prove what exactly?

Chloe wasn't a threat to him or the club. In fact, the more time he spent with her, he actually adored her.

She was sweet, especially when she smiled, which wasn't often enough for him. The moment she stopped worrying about the bullying, and doubting him, she'd really started to shine, and her glow, he adored it, relished it, and knew he wanted to help her to keep on shining.

Closing the corridor, he missed the creaky floorboards, and without knocking, let himself into Chloe's room.

What had started out as a trick to hurt her had turned into him seeking her out. Sitting with her in class was no longer an act for him.

Sure, it hadn't exactly lasted long, but now, he didn't want to stop.

How crazy was that?

Another change that had been made was that his boys sat with her as well. He'd moved her from her small little table in the corner of the room, to the one he sat at with his boys. At first there had been animosity, but like he had, they'd come to see that Chloe didn't have a mean bone in her body. Far from it, she was just … shy.

Yes, shy, for the most part.

The lamp was on, and she had a book in her hand. "Alfie, what are you doing here?" she asked.

"I wanted to come and see you. I couldn't sleep."

She put the book down as he approached the bed. Lifting the covers, he slid in right alongside her.

"You can't sleep here," she said with a giggle. "Your feet are cold."

"Our parents are getting close."

"I know. Mom started singing as she baked cookies. It has been so long since she did that, and I know it's because your dad makes her happy." She touched his cheek, then the tip of his nose. "Your nose is cold as well."

"What are you wearing? Old lady pajamas."

She giggled. "I get so cold." She let out a little shiver.

He wrapped his arms around her. "I'll warm you up."

He kissed her lips, feeling a stirring in his cock.

"Will you still be my friend when I'm your stepsister?"

"We're not just friends. We're dating, and I'm not going to stop just because our parents decide to do the whole grinding thing."

Silence met his joke.

"What's it like?" Chloe asked.

"What?"

"Sex."

He pulled back a little to stare into her eyes. They were so blue. "You want to know what sex is like?"

"I don't want to actually do it yet. I'm not ready, you know, but I'm curious to know what it's like. Forget it."

"You look so cute with your blush. It's the nicest shade on you."

"Stop it."

"I'm not joking. We've got a blusher here." He whispered as if to tell everyone in a joking voice.

"Stop it. They'll hear you."

"Do you think they're making out?" he asked.

She giggled. "I have no idea. Would they really do that?"

He snorted. "Of course they would." He ran his fingers through her hair. "It…" He didn't know how to find the right words to make it sound. "I don't know what it's like for a girl, but for me, I mean, I haven't been with anyone special."

"Alfie, you don't have to worry about me being upset or anything. I won't be. I promise."

"Fine, sex is nice. Orgasms are nice. It's sex, so yeah, it's good."

"You're not really selling me on the idea of sex."

"Because it's not always good. You can sleep with someone and it can mean absolutely nothing. It can be empty with no meaning, nothing."

"You've had a lot of meaningless sex?"

"Yeah, I have, and believe me, it's not exactly something to enjoy, you know." He kissed her hard, and she moaned. "You feel that?" He pushed his cock against her. "It's what you do to me. All the time."

"All the time?" she asked.

He took her hand, and she didn't fight him as she touched him.

"I don't know how sex is going to be for you, or for us. I know I want you, and I'm going to make everything perfect for your first time."

She giggled. "You're a little sure of yourself."

"I know you're a virgin, Chloe."

She didn't stop smiling though.

"And you're the master at knowing everything."

"When it comes to you, I do know everything." He winked at her. Slowly, he moved his hand from her hair, sliding down her body until he got to her tit. He rested it there, waiting for her. "I won't pressure you, Chloe. I won't do anything you don't want me to do."

"You'll be the perfect gentleman?"

"Yes." He took possession of her lips once again, and she moaned. He swallowed it down, not knowing if his father had Lily distracted or not. "Tell me to stop."

"I don't want to. Not yet. It feels good." She ran her hand up and down his length, and he knew it felt good to him.

Stroking over her nipple, he gave the point a squeeze, before sliding down her shirt to the edge of her pajama pants. She still didn't push him away, and he took his chance, pushing his hand inside, cupping her pussy.

She wasn't wearing any panties, and as he slid a finger between her slit, he felt how wet she was.

He found her clit and began to tease her back and forth, wanting to watch her come, to see her let go for him.

"Does it feel good?" he asked.

"Yes."

"I want you to come for me. You're going to have to be quiet though. I don't want anyone to hear."

She pressed her lips together, and he chuckled.

Kissing her mouth, he ran his tongue across the seam, and slid inside. Chloe didn't let go of his cock as he fingered her pussy.

He wanted to hear her come, and one day soon, they would be alone in a bed, and he wouldn't have to be quiet or consider his father downstairs.

Whatever he did, he couldn't break Chloe's heart.

Eagle, being club prez, could make his life a total misery, and he wanted his father to be happy. Besides, he didn't see Chloe as a means to an end, or someone to hurt.

He truly was starting to care for her. The feelings he had were real.

He'd even told Ian and Riley about them, and they had both said it must be an occupational hazard or something.

Either way, he wasn't walking away from her.

He felt the change begin to stir within Chloe. She moaned his name, and he swallowed it down as she came on his fingers.

He wanted to taste her, but for now, he'd tease her.

His own release wasn't far off, and as she brought him to climax, he filled the fabric of his boxer briefs.

They were both panting afterward. He didn't pull away completely from her. He rested his palm flat against her mound.

"That's how it can be between us. Just the start. It may not always be like that."

"I enjoyed that." She kissed him again.

"I'm never going to get bored of this, am I?" he asked.

She frowned. "I don't know if you meant to ask me that."

"I had no idea just how special you were."

"Alfie, you already have your hand in my pants. You don't need to keep worrying about more."

"When will you tell me your plans?" he asked. He had to change the subject as he was having another of those moments when he could see Chloe being by his side for a lot longer than high school.

"You keep asking about them."

"Because I'm curious and I want to know what makes my girlfriend tick."

Whenever he called her his girlfriend, she always looked a little uneasy.

"Come on, you know I plan to prospect and become a full patched in member at the Satan's Crew MC. What about you?"

She took a deep breath. "Okay, fine. I plan to leave town."

"What?"

"Yes. You heard me."

"Does your mom know?"

"She does, and she's even helping me. I'm going to a culinary college."

"Cooking?"

"That's the one. We've been saving up for me to go since I started cooking when I was ten."

"I've never seen you cook."

"You have, you just didn't realize it was me as well as my mother."

"You don't brag about your cooking," he said.

"I don't want to. Anyway, that's my plan."

"You're going to be a chef?"

She nodded. "Or something. We'll see."

"You're going to leave Satan's Croft."

"Yes."

"Is Lily going with you?"

"No. I think if I become a rich millionaire with all my own shows, maybe, but she's staying here. She wants to have a place for me to come back to. I don't have many other plans outside of that one. So now you know my little secret."

"And that's why you've not been applying to other colleges."

"I already got in. I've got to bring my bad self to the college in late August." She nibbled her lip. "And now there's you."

"No, you can't not go because of me."

"What about us?" she asked.

"You didn't say that there would be no chance of long distance? You could come back during the weekends."

"Are we really doing this? Considering ourselves together as, like, a couple? The bully and the bullied."

Alfie kissed her again. "I wish I'd never bullied you."

"You've got votes from me to never do it again."

"I will spend a lifetime making amends to you," he said.

"You don't need to make amends. I think we both messed up. If my mom and your dad keep dating, we're going to be family."

"True. I can spend a lifetime making it up to you."

"Alfie, there's nothing to make up for because I forgive you."

Chapter Eight

"You guys have gone all silent on me," Alfie said, throwing another stone at the frozen lake.

"It's kind of a lot to take in," Riley said.

Ian was sitting on the ground with his knees up to his chest. There was a party going on at the clubhouse. Lily was sick, and Chloe had stayed home. His dad had no choice but to stay at the clubhouse as there was a patching in ceremony. Once that was all done, Alfie was following his father to Lily's house.

He'd been sharing Chloe's bed now for a couple of weeks, especially over Christmas break when his father spent a lot of spare time there.

"What's to take in? When we decided not to go through with the plan, we knew it was either going to end up with Alfie dating her, or just being friends. Is this a fake dating or an actual dating?" Ian asked.

"It's real, man. So real."

"Wow, I can't believe you've gone from hating this chick, to actually liking her," Riley said.

"I got everything wrong with her. She's not a bitch, and she doesn't think she's better than us. Far from it, in fact. I was the one that fucked this all up, not her." Alfie couldn't believe he was having this conversation. "What I asked you guys here for is to make sure none of you talk about what we were going to do."

"It's dead in the water," Riley said.

"Yeah, have you guys watched Eagle lately? That man is like a cat that got the fucking cream. I am not shitting on his parade with Lily. If any of this comes out, our patch could be kissed goodbye," Ian said.

"It wouldn't be kissed goodbye," Alfie said. "We'd be punished for it."

"Hello, if it came out and Eagle was married to

Lily, it would be over for us," Ian said. "You think he'd allow the kind of shit we had planned to slide in some kind of punishment? You're deluding yourself there." Ian held his hands up. "I'm taking it to my grave. I don't want any of this shit to ever come out. It's got to stay between all of us. No one can ever know."

"Neither can Chloe. I don't want to hurt her."

"Are you falling in love?" Riley asked.

"Don't take the piss right now. I'm not in the mood. I mean what I say. I don't want to hurt her. I've already done enough of that over the years."

"Then don't film yourself having sex with her. Whatever you do with Chloe is now on your own time," Ian said. "My lips are sealed. This will stay between us."

"Agreed," Riley said. "So, be honest with us, you like her?"

"Yes, I like her. I like her a lot." He rubbed the back of his head, feeling a little uncomfortable with how honest he was being. "It's crazy to think I spent so much time hurting her, you know. It makes me feel a little sick inside."

"I bet."

"Alfie, it's time to go," Eagle said, coming to the edge of the fence.

"That's my cue." He shook Riley and Ian's hands. "Love you guys."

"Aw, he loves us. Maybe we should pin him down and start fucking him," Ian said.

"Fuckers."

He left them out there laughing as he saw his father.

"Did you drink?" Alfie asked.

"Not a drop. I'm good to drive us. Come on."

They climbed into his dad's truck, and he saw a couple of the club whores pouting. Lily had never been liked by the club whores, and Alfie imagined it was because of his father's infatuation with her. Other women had some kind of intuition when it came to that shit.

"So, son, how do you like Lily?" Eagle asked.

"I think she's great. Do you know what has happened to Kurt?" Alfie asked.

"Not heard a peep out of him. He left the club and said he was taking off, needed to clear his head. He's probably trying to convince another club to take his cowardly ass in."

Alfie nodded.

"I want to ask Lily to marry me."

"You do?"

"Yes. I love her, son, and well, I've been waiting a long time to finally have her."

"I know you loved her. Even when she was with Kurt."

"Why didn't you ever ask me about it?" Eagle asked.

"I figured you'd tell me when you were ready. It's what you always told me growing up. That when I was ready to be a man or to tell you something, I'd man up and do it."

"Shit, I fucked up with you, didn't I?"

Alfie laughed. "I think I've come out all right. To some I'm a pain in the ass, but for the most part, I'm adorable."

"Thank you," Eagle said.

"What for?"

"For being a damn good son. You've made me proud so many times over the years. Not when you nearly killed your friend, but I was so fucking scared that day. I knew I shouldn't have whipped your ass, and after I done it, I knew I was wrong. I've always been told that when you have a son, you've got to push him to be the good man. The right kind of man to take over at the club. If not, if I was too soft on you, they'd crush you. That's club life. I want you to know that I do love you, Alfie."

"I think you should propose to Lily more often."

"Shut up, you little shit," Eagle said, laughing. "So this thing with Chloe? Is it the real deal?"

"Yeah, it's the real deal." There was no hesitation.

"Seems kind of sudden."

"Not really. I've been friends with her for a couple of months, so it makes sense."

Eagle chuckled. "Well, treat her right. If she's anything like her mother, she's one of the good ones," he said.

Alfie didn't say anything. There was nothing more to say.

When they got to Lily's place, the lights were still on. Eagle had been given a key, which he used to let himself in.

Lily was on the sofa, and she let out a moan. "Could you please check on Chloe? She didn't look so good an hour ago."

"I'm on it," Alfie said. He left his father to be with Lily. He found Chloe curled up around the toilet, vomiting.

"You shouldn't be here," she said. "You're going to get sick. It's contagious."

"I'm not leaving you."

She started to throw up again, and he put a hand on her back, rubbing. When he pulled her hair back from her face, the stench of vomit was overpowering.

"Please, go."

"Not going to happen."

"This isn't sexy."

"I don't need sexy." He glanced around the

bathroom. "You're burning up."

"I'm never going to be able to look at you again."

"Don't worry. I can look at you all I want." He pulled her sweater off, and she wore a shirt that was soaking wet. "We need to get you cleaned up."

She finished vomiting, and he got to filling the tub with water.

Next, he worked on stripping off her clothes, and she tried to fight him. It was really cute of her to attempt it, but there was no getting away from him.

"Please, leave me alone."

"Not happening."

"I could scream."

"Go ahead. Your mother looks like death, and that would mean my dad would be in here to help you."

"None of them sound like good options."

"Exactly, let me help you, and I can fix this."

"I'm sick, Alfie, not broken."

"True, but maybe after this you'll start to trust me." He got her naked and tried not to pay attention to her body. She was sick, and thinking about her, sex, and more sex, wasn't going to help the situation.

He'd not been with another chick since he'd started to be with Chloe. Women complicated things, and he often spent as little time around people as was humanly possible for him.

With her naked, he grabbed the soap, and the bubbles he'd put into the water hid her from view.

"You've seen me naked now," she said, sniffling. "It's bad, isn't it?"

"What's bad is I'm going to have to make it up to you."

"What?"

"One day you're going to see me naked."

"You still think we're going to have sex?"

"And you don't? This is all about the trust thing, isn't it? You don't trust me, and you never will."

"Alfie?"

He got up. "Look, I've not been a good guy. I know that. I've not even had amazing intentions when it has come to you. I've fucked up at every single turn, but I'm not going to do that now. I'm here, Chloe. I'm here, and there's nowhere else I'd want to be. I've not been with anyone else, and I never will. How about that for commitment?"

"What exactly are you saying, Alfie? Be careful, I may not remember it all."

He smiled. "I'm saying, Chloe Decker, that you and I are officially dating and have been an item for some time. You're my girl, and I'm your guy." He leaned in close but then thought better of it. "I'm not going to kiss you."

"Probably for the best."

"This makes me your first kiss, your first orgasm, and now your first boyfriend. You know I'm going to be your first dick as well."

"You say something so sweet and then screw it up. I find it surreal you've gone from hating me, to liking me."

"I guess spending time with you, I was able to see the error of my ways."

"You know I never thought of myself as better than you or the club." Her voice was croaky from all the heaving.

"I know now."

"I don't make friends easy. I'm awkward, weird, and I'm not a lot of fun to be around. I like to cook and read books."

"I know. I think it's sexy to watch you read."

She laughed and then groaned. "I hope this is all a

dream when I wake up."

"Don't worry. I'm going to go and make you some soup when we're done."

"Do you know how to cook?" she asked.

"Not a chance. I know how to walk to the diner, order soup, and come back and take care of you."

She rested her head back against the bath. "Thank you, Alfie. You know, you're my very first friend as well." She took his hand, linking their fingers together.

"I need to wash your hair." Alfie didn't like the guilt that flooded him from her saying he was her first friend.

"I always wanted to be, you know," she said, sounding more tired than he could recall.

"You always wanted to be what?"

"Your friend. I would wish to be included in your gang. I know I was a girl and my father was branded the way he was, but I knew I'd make a very loyal friend. No one ever gave me the chance to prove it though." She sighed. "Thank you for giving me the chance and not letting me push you away."

"You can't sleep in the bath, princess."

"I'm going to treasure this with you always."

Alfie finished getting her cleaned up, and put her to bed.

On the way downstairs, he offered to go out and get some soup. He needed to clear his head.

He didn't know what was happening to him anymore. Not when it came to Chloe. What had started out as a revenge trick was becoming a little more complicated.

Alfie knew deep down he should just walk away. With his dad now involved, his options were limited. The moment his dad proposed, Alfie didn't have any way out.

Do you want to?

This again was fucking irritating. Whenever he was away from Chloe, he couldn't stop thinking about her, and imagining life without her sucked, which in itself was fucking insane. Crazy insane. He'd spent so much of his life hating this chick, and now, he actually enjoyed spending time with her.

When did it all change?

What the fuck happened to him?

Nothing made any sense, and now he was walking to the diner to go and get soup.

Ian and Riley, even they didn't mind hanging out with Chloe.

Entering the diner, he ordered a couple of cartons of their chicken soup and some burgers for him and his dad.

The club had noticed a change in Eagle though as well. He spent a great deal of time with Lily, and it would seem that woman would make a good, honest man out of anyone.

Waiting for his order, he noticed Kurt lurking around outside on his cell phone. It was the first time he'd seen the man since his apparent cheating.

Grabbing his order, Alfie headed outside just as Kurt finished up a call.

"Hey, kid," he said.

"Kurt."

"What are you doing?"

"I'm taking some food to—" He didn't know what to say. "What are you doing here?"

"I can't do it. I've got to try and win Lily back, man." Kurt ran fingers through his hair. "I'm not going to come crawling back to the club."

"Are you high?"

"No. I mean, I've had a couple of joints."

Alfie looked toward his arms, but in the darkness

couldn't see any signs of track marks. It didn't look good.

"I've got to go."

"I'm heading over to Lily's. I bet she's missed me. She always loved me, and I know I can win back her love."

Alfie paused, counted to ten, and turned. "It's not a good idea for you to go to Lily's."

"Why the fuck not? Look, kid, you may be Eagle's brat, but I don't have to sit around and put up with your shit."

"She's moved on, and you need to get out of town."

"Moved on? That's not possible."

"She has. You coming back here, it's only going to upset her."

"Who?" Kurt asked.

Alfie stared at the man. If Kurt decided to start something, he would be able to take him, no doubt about it. Kurt wasn't a fighter. He acted all hard, but he'd also seen this guy curl up into a ball and beg for whoever it was to stop hurting him. He'd cried like a little girl, and what made it worse, it had been a friendly play fight and Kurt had gotten knocked down by accident as he'd not even been part of it. That was why none of the club liked him, why they tried to avoid him like the fucking plague.

"You need to leave."

"It's Eagle, isn't it?" Kurt asked.

Alfie said nothing. If Eagle married Lily one day, the entire town would know. With Kurt here now, he was surprised he didn't already know.

"You think I didn't notice the way he'd look at her? How he'd react whenever she was around? That piece of shit couldn't stand that I had her. Could he? I knew he had a thing for her, but I figured he got over that shit when he was banging all the other women he liked to party. If he thinks Lily will go to him, pick him over me, he's got another think coming. There's no way, and I mean no way, I'm letting that happen. He couldn't keep his dick in his pants for two minutes."

"Neither could you, and last I checked, my dad is being faithful. You don't have a chance at this, Kurt. You should back the fuck away. Or you will get hurt."

"Is there a problem here?" Eagle asked, coming toward them.

His father looked menacing.

"You took way too long with the soup, son. Lily said to check on you."

Alfie nodded toward Kurt.

"You should get out of town, Kurt. You're not wanted here."

"You mean because you're so busy fucking my wife."

"She's your ex-wife, and I always knew she deserved better than you."

"You're going to regret this, you piece of shit. Both of you. You think you can do that to me, ruin my life and then take my place in my family? You've got another think coming."

Alfie tensed up, ready for a fight, but instead, Kurt got into his car and left, without even throwing a punch.

"He was heading over to Lily's. I didn't know what to say," Alfie said.

"It's fine, son. He didn't hurt you?"

"Please, Kurt couldn't hurt anyone."

"He could if he really wanted to. A coward he is, and he'll always take the easy way out. That's who he is. It's why I've always kept a close eye on him. I'm going to have to keep a couple of guys on his ass. I wouldn't put it past him to go and tell another club our secrets."

"He'd do that? Seriously? Being a rat, he'd be killed within seconds."

"True, but I'll see how he reacts. Come on, let's get this to the girls before the soup is cold."

By the time he got to Lily's house, the soup was just warm enough for them to eat. He left Eagle to tend to Lily while he went upstairs to Chloe's bedroom.

She was curled up, looking so pitiful and exhausted.

"Hello, beautiful," he said, waking her.

Chloe opened her eyes and gave him a smile. It was so fucking sweet.

"You look like death."

"That's what every single girl wants to hear, just how bad they look. You're so sweet."

"I am sweet. I'm here with you, aren't I? I come bearing offerings."

"Of?"

"Soup." He helped her to sit up, and even sick, he could see a beauty to her. Why hadn't he noticed this before? His hatred of her had really gotten to him, and he'd fucked up in so many different ways.

"You went to the diner?"

"Yes."

"They have good soup."

"That they do, and now you get to have it. Open up for Alfie."

She chuckled, opening her mouth as he fed her. "This is so surreal."

"Why?"

"I'm sorry, I just, it's like I've stepped into an alternate reality."

"Where I, the king of the bikers, am feeding you?" he asked.

"My bully is feeding me. You're here in my room, and you're not trying to hurt me."

I was. I was going to make sure the entire world saw you, and now I know how fucked up that was.

"I like your company so much, Alfie," she said.

"I saw your dad today." The guilt was too much.

"Kurt?"

"Do you have any other dad?"

She chuckled. "Fair point. I've not seen him in so long. How is he?"

"He knows about Eagle and Lily."

"Is that a good thing?"

"I don't know. I honestly don't fucking know anything anymore. Do you think he'll do anything stupid?"

"I have no idea. I'd say no because he loves Mom, but now, I mean, she told me she caught him in bed with strippers."

"You and your mom share everything, don't you?"

"Yeah, we're close. She's my best friend. You're not close with your dad?"

"He's got to be president. He has to show the club he's the right one to lead them. It makes any kind of a relationship tough."

"I'm sorry."

"Don't be. I'm not. I'm happy."

"I'm happy you're here and that we're no longer fighting."

"I'm happy to call you mine," he said. "It's still nice to see that no matter how sick you are, I can still get you to blush."

"It's not hard to do," she said, laughing.

"Eat up. You've got to get well so we can get back to scaring the school."

"It is fun to walk down the main corridor, holding hands, while the entire student body looks on with their mouths open. I always wonder if a fly is caught or something."

He chuckled. "Who would have thought out of everything I can do, it would be this, with you, that has them the most shocked."

"I'm guessing, and it is just a guess, they already had a girlfriend in mind for you to pick."

"So you are admitting to being my girlfriend?" he asked.

"You told me I should, remember. I'm simply trying it out."

"And? Do you like it?"

"I could get used to it."

That was fine by him.

Chapter Nine

Three months later

Chloe entered her home on Saturday feeling a little … different. She'd been dating Alfie, officially, for three entire months, and had decided to trust him the night he fed her soup. Well, she had taken their relationship to the next level as she'd just snuck out of Ian's bedroom, but it hadn't been Ian she'd been with. It had been Alfie.

He'd taken another first from her.

Many firsts last night.

Her virginity now belonged to him.

As did her first real party.

Sex at a party.

Sex in a stranger's bed.

Sex in his best friend's bed.

Drinking.

Dancing.

He'd made sure she had fun, and well, the soreness between her thighs was a testament to that.

"You stayed out all night," Lily said, leaning against the doorway in the hall.

"Hey, Mom." Her hands were shaking, so she clenched them into fists. "Morning."

"You were out all night. Ian's party must have been really something."

"There were kids from high school, and it was fun."

"Fun?" Lily asked.

She couldn't do it anymore. It was like her mother knew and all this was for her was the torture she intended to inflict until she knew the truth. "I had sex with Alfie last night."

The moment she said it she slapped a hand across

her mouth. She wanted to run to her bedroom and hide, but she stayed perfectly still, rooted to the spot, unable to move.

Lily paused and didn't say anything.

They stared at each other, neither of them breaking their silence.

Finally, a knock at the door interrupted them.

"I'll get it."

Her mother put the coffee in Chloe's hand and opened the door, only to find the guy of the night before, standing right there.

"Hello, Lily, I'm here to see Chloe."

"Hello, Alfie. It would seem my daughter has more to tell me than I realized. You have two minutes with her, and then I want her in the kitchen and you're to go home. You both better hope you used protection last night." Lily took her cup from Chloe's hand, leaving them both alone.

Alfie stepped into the hallway and closed the door.

"You snuck out."

"Yes."

"Look at me, Chloe. Don't hide from this."

"I wasn't quiet enough. I only just got home." She tucked some of her hair behind her ear and wrapped her arms around herself. "I wasn't going to sleep with you last night."

"Neither was I. I just wanted us to have some fun, and I don't want you to freak out about last night."

"I'm already there." She pressed her lips together. "I don't know what you want from me, Alfie."

He stepped toward her.

She didn't move.

He stroked his fingers down her cheek. "I'd like you to look at me and realize that … last night meant everything to me."

She stared into his eyes, wanting to believe, and as he looked right back at her, she saw it.

"You did?"

"Chloe, I'm not a great guy. There are things you don't know about me. What I've done. What I'm capable of, but believe me when I say, when it comes to you and this now, I'm one hundred percent committed. I want this. I want you. Being your first everything is all I want from you." He cupped her face, tilting her head back so she had no choice but to look him in the eye. "You're my girl, just as I'm your guy." He slammed his lips down on hers, and she let out a little moan.

"Do not have sex in my hallway," Lily said, calling from the kitchen.

Chloe tensed up, and Alfie laughed.

"We won't," he said. "Can I come by later?"

"I have a feeling I'm going to be grounded."

"So, I can get Dad to distract her, and I can sneak in."

"This is so wrong, but yes, I want to see you." This time she held him as she kissed him hard.

He groaned. "I better go, as otherwise I will be taking you." He stepped out of the door and smiled at her. "Last night was the best night I ever had. No doubt about it, and I'm going to want to repeat it."

"I'm kind of sore."

"I won't repeat tonight. I'll let you rest." He held her hand, giving it a squeeze, before letting her go. She watched him walk away, on cloud nine, dizzy with desire, and happiness, and just everything in between.

Closing the door, she found a coffee waiting for her in the dining room.

She took a seat and waited. Lily hadn't spoken yet. Picking up the cup of coffee, Chloe took a sip. It was red-hot.

"We used protection," she said.

"And it didn't break?"

"No, it didn't."

Lily took a breath.

"I … I wanted to. Alfie didn't force me or convince me. I really did enjoy last night, Mom."

Lily turned to her with a smile, and there were tears in her eyes. "You reminded me so much of what it was like the first time with your father."

"Ew, Mom."

"I know. I know. I had no one to talk to. Of course, everyone thought I was insane. Your father, he wore the leather cut, and he'd brag all day about how he was going to prospect and earn his patch. I didn't care about the biker element. My parents hated it, but I didn't. I knew his heart was sweet, at the time. He had so many plans for all of us." Lily put her hands against her face. "I know you and Alfie have come a long way, but is this really what you want? Have your plans changed for leaving town when you graduate? To go to culinary school? It's what you've dreamed about for so long. Has it all changed?"

"I don't know," Chloe said. "When he first started to hang out with me, I thought he was faking it, you know. Trying to trick me or something. Now, I don't know."

"You still think he's trying to trick you after everything?"

"No, no, of course not. I do believe he cares, a lot. I just don't know if this is something he cares about long-term." She shrugged. "I don't know what to do."

"What does it feel like when you're with him?"

"Like we're the only two people in the world and for the first time in my life, I don't have to care what anyone else thinks or feels about me. It feels real to me. Last night was the best night of my life, and I don't know if I can walk away from that. Do you think I could be … falling for him?"

"I think that's something only you can know."

"I don't know if I can handle this. What if it's not long-term? What if he likes the club women more?"

Lily reached out, taking her hand. "Not all men need more than one woman to satisfy them. Some need just one."

Chloe stared down at her mother's wedding ring finger. "Dad never got you a diamond engagement ring."

Lily pulled her hand away, and Chloe watched as she teased the ring across her finger. "Eagle was here last night."

She was surprised. Unless it was serious club business or he had to go out of town for whatever reason, Eagle was always home.

"And?"

"He proposed."

"He did?"

"Yeah, and I said yes. He told me he'd been in love with me for a while, and well, I feel differently when I'm around him."

"You don't think it's too soon, after Dad?" Chloe asked.

"I said to Eagle I haven't been a divorced woman for long and I loved Kurt so deeply."

"He still wanted to marry you?"

"He said that he'd seen my marriage decline and knew it was going to end. No way could a woman take that kind of pain and betrayal. He's willing to wait for as long as I am to make sure my feelings are in the same place," she said. "How can you not love a man with patience, Chloe? This shouldn't be about me. This is all about you."

"No. No. This is about you," Chloe said. The less they talked about her and Alfie the better. "This is a huge step. Do you love Eagle?"

"I think I do. I … he's … different."

"Different?"

"From your father. I really shouldn't be talking to you about this. I loved your father."

"Mom, you don't have to justify my feelings when it comes to Dad. You know that. He broke your heart more than once, and I had to see how upset he made you. I've never seen you smile as much as you do when you're with Eagle. He makes you happy, doesn't he?"

"He does, but … he's a biker. He's got huge responsibilities, and I don't know if I want to be part of that, and it sounds so selfish to me."

"No, of course it doesn't. You're not a selfish person at all." She hugged her mom. "You have a right to be happy."

"I do?" Lily asked.

Chloe laughed. "Do you think you don't have any right to be happy?"

"Your father."

"Mom, don't try and do this because you think you owe him or me, or anyone else. If Eagle makes you happy, then trust in your feelings. I've seen the way he is around you, and I think it's amazing how sweet he is."

Lily smiled. "He does make me feel … alive. Is that weird? He even took me on his bike the other day, and I've never felt such a rush before in my life."

"Then don't worry about it, or me, or anything else. Be happy. I know I am."

"And what does this mean for you and leaving?"

"It means … I don't know what it means. Part of

me thinks I should just carry on. What if it doesn't last the rest of the year and I change my plans?"

"And what is the other part of you saying? I know my daughter, and she will always have two sides of herself competing in this race."

She sighed. "She's wondering if she should stay and give this a try. I'm so confused."

"Honey, you don't have to make any decisions right away."

"I don't?"

"No, do what you have to do. Let this run its course. You know you want to." Lily took her hand. "We're just a couple of silly women overthinking every single aspect of our lives, and we should just enjoy what we've got."

"You're right. I love you, Mom."

"I love you too, sweetie."

****

Later that night Alfie climbed through Chloe's bedroom window. His father was downstairs with Lily and he couldn't exactly sneak into the house, so he had no choice but to come to his girl through her bedroom window.

"I don't know how they do it in the movies to make it look so effortless."

"You know they're not really climbing up a building. It's all green rooms, props, ladders."

"It would have been easier with a ladder." He grabbed her hips and pulled her closer. "I missed you."

"You've been busy, so how is that possible?"

"Simple, I thought of you every single second today and wondered how you were." He pulled away from her to get a good look at her. "Are you okay? Are you sore? How are you feeling?"

"A lot of questions."

"You skipped out on me and you think I wouldn't have any questions."

"I didn't want to skip out. I woke up, realized what we did, and had a little panic attack." She stepped away from him, sitting on the edge of her bed. She wore a pair of red shorts and a white T-shirt. He took a seat beside her, taking hold of her hand so she didn't have a single excuse to pull away from him.

"Do you regret us being together?" he asked.

"No. I don't regret that. I told you I was ready, and I wouldn't lie to you." She lifted up his hand and kissed his knuckles. "Last night was so magical and fantastic, and I woke up this morning and I freaked. I didn't even mean to freak. I know it sounds crazy, but I honestly just had to get out of there. I thought you'd regret it or something."

"There's no chance in hell of me ever regretting what you and I had last night. I know I've not always been a great guy to you, Chloe."

"You don't have to keep bringing it up."

"I want to. I want you to know that I'm doing everything to prove to you I'm the man for you."

She smiled. "Again, you really need to stop. It's really not necessary. I know you've got a big heart, and you thought I was stuck up. I get it. I do. I trust you."

Now he felt the guilt, the wave upon wave of it as if it was crushing him.

"You do, just like that, forgive me?"

"Of course. Why wouldn't I? I mean, when you first started hanging around with me, yeah, I had my doubts. I'm sure any woman would have. Now though, after everything, I believe you. I trust you."

Trust and loyalty, the two rules of the club.

He didn't start out with good intentions, though, and she didn't know that. After what he felt last night, claiming her virginity as his own, he couldn't ever let her know the truth of what he'd really intended for her.

Ian and Riley, he'd already seen them, and they agreed.

Trust and loyalty came before everything else within the club. This was their chance to prove to each other they have their backs, and under no circumstances would that news ever come out. Not ever. Not even a slither.

"I'm glad you could trust me." He stared down at their hands. "I won't do anything to let you down."

"Alfie, please stop. I meant it. I trust you." She giggled. "I don't know what this is. Are you feeling guilty because of … last night?"

"You *did* give me your virginity."

"You haven't slept with a virgin before?" Her cheeks were bright red.

"No."

"No?"

"You're my first and last virgin." He leaned in to take her lips, but she placed her hand on his lips, halting him. "What is it?"

"I planned to leave at the end of high school. There's a culinary school in the city, Mom signed me up for it before we started this last year."

"You told me."

"I don't know if I should go," she said.

Now he pulled back and didn't try to steal another kiss. "You don't know if you should go? Because of me?"

She nodded. "I'm a little confused. I wasn't going to talk about this."

"You want this though, right? I can move to the city. Come with you. Or I'll visit if you're in one of those girly dorms and can't have visitors. I could be your sexy ass biker boyfriend. You know, the kind that makes people squeal and go crazy. You will be the talk of the entire college."

"It's not a college per se. It's a culinary school. I'm not going to a dorm. I'm going to be renting a small apartment. My mom and I already checked it over, and the school owns the building and we've reserved me a spot."

Alfie held her hands. "Don't stop your plans for me. We'll make this work."

"Long distance?"

"We've made it work after I've bullied you. I'd say we'd call it even." He had to find any way to make this up to her, in his own mind. She would never know the truth, not while he was in charge, and it was the only way he could be.

"When did you get so perfect?" she asked.

"It would seem you really do bring out the best in people."

This time, Chloe kissed him. "There is something I want to ask you."

It took every single ounce of willpower not to freak out at that one tiny little question. He smiled, and pretended all was normal in the world and in his life. "You can ask me anything."

"The time on the bench. Start of school. The banana peel thrown at me. You know, when my dad was supposed to pick me up?"

Oh, he knew all right. It was the time he started to put his whole plan in motion. "I remember."

"You tackled me to the ground and held me down. I was just wondering how far you were willing to go before my mom showed up."

He'd every intention of scaring her away. "I'm not a rapist, just so you know. Erm, I wanted to scare you. I had no intention of following through with what you thought I was going to do."

"You weren't?"

"No, so you shouldn't worry. I won't ever hurt you because now I know the truth, and I only regret what I made you feel."

"I feel like I've walked into a strange alternate reality. You really thought that *I* thought I was better than you and the club?"

"Yes."

She chuckled. "Wow. I never thought that, ever. I told you before I hated the way my dad always wanted your guys' approval and to be a patched in member, but other than that, I didn't care." She rested her head on his shoulder. "Your dad finally proposed to my mother."

"Good. She makes him so happy."

"What will happen once my dad finds out?" She lifted her head.

"Have you seen him?"

Eagle put out a little search for Kurt within the club. If anyone saw him lurking around town, or near Lily, they had to contact him immediately. Other than the time near the diner, Alfie hadn't seen him since.

"No, I haven't. I wonder if he's moved on, you know. Found a new place somewhere. Do you miss him?"

"Sometimes. When I was a kid, he did miss important stuff, but he'd come back with a toy or he'd take me out, and we'd laugh before it all happened again. It wasn't an entirely bad experience growing up. I had my mom, and she had my dad. It's only in the past few years has it gotten so bad." She shrugged.

"Will you want to see him again?" Alfie asked.

"I don't know. I'm still a little mad at him for what he did. I know that my mom found him cheating on her, but at the same time, they weren't together. I don't know. That's a little grey area, seeing as they hadn't divorced yet, and knowing my mom, she'd have wanted to make it work. Forget it, I just blah out of my mouth."

He chuckled and held her close. "You can talk to me any time you want and blah out your feelings."

"You can't stay the night."

"I know. My dad said he'd be home as well."

"How has he been since he's been dating my mom?" she asked.

"He's been … like a real dad. How is that for weird?"

"Do you like it?"

"I'm not sure. He asked me three days ago if I had any homework."

She giggled. "Yeah?"

"Yeah, I kind of freaked out. I asked him if he wasn't feeling well. He said he was feeling fine, but you know what it's like."

"I think so."

"Come on. I want to hold you while you go to sleep."

"You think I can sleep through you climbing out of my window?"

"Yes, I'm hoping to do it, stealthily."

She laughed again, and he loved the sound.

He pushed off his boots, making sure they didn't make a sound. Leaning back on her bed, Chloe got under the covers and snuggled up against him.

"I think I could get used to this."

He wrapped his arms around her, not wanting to let her go. She felt so amazing against him, and last night was the best night of his life. The sex, it hadn't been the best because she'd hurt, and seeing those tears in her eyes as he'd filled her with his cock, he'd never felt so protective in his life.

These new emotions were all inspired because of his feelings for Chloe. He'd told Ian and Riley it wasn't about revenge anymore or keeping up appearances for his dad. He did, in fact, have feelings for her, and he needed for them to keep his secret about the truth of what they had once planned.

They had both promised, and he would do whatever it took to keep Chloe.

He finally knew what it was like to have a woman worth keeping, and Chloe, she was worth every single second of it.

Chapter Ten

Two months later

Lily had already left with Eagle, and Chloe waited for Alfie to turn up. She opened her cell phone and didn't see any other text from him.

The fair had come to town, and with it, everyone that she knew was heading toward the large field to do some dancing, partying, and to just have a good time. Every single year the fair came with rides and special booths to win prizes. It was a big deal in the Satan's Croft tourist calendar, as it stayed for a couple of weeks, brought tourists, and it was a chance to put themselves out there on the map of places people wanted to visit.

It was also the one time the MC kind of stayed at home. The leather cuts were sometimes worn, but for the most part, they mingled with the town and just had fun. The fair was kind of like the only place they couldn't bring a fight.

Alfie had asked for her to wait for him to enter as he wanted to take her on the back of his bike.

He'd gotten it last month, and since then, he'd been promising to take her for a ride, and tonight it would seem would be her night.

Most kids got a car; Alfie got a bike.

He'd told her he'd been promised the bike months ago, and Eagle had been waiting for the guy to finish it up, and Chloe could see why. It was a damn sexy machine, and the way Alfie stroked it as he showed the bike off, well, she'd been a little, tiny bit jealous.

Not anymore as he said he needed to break his bike in to make sure it was safe to take his most precious cargo, which would be her.

How could a girl not swoon over that?

She had, and now she was waiting.

She'd even worn jeans for the occasion.

The rumble of the bike made her smile, and she walked outside, being careful to close and lock the door behind her.

Alfie was at the curb. He wasn't wearing a helmet, and he turned off the bike and winked at her.

"Hello there, little lady, I hear you're waiting for a ride?"

"That I am, sir. I'm a damsel in distress, and my boyfriend totally forgot about me." She played along.

"Well, if I was your boyfriend, you'd never be forgotten."

"Oh, promises."

"Jump on, hot stuff," he said.

She climbed on the back of the bike.

"Wait, you get to wear the helmet," he said.

"You're kidding me, right?"

"Nope. Dad's rules. Take it up with him. When we're a little older I'll take you for a ride without a helmet, but until then, you've got to wear the helmet."

"I hate this. A lot." She put the helmet on. "Does it look okay?"

"You look sexy as fuck, and I just knew you would. Climb on, sexy lady."

She laughed, but did as he asked. She didn't have a clue where to put her hands.

"They, sexy, need to go around me." He pulled her hands around his waist, and she rolled her eyes.

"Like this?" she asked.

"Yes, exactly like that. Now hold on tight."

He started the bike, and she let out a little cry.

"Don't you worry about a thing."

He pulled away from the curb, and she burst out laughing as he started to ride. He couldn't have been going faster than ten.

"You know, a baby could out-crawl us at this rate," she said.

"I'm not having anything bad happen to you."

Whenever he said sweet words like that, it always made her ache everywhere. He was always so sweet, attentive, affectionate, and he always surprised her, which she truly didn't think was possible, but when it came to Alfie, he did, at everything.

Finally, he started to ride properly.

"We'll make it before the fair packs up and moves onto the next town."

"I know, but here I was thinking you'd like to spend the time at home, alone, you know, having sex."

She held him a little tighter. "Another time." She wanted to kiss him, but the helmet was in the way.

They were no longer the talk of the entire school when he'd kiss her, and he walked her to every single class, even when it was far out of his way. Of course, there were also a few classes where the teachers had to tell him to let her go so she could sit in her own seat. No matter how many times she argued with Alfie to let her go, he'd always keep on holding her. It was always the teachers' job to spoil his fun, and he made it known to the teachers they were doing exactly that.

He didn't like to be told what to do, by anyone.

She couldn't believe how far they'd come. From two enemies, to a couple. He'd even presented her with a rose on Valentine's Day, the day of romance, and the school had been humming with that little detail in their relationship.

There were still moments, she felt she had to pinch herself as they didn't feel real, but they were.

Her feelings for Alfie over the past couple of months had grown to a fever pitch. She'd been tempted multiple times to cancel her place at the culinary school to give someone else the chance to take her spot. Each time, he'd tell her not to, that he'd find some way to make it work with her.

She'd always have her doubts, but then he'd start talking about riding around the city, going out to dinner, and showing her he could make it work.

Pushing all those thoughts aside, she saw the fair up ahead. The large movie screen was blaring out some holiday movie. It was always there for the kids to enjoy when they were screaming or on one of the rides. There was always an attendant there, monitoring it.

Alfie parked his bike, and she climbed off. Her legs felt a little like jelly, but they'd not ridden far and she didn't have to worry about falling on her ass.

Removing the helmet, she ran her fingers through her hair, working out the flatness because of the helmet.

"You look stunning," Alfie said, wrapping his arms around her waist, going straight to her ass and pulling her close.

"You know how to say the right things."

"I told you, I'm not interested in how you look. I'm only interested in you." He pressed a kiss to her lips. "And a couple of other things."

"Alfie, it's safe to say you're always thinking about sex."

"That I am. When it comes to you, I just can't help it." He pressed a kiss to her lips, and seconds later, she heard the male whistling and catcalling.

Alfie broke the kiss with a groan.

Ian and Riley were waiting for them. "I can find new friends."

"We heard that, and you wish you could find new friends," Ian said.

"What have you done with our friend, Chloe? I swear there was a time he used to like us."

"He still does, but he likes me just a little more."

Alfie took her hand and led her into the fair toward his friends.

He didn't let her go as he did some friendly handshake with each of them, hugging them.

"You don't have dates?" Alfie asked.

"Nah, only you seem happy with the one kind of girl. No offense, Chloe," Riley said.

"None taken. Believe me."

"We're going to see what chick comes to us. Be it three or four, we're not picky," Ian said.

Chloe laughed as they made their way through the maze of people. She spotted her mother near the guns, shooting at targets, and gave her a wave. Lily gave her two thumbs up before going back to the game.

"I want to win you a giant teddy bear," Alfie said.

"A giant teddy?"

"Yes. It's only fair. When you're off at your fancy culinary school, which I love because it means you'll feed me everything you cook, and I won't have to guess who cooked it, you can cuddle up with the bear, and pretend it's me."

She rolled her eyes. "I don't need a bear. I will remember who you are, Alfie."

"I know, and I'll be reassured with the bear. I'll buy it a leather jacket."

He pulled her toward several games, none of which had any kind of giant bear, but she played along with him. They lost nearly every single game they played. Afterward, they needed to get more change so they could play, and they shared some cotton candy.

"Does the culinary school bother you?" she asked.

"No. I just don't want you to forget about me."

"Alfie, that's not possible. We're dating."

"I know."

He dumped their empty cotton candy containers into the trash can and held her close, hugging her.

She forgot everything and everyone as he kissed her hard, making love to her mouth with a passion that completely stole her breath.

When he broke the kiss, she heard giggling, and glancing around, she saw some people were looking at them and then pointing at the screen.

"What the fuck is going on?" Alfie asked.

She looked toward the screen, and her heart started to pound.

No way.

It wasn't possible.

She would never forget that night.

Alfie spun and looked up at the screen.

"Holy shit," he said.

"It hurts," she said, gasping.

"I know. The pain will go. Believe me, it will. I've got you, Chloe. You feel so fucking amazing."

He'd told her he'd never felt anything like it, but right now, the entire town was seeing this. It was playing for all to see. There was no doubt in anyone's mind what was going on.

Words ran across the bottom of the screen: *She believed it all, but it's a lie. How could the fatty be with the biker?*

Tears filled Chloe's eyes as she stared up at the big screen. This couldn't be happening to her. Not now. Not in front of everyone in town. No matter how she pinched her arm, or wiped away the tears, or hoped it would all stop, the images kept on changing, between the night she lost her virginity, her cries, gasps, moans, even Alfie's. It was all there for others to see.

Alfie stood beside her, and the club was there as

well just without their patch. Her mother was having to see this. Ian and Riley, everyone from school.

It was the fair that came to town every single year and was the highlight of Satan's Croft, and brought in tourists. It was the fair she adored, loved, and this year, she had decided to come with her boyfriend, only, he wasn't her boyfriend. There was usually a movie playing on the big screen for those to enjoy while they weren't taking their turn on the rides, mostly for the kids, and where was it? Why was everyone watching this? This was so humiliating.

"Chloe," Alfie said. She pulled away from him as different shots of her with him showed up. The changes over the past six months as she came to feel about him. At first it showed her being hesitant with him, and gradually, she saw herself change. Rather than brush off his touch, she basked in it.

Everyone saw her fall for him.

The entire town.

"All of this was a lie?" she asked. "You planned this?"

She couldn't look. The tears kept on falling, and no matter how many times she tried to swat them away, she just couldn't make it stop.

"Please, I didn't do this. We were being filmed without my knowledge."

"You wanted to do something like this, though. Make me pay, for what? For not understanding my dad's love of your stupid club!" She screamed the last bit. "I told you the truth. I told you everything, and this is what it was all along. Some stupid lesson because you couldn't handle that I was different? That I wasn't searching for some kind of ticket to make me part of your fucking world."

"Chloe, I swear—"

"What? You swear what? This wasn't all part of your plan?"

"Not anymore, okay? Yes, it started out as punishment. As me wanting to show you that you weren't better than us. But I never made that tape, and I never wanted this!"

"Congratulations, you got your wish. Now everyone knows." She turned on her heel, needing to get away. People were laughing, smirking and it was still playing in the background.

She got it.

Message received, loud and clear.

"Chloe, don't go." Alfie reached out to grab her arm, but she pulled away.

More than anything, she wanted to smack him across his smug face, and tell him to go and eat shit, and to hurt him. The pain inside herself was more than anything she could bear. She felt the betrayal everywhere.

"The entire town," she said, gritting her teeth. "Don't come near me."

"Chloe, please, I swear to you, this wasn't me. I fell in love with you."

She laughed. "You really expect me to believe that?"

"Not after what you just saw, but everything was real."

"No, it wasn't real, Alfie. I don't know when you changed your mind, or if you ever did and it was changed for you. I don't know. What we started, it's not real. You only did this to hurt me. Your main ambition in getting close to me was to cause me pain. Congratulations, you achieved what you set out to do. I'm not some virginal girl anymore. You fucked me, loud and clear. Now stay away from me. I mean it."

She backed away, and turned, not daring to look at anyone as she pushed her way out of the crowd, and away from him.

In her head, she kept on chanting the same thing.

She should have known. Shame on her.

****

"Shit, dude," Ian said.

"Find out who filmed us, and bring them to me." Alfie wanted blood.

Lily and Eagle broke through the crowd, and the fire in her eyes made Alfie's blood turn cold.

"Where is she?" she asked.

"Lily, sweetie, we can handle this."

"She didn't trust you, you know. She was scared that you would try something like this, and I told her that she was too cynical. You will stay away from my daughter," Lily said.

He'd never seen such hatred in Lily's eyes in all of his life. He'd put that there because of what he'd done.

He watched, and it was like he was having an out-of-body experience.

"I can fix this," Eagle said.

"No, you can't. You can't turn back the clock and stop that. I can't marry you, Eagle. I can't be with someone who raises a son to do that kind of thing to my daughter, and I would never put her through the kind of pain your son did. We're through."

Alfie watched with a sinking heart as Lily removed the engagement ring she'd not long ago slid on her finger and gave it back to his father.

This shit wasn't going to end well.

Whoever had filmed him, done this, well, they had a death wish.

Lily turned on her heel and went the exact same way her daughter did.

Alfie watched her go.

"Dude, you need to leave," Ian said.

Eagle approached them. "I suggest you three get your fucking asses to the club, now. If I have to come hunting for you, I will personally cut your dicks off and make you eat them."

Alfie watched his father go.

They were still alive.

For now.

He didn't know exactly how long that would last.

Probably not very long.

"Fuck!" Alfie rushed toward the back of the movie screen to see the man in charge fast asleep.

"You think he's been drugged?"

Alfie didn't know what to do. He grabbed the equipment and pulled out the tape. Whoever had filmed him better leave town. He was going to come for them.

With the tape in his hand, he tucked it into his jacket.

He'd lost her.

Alfie just stood there, staring at the ground, completely fucking lost.

"Dude, you're starting to scare me," Riley said, grabbing his shoulder.

Alfie shoved him away hard. "Did any of you two know about this?" he asked.

"Whoa, whoa, you be careful, Alfie," Ian said. "We're your brothers. Your best friends, we wouldn't do this. You know that."

"Then how the fuck did it get on there? It was at your party."

"There were a lot of people at my party," Ian said, yelling right back. "We've got to get to the clubhouse and deal with Eagle."

"We're all fucking dead, you know that, right?"

Alfie didn't know if he could face his father, not with lies or promises to make it better. "I've lost her. I've lost Chloe. She'll never forgive me."

"We can fix this."

"There is a lot of shit in life we can't fix that is exactly like this, Ian. I don't know how I'm going to win her back."

"We'll help," Riley said. "We saw what she means to you, and we won't let you down."

Alfie laughed. "No, there's no coming back from this."

"It's not over until it's over," Ian said.

"We've got to face your father, and we've got to find out who filmed you" Riley said. "Then we'll figure out a way for you to win Chloe back."

Alfie nodded, running a hand down his face. He followed his friends, heading back to the car park.

"Nice, Alfie. You really know how to stick it to the fat girl." One of the guys, he didn't know who, from the football team teased as he walked past.

Alfie didn't stop to think. He charged the group, to the guy that had shot that shit at him. Grabbing him around the throat, he pinned him against one of the games. People gasped.

"You think that's funny?" Alfie asked, squeezing the very life from him. He wasn't a man to be played with.

His entire plan and life had been fucked up, and he was gunning for everyone who dared to speak against Chloe to him.

"Dude, not today. We can't do this today," Ian said, coming to put a hand on his shoulder.

Even though he knew it was hopeless, he couldn't allow his feelings to get in the way, not right now.

"You're lucky. I hear anything about Chloe or

me, or this, and I will personally cut out your tongue." He gave another squeeze and shoved the man to the ground. Leaving the fair, he climbed on his bike. The helmet sat mocking him as he'd wanted to take Chloe out for a ride after the fair.

He was so fucking pissed off. Straddling his bike, he rode across town to the MC clubhouse.

There were several bikes parked, but only a few men lingered. None of them spoke as he, Ian, and Riley each made their way inside.

Whatever was about to happen, it wasn't going to be good for any of them. Entering the clubhouse, he saw several tables were overturned and the bar was smashed up.

"So, do you want to tell me what you boys think to completely disregard what I demanded. Not only am I your father, Alfie, I'm your fucking president."

"I wasn't going to go through with that."

"Do you know how this makes me look?"

"Dad," Alfie said.

"No. You don't get to dad me. Not right now." Eagle stepped up to him and glared at him. "I've killed men for less than what you did today."

"We didn't do the tape," Ian said.

"Shut up, Ian," Alfie said.

"You didn't do the tape? You know what makes that worse? You boys were so fucking sloppy. You couldn't even tell when you were being filmed. Ask yourself why I should even allow you in my club."

"I'm in love with Chloe," Alfie said. "I can fix this."

This time, Eagle burst out laughing. "News flash, son, she's not going to forgive you. In front of the entire town, they saw her lose her virginity. Do you think there is any way for you to come back from this? That girl is no club whore. She's not the kind of woman who fucks multiple men and is happy for it to be played to thousands of people." Eagle shook his head. "If I touch you right now, if I react, I will fucking kill you. You are all banned from the club indefinitely."

"Dad?"

"No. What I see before me is three traitors. To this club and to me personally. You knew what Lily meant to me. I care, Alfie. I fucking love that woman, and I told you, all of you, to leave Chloe alone. You disregarded that, and now, you can pay the price. You're not even prospects yet, but if you can't take a single instruction in high school, then I don't want you in my club. Get out."

Chapter Eleven

One week later

"Please, Chloe, open the door. I know you're in here." Alfie gripped the doorway, knocking and hoping against hope she'd open the motherfucking door. So far, nothing.

He'd been trying to see her every single chance he had. For now, he wasn't allowed in the club, and when his father returned home, he wouldn't even talk to him. Ian and Riley were experiencing the same level of abandonment, and they only had themselves to blame. He'd fucked up big time, and he'd ended up taking his friends with him, which he didn't like.

Lily wouldn't even look at him.

Chloe hadn't returned to school.

The bad shit on her locker had, and each day, he cleaned it for her, and if he found whoever did it, he would beat the shit out of them, boy or girl. He'd get one of the club whores to handle the girls, or something. He'd not figured out everything yet, but he would, he had no doubt.

"Come on. I know you're there."

Her locker had been cleaned out earlier today. He'd seen the principal taking all of her stuff, and he'd heard through the rumor mill she wasn't ever coming back to school.

A week without seeing her.

It was killing him.

"I'm not going to leave. You can call the cops and I'll be back once they remove me. Please, Chloe, shit, this wasn't supposed to be this way."

The door opened. "Then what was it supposed to be like?"

She looked a mess. Her eyes were bright red, skin

pale. She looked sick.

"Chloe."

She held her hand up, making him stop. "No. You don't get to come near me. I want nothing to do with you."

"Please, let me try and make it up to you. Let me try to explain, it wasn't how it went down."

"It wasn't how it went down? Are you freaking kidding me right now? Okay, hotshot, tell me how it was supposed to go down? Were you and Ian going to take turns while Riley held the camera? What was going to happen? Not only do I sleep with you, it's exactly what you intended." She slapped her hand to her forehead. "I even knew you were lying. The moment you started to show any kind of interest, I knew it, and what's worse, I still went along with it. I started to think I was going crazy, that it was clearly all in my head, but it wasn't, was it? You wanted to hurt me. To bring me down a peg or maybe drag me to the floor kicking and screaming. That's what you wanted."

"It was in the beginning, but it changed. *I* changed."

"Really? You're going to start telling me how you saw the error of your ways."

"It started to feel real, Chloe. You, me, this, us."

"There is no us."

"I didn't film us. That night and every single night since then with you has been amazing, incredible. I would never do anything to hurt you."

"But you did," she said.

He saw the tears, and it broke him apart.

"Chloe, I can fix this."

"You can't. I can't go to school. Everyone saw that tape, and I don't trust you."

"I didn't do it."

"But someone did. Someone you don't know got the proof." She pressed her lips together.

"Don't cry, Chloe, please don't cry."

"I … I didn't trust you. I didn't think there was a single nice bone in your body." She took a deep breath. "But I started to see something amazing in you. Something that thrilled me, and made everything exciting. I truly started to believe you."

"Don't give up on me. I'm begging you. I can make this work."

"You can? You can stop people moaning or pointing. Laughing. I went to the grocery store today, and I got all that. I never ever thought of myself as better than you, or any of you." She was sobbing. "If you want to know the truth, all I ever wanted was to be able to fit in, to be part of you and your group. You all treated me as if I was an extension of my dad, but you're not even a friend because someone who cares, who loves you, wouldn't be looking for ways to bring you down. I'm finishing my schooling, and then I'm out of here."

"Chloe."

"If you care at all for me, you will leave me alone. You will go and let me live my life. You won, Alfie. Take the win and leave me the fuck alone." She slammed the door closed, and he heard the lock click.

"I love you, Chloe. No matter where you go or what happens, I will always love you, and there's nothing you can do to change that." He rested his head on the door, wishing he could think of the right words to say, or something that would make her see sense.

"You need to leave," Lily said.

He turned to see her in the driveway. She looked just as pale and sad. "My dad had nothing to do with this, Lily, I swear. He told me not to bully Chloe, and I stopped. I stopped … doing everything. I promise you, I love her, and I want to do whatever it takes to make it right. You don't have to call the wedding off or the engagement, or anything."

"You know I told my daughter to be fairer to you. To give you a chance and then I had to see what I did. I'm not going to force my daughter to do anything she doesn't want to do, and you need to leave."

"Lily, I promise you, my dad—"

"It doesn't matter. My daughter will always come first, and if I were to marry Eagle, it would mean being close to you. Every time she sees Eagle, she'll remember you. I'm not going to do that to my daughter, and neither are you. You will leave her alone." Lily pushed past him, and he watched her step into the house.

This was useless. He knew that.

Leaving Chloe's house, it tore his world apart as he didn't want to leave her behind.

They were going to make this work. He'd stay at Satan's Croft as a prospect to the club, she'd get her culinary qualification or whatever it was she wanted, and she'd come back here, open her own place, and it would all work.

Everything was perfectly mapped out, at least in his head, and now, it was all fucked up because of him.

Ian and Riley met up with him as he crossed the road heading into town.

"You okay?"

"No. Do I look okay?"

"You don't need to bite my head off, just asking is all," Riley said.

"You're right. I'm not okay. Any of your folks talking to you?" Alfie asked.

"Nope," Ian said. "My house is completely silent. Even my mom won't talk to me, and she's not even cooking for me either."

"I've got nothing. Dad took my bike and my credit card," Riley said. "I've already put in a couple of applications for a job. They won't support me. I've got a bed, and that's it."

"My bike's gone. Dad trashed it with a bat," Alfie said. "It's nothing but a pile of metal in the back yard."

"Welcome to being the assholes that we are," Ian said.

"I need to know who was at your party. Who had a beef with us, and who would film that shit," Alfie said. "I've got to fix this one way or the other."

"You know I didn't exactly send out invitations. Anyone could have been filming us at any given time." Ian shrugged. "I've gone all over my bedroom, and the only way they would have gotten away with that was by standing at the window, filming you guys. You didn't see anything?" Ian asked. "I've got a little cabinet next to the window. Someone must have planted a camera on the cabinet, filming you. Then when you were asleep, they took the camera back. I don't know. It sounds too perfect."

Alfie rubbed at his eyes. "I can't do this right now. I fucked up, but I never thought I'd lose her to this."

"We'll help you, man. We'll get her back for you."

He knew it wasn't going to be easy, but he was more than willing to fight for it.

****

"I don't want you losing Eagle because of me," Chloe said as her mother entered. She sat on the bottom step, and it overlooked the doorway. She got another glance of Alfie, and he looked heartbroken.

She hated seeing him like this, but there was no way she could forgive this.

161

"I do."

"No, Mom, you don't. I'm not going to let you sacrifice your happiness for me or because of me. I love you too much to let you do something like this."

"Sweetheart, it's not your decision. This is mine, and you think I could stand to see you go after what happened?"

"You heard Alfie. It wasn't Eagle."

"I know, but I can't do it. What would people think if I married him?"

"Who cares what people think?"

"I care what people think of you." Lily put her shopping down and walked over to her, cupping her face. "Now, I know you don't think all that much of yourself, and I don't care. I really don't because I love you, and I know how amazing, beautiful, sweet, and wonderful you really are. I love you more than anyone else in this world, and so, I'm not going to let a man or anything come between us."

"Mom, you deserve to be happy."

"And I will be."

"You were falling for Eagle, don't lie to me."

"I was falling, yes, but I wasn't there. I'm not going to budge on this. Now, did you do all of your school work?"

"Yes."

"What are your plans?" Lily asked. "We've got your accommodation arranged. School is not far from graduation. You've done all your tests. It's now just a formality."

"After I graduate, I'm leaving town. Will you come with me? We can make a new life together away from here."

"I wish I could, sweetie, but I'm going to stay here."

"Mom?"

"No, listen to me, I love it here. Sure, it has some horrible people in it, but no matter where you go, you'll find them, or they will find you. I love it here. I'm staying here." Lily pressed a kiss to her cheeks. "Now, what next?"

Chloe told her mother of her plan to leave after graduation. She'd intended to stick around the summer to spend as much time with Alfie, but now her plans had changed. She wasn't going to be in a town that pointed and laughed and mocked.

She was done.

This town was going to see the last of her, and she was never going to return.

Alfie had told her he loved her, and she really wished she could believe him.

"I think I was falling in love with him, Mom," she said.

"I know, honey. You were. I could see it, and I'm so sorry he treated you this way."

"I feel like everything I thought I knew is falling apart, and I don't know anything anymore. Please, help me make it stop."

Her mother couldn't make it stop. All she could do was hold her, love her, and for now, it was the only thing that was going to be enough. She was never going to let another man do this to her.

She'd start a new life and never look back.

PART TWO
Chapter Twelve

Five years later

"I don't think I should go on a date," Chloe said, lifting up onto her toes and pushing some of the sauces around.

"What are you doing?" Lily asked.

"Looking for the soy sauce, I know I put it in this cupboard. I really need to go through everything, you know. I've got to move out in a couple of months, especially when I hand in my notice."

As part of her culinary course, she'd been working on several of the restaurants that donated and supported key students and chefs. This was one of the first start-up culinary schools to offer this kind of program that not only trained students, taught them everything about food and management, but also supplied them with culinary scholarships at local delis, restaurants, and food chains.

Since leaving Satan's Croft with her heart and reputation in tatters, she'd thrown herself into her work, and did what her mother asked, forgot about everything she once knew. In the past five years, her mother would travel to her, and they'd spend all the holidays and vacations together, and she didn't have to go back to town.

This was all Lily's choice, not her own.

Also, neither of them spoke about Eagle or Alfie.

She felt a little pain rush through her at the mere thought of Alfie. When it came to her mother, guilt was never far behind.

Lily always tried to put on a brave face, even though her love for Eagle was there, without any doubt at all.

"Do you have somewhere else to move to?" Lily asked.

"Not yet, but I've also been applying for a sous chef position at a couple of places. Demand is not really there, and the competition is fierce. I've heard several of the guys are doing the whole food blog thing, and I may have to consider it. People just don't eat out anymore." She shrugged. Her mother couldn't see it. "For now, I'm the vegetable prepper, and at least I have a position, you know."

"You want more though."

"Yes. I do. Aha, soy sauce. Yum." She quickly drizzled it over her vegetables in the stir-fry, and gave it a toss with a flick of her wrist. "Done."

She didn't bother with a bowl but took a mat to rest the pan on the surface, and started to eat the garlic and ginger vegetables she'd made.

"So, what were we talking about before we got into the soy sauce conundrum?" Lily asked.

"A date. One of the head chefs has asked me out on a date, and I'm not sure. He's not the owner of the restaurant, but he's kind of a big deal. I don't know if I want to go on it." It wasn't like she was given much of a choice in the dating element with Reginald. He'd walked up to her as she was chopping, and pretty much told her they were going on a date. There was never a chance to dispute their potential date.

He was busy.

She didn't want to bring it up at work, so that meant she was now only hours away from going on said date. This was one of the few days she had off, and she liked to spend it researching or talking to her mother.

"You're not going to stand him up. You need to go out and date more."

"Mom, me and dating, please."

"You haven't dated in five years, and this is the first time I've ever heard you talk about a guy."

"There's a reason for that. I've been focusing on my studies, you know that." And she'd been suffering from a broken heart, and well, going out with any guy just didn't appeal to her, not that thinking about Alfie helped.

She'd left Satan's Croft and never returned. Sometimes she felt so alone in the big city. Then her mom would come and visit and everything would be magical again. She'd stop feeling sorry for herself and think about the future she had planned.

Alfie was a difficult subject for her to forget.

Even though her mother promised her no one talked about that dreadful night, she hadn't been able to leave the house during the last month before graduation.

"Honey, I'm not stupid. You and I both know the reason you don't date. I get it. I really do, but you've got to do something about this. You can't spend your entire life judging other men because of him."

"Is *he* still in town?" she asked.

"Yes, and he's also a prospect now as well."

"He is?"

"Yes. I don't know how he earned his patch, but he did. As did Ian and Riley. I told you, I've got no reason to know anything more. I've seen their leather cuts. Alfie tries to talk to me, but I ignore him."

"You're being rude to him?" Chloe asked. "I know you hate being that way, and you shouldn't be that way with him, or with anyone. It makes you uncomfortable."

"I'm not going to lie, it does, but I can't help it. I remember how sad and broken you looked."

"Maybe I should come home. Face my fears," Chloe said. The very thought of it turned her stomach.

Leaving Satan's Croft was the best thing she ever did, and her mother never judged her for it.

"I can hear the panic in you, Chloe. You're not ready. One day you'll be ready, and when you are, I'll be waiting for you."

Chloe released a breath. "You should date Eagle. Is he seeing anyone?"

"No, he's not seeing anyone, and well, the last time we spoke, it didn't go well."

"Mom?"

"No, I'm not telling you any of my business. You don't need to worry or to know about it. I'm your mother, yes, but I also can have a life of my own. Now as your parent, I'm ordering you to go on this date. To be sensible and to also have fun."

"You know those two things don't go hand in hand."

"You're my daughter, and I know you'll make it work."

"Speaking of the whole parent thing, have you heard from *him?*" Kurt had been around a couple of times in the last five years, but from what Lily would tell her, nothing had come from it.

He wanted to get back together and he'd made the usual promises, but after everything that happened with Kurt, then with Eagle, her mother had sworn off men, all men, for a lifetime.

She personally felt it was a little too harsh, but again, this was her mother's life, not hers, and there was nothing she could do to change Lily's mind.

"No, sweetie. I'm sorry."

During the time he'd been around, not once had Kurt asked about her, or paid any attention to her.

He'd ignored her very existence. She didn't want to see him either, and it was childish of her to behave that way, but she wasn't changing her mind.

"I better go. Get ready. I'll send you a picture of what I look like." She blew her mother a kiss, promised to talk soon, and hung up.

The stir-fried vegetables held no appeal anymore. She boxed them up and would probably eat them another day. She hated waste.

Her date wasn't for a few hours, so she sat down on the sofa, picked up a good book, and tried to allow the time to pass, while also not thinking about Alfie.

He'd tried, and she'd left.

There were times she was flooded with regret when it came to him.

She had been falling for him, and he'd broken her heart.

"You're not going to think about him. It was five years ago. Get over it already." If she really regretted leaving him behind, she could have easily gotten a cab and gone home.

She'd been tempted to, but each time, she'd found herself just back where she started from.

Forgiving Alfie … could she do it?

He'd not taken and shown the video—that much she did know. And her mother had said about someone else filming it, Daniel, the guy he'd beaten up at school, but it had been too late. The video aside, Alfie's initial intentions were what broke her heart. He'd been planning to hurt her, but she also knew, he had changed his mind. This was what made it so hard for her. The bully she had known was gone, and in his place stood a guy she had fallen for—but it had started out as a plan to hurt her even more. Ugh, this was so hard for her because she knew he was both kinds of guy, the good and the bad. She wanted to just forget about everything and move on. But how could she move on without him?

Running fingers through her hair, she pressed her face against her hands and wondered what the hell she was going to do. Her life wasn't complicated here. She worked, read, and worked some more.

She still didn't make friends easily, which was why she still lived alone and hadn't been able to find a place with a roommate. It would be the only way she could afford anything anyway.

Going home for now was out of the question. She'd already made the decision that if she was to go home, she'd do so only when she'd made a success of her life so she could look back on what happened, and laugh.

There was no other way forward for her.

Had Alfie moved on?

He was still in Satan's Croft, so he must have.

She'd not seen him in five years. Had the time been good for him? Bad?

"Just get that out of your head. Enough already." She slammed the book closed and decided to get ready for her date.

****

Alfie lifted up the empty metal beer keg and loaded it up onto the truck. This was his job as prospect, doing all the heavy lifting.

"You've been lifting those weights for five years, and now it's time to put your super muscles to the test."

That was his father a week ago when he'd given him every single job he could think of that would require him to use nothing but brute strength.

So far, he'd been able to do every task from lifting beers, tires, bikes, holding cars, and even just standing, holding out beers.

In the past five years since his life went to shit, he'd been working harder than ever to prove to his dad and the club that he was trustworthy and loyal.

"Hey, man," Ian said, entering the parking lot.

"Hey," he said.

Riley and Ian had been with the club when they had to go out of town on a drug run. It had gone bad, and all three of them had protected the club. Riley took a bullet to the chest, Ian to the shoulder, and Alfie had taken one in the leg, but none of the clubmen had been hurt.

It was during that time Eagle had changed his mind and allowed them to become prospects. Now, they had the grueling challenge of earning the club's respect. This part should have been a piece of cake, but he'd fucked up by going against his father's wishes all those years ago.

He'd been able to track down who made the fucking tape. Daniel had paid one of the tech people in the media department of a local college.

All the evidence had been on his cell phone, and he'd uploaded it onto the tape. If it hadn't been for the little sticky tape inside the VHS tape, Alfie would never have found the college, and gotten Daniel.

In doing so, he'd run Daniel out of town, after getting the bastard to apologize to Lily. He'd hoped she'd bring Chloe back to town, but her daughter had never arrived.

All of Daniel's family had been pushed out, and he'd not seen them since. It was probably a good thing. Whenever the fair came to town, it only served to remind him of all he'd lost five years ago.

"Your dad got you lifting shit?" Ian asked.

His relationship with his father was a tense one. He'd finally moved out as he couldn't handle the stony silence. While Eagle had been willing to give him a chance at the club, his father wouldn't give him the time of day outside.

He didn't know what was worse, having Eagle, or not having his father. For a short time, while he was with Lily, Eagle had been the kind of father Alfie always wanted.

Now, they were back to hating each other.

"You know the drill. All the prospects get the shitty jobs."

"Yeah, I don't know if this is as shitty as the stuff Kurt had to put up with," Ian said. "You ever miss that motherfucker?"

"Only when I'm the one they want to dress up like a girl and spank." Alfie shook his head. He didn't even want to understand that one, but the guys had done it. Eagle had told him it was all about trust, and Alfie had been around the club all of his life to know shit like that happened in the club.

Sure, it made no sense and was so fucking embarrassing, but if you can dress up in ladies' underwear and trust the club, then you'll take a bullet.

He'd already taken a bullet, but Eagle was paying close attention to the three of them. Some of the other club friends had already been a prospect for longer than they had.

"What are you doing here, Ian?" he asked.

"Wondered if you wanted to hang out? It hasn't been the same since Riley quit, you know."

"Oh, he really did quit the job at the DIY store?"

"Yep."

While he'd taken a job at the garage fixing cars, Ian and Riley could only get work at the DIY store. From what he knew, the owner hated Riley's dad, so he'd made it his personal mission to make Riley miserable, especially as the town had discovered they were all enemies of the club, until they were patched in. Riley still continued to work at the store until last Friday, when he'd nearly been killed due to a lack of safety equipment. He'd threatened to sue, and walked right on out of the store.

"Anyway, it's kind of boring without him there."

"I think he was planning to work at the titty place, you know?"

"Yeah, as a guard. Please, as if that's a fun job."

"The point of it being a job is not fun."

"I suppose being close to that much pussy would be a benefit."

"If you say so."

"You seriously don't miss having sex?"

"I'm not talking to you about who I fuck," he said. The truth was, he didn't fuck anyone and hadn't in over five years.

How stupid was that of him? Or lame? He'd not been with another woman since Chloe. Being with anyone else didn't appeal to him. Maybe it was time he tried, but he didn't want anyone else.

He'd accepted what he'd done and how he'd fucked up. One day, he'd make it up to Chloe. He couldn't imagine being with anyone else.

"She's not coming back, Alfie," he said. Ian spoke quietly, softly, and Alfie stared at his friend.

"We're not talking about this."

"Look, it has been five years, and you're not letting this go."

"Ian, enough already. I have no interest in other women." He just wanted to get his work done, and go home. He'd really had enough for the day and couldn't handle anymore.

"I'm sorry for bringing it up," Ian said. "I'm meeting up with Riley, and we're heading to the strip place. I'm hoping you could come."

"Go on ahead without me."

"You're sure."

"Yeah, I've got stuff to do." He had nothing to do, but the last thing he wanted was to stare at naked women as they danced and flashed all day and night.

"If you're sure."

"Totally sure," he said. When it came to hanging out at the titty place, he only ever went there if he really had to. Otherwise he avoided it.

"Well, if you're okay with me and Riley going on our own."

He nodded his head, not really caring about what his friends were doing. Just as he'd finished loading up the last empty metal beer keg, his father arrived, or should he say, Eagle arrived.

"What are you two doing here?" he asked. "You've got your own work to be doing."

"Sorry," Ian said. "Just wanted to hang out with Alfie, but he's got plans."

"When you're on club time, it's Rock," Eagle said.

Out of the three of them, he'd earned his club name for being a Rock when it came to the club. No matter what was asked for him, he did it. He wouldn't let them forget about him, not once.

He'd been a complete rock for all of them.

"When you're done with this, I need you back at the clubhouse," Eagle said.

"Okay." He wasn't going to argue. He'd intended to go home and just relax, but if the club needed him, he'd do whatever it took for them.

He didn't know why his father didn't just call him, but he imagined it was to check up on him. There were times he thought he was really starting to agree with his father on some level, but then Eagle would show up. Just as Eagle was about to leave again, the sheriff showed up. Ryan was a good guy, but he didn't know how to handle any of the bad shit that came to town, and he didn't have a problem with calling the club for help. Rarely anything happened in Satan's Croft as the club was a nice little deterrent for them all.

"You okay there, Sheriff?" Eagle asked.

"You told me to come to you if there was ever a need; well, there's a need. Lily's at the hospital. She's been hurt real bad."

"What?"

"Someone ran her down. No one saw the car, and it's just near the library."

"Alfie, get in the car," Eagle said.

He rushed toward his dad's car, and it only just dawned on him that his father was actually driving a car, not his bike.

Pulling out of the parking lot, they rode toward the hospital with Ryan hot on their heels.

"She'll be okay, Dad."

"Don't, Alfie. You and I both know that I'm not ready to talk about this yet."

"It has been five years."

"I know, and in those five years she's spoken to me three times, that's it. She was going to marry me, and now, I've got nothing."

"Dad, you really shouldn't worry about this."

"How about you shut up and let me drive."

If Lily was in the hospital, they were going to have to call Chloe back home. Alfie didn't speak again. He didn't make a sound.

Eagle parked the car, not that anyone would call that parking, and rushed out into the main reception. With Ryan at their side, the staff didn't give them shit, and Eagle announced he was her fiancé.

They were shown to Lily's room, and it didn't look good. Both of her legs were broken, and her face was badly bruised. She was also in a coma, which was the tricky part. The doctor kept on speaking, but Alfie had stopped listening.

By the window, he noticed her bag of stuff the hospital had gathered together, and he grabbed the cell phone. They needed to call Chloe.

They were ushered out of the room, and Alfie kept the cell phone in his hand until they got to the main reception where they were handed several stacks of paper for them all to go through and complete.

"You okay, Dad?"

"No, I'm not. Did you hear what they said about the coma?"

"It's going to be okay. It has to be. Lily's a strong woman, but you know who she needs now?"

"Chloe," Eagle said.

Alfie handed him the cell phone. "I got this. You've got to call her. This could be your chance of winning her back." He had no idea Eagle had gotten the Sheriff to contact him in the event of an emergency when it came to Lily.

He didn't want to put too much hope in this moment, but this could be his chance as well. So far, his father hadn't threatened to murder him, which was a step up for him.

Eagle opened the phone and smiled as he broke the password. "She always puts everything as Chloe's birthday."

Alfie nodded, and he wouldn't be retaining any of that information.

"That's her," he said, thumb hovering over Chloe's name.

Alfie waited, worried about her.

"Call her, Dad," he said.

Eagle pressed the name, and the phone started to ring.

Alfie let out a breath and smiled, trying to contain his excitement. Eagle put the call to speakerphone, and he waited.

"Hey, Mom," Chloe said, answering a few seconds later. Her voice sounded amazing, and Alfie could just listen to her all night long. "So, I went on that date, and you were right. I mean, it was okay, but it wasn't great. He kept on talking about the perfect Hollandaise sauce and I totally kept up, but after two hours of him telling me how he perfected it, I was a little bored."

"Chloe," Eagle said.

"Who is this?"

"It's Eagle."

"What are you doing with my mom's phone?" she asked.

"There has been an accident, and you need to come down here."

"An accident?"

"Yes. Your mother, she's stable, but I know she'll want you."

"Wait, what?"

"Someone ran your mother over."

"It's Satan's Croft. How is that possible?"

"I promise you, I'll find out." Eagle hung up the phone, and Alfie wasn't ready to say goodbye.

"You're just going to leave it like that?" he asked.

"I've just given her bad news. I know what you're thinking, Alfie, but you're going to have to put your hopes to one side on this. This is all for Lily. I've got to find out what Ryan knows, and get this shit fucking handled." Eagle handed him the cell phone and walked back out to where Ryan was having a smoke.

Alfie wasn't going to do anything stupid, but he also wasn't going to allow Chloe to leave town again.

Chapter Thirteen

Chloe arrived at the hospital four hours after the first phone call. She had phoned the hospital to make sure it wasn't a prank, and they'd told her Lily was indeed a patient.

She hated doubting Eagle, and couldn't believe she had. Walking up to the desk, she took a deep breath.

"Hi, I'm Chloe Decker. My mom is Lily Decker. She was run over and is in a coma." That was all the information she could find out over the phone. Her heart raced as she thought of her mother in some hospital bed, hurt, and possibly in so much pain. She was so nervous.

"Down the hall and follow the direction for Trauma."

"Thank you."

She turned and walked several steps before realizing Alfie stood right in front of her. Chloe stopped and took him in.

He'd changed a lot.

In high school he'd always been the bad boy biker with the smoking hot body, but now it was more than that, and her mouth went dry.

"Alfie," she said.

"Chloe."

He rubbed the back of his head, and he'd gotten even more tattoos than the ones in high school.

"You were with your dad when he called?"

"Yes. We were both alerted to what happened to Lily. I'm so sorry."

"Where is your dad now?"

"He's with her. I can take you to her."

She wanted to tell him no, to leave her alone, but this was her mother, and she hated coming to hospitals. "Please do."

Since the phone call she'd been feeling sick to her stomach about what it could all mean.

Biting her lip, she waited, trying to remain calm and completely failing.

"It's good to see you," Alfie said.

She didn't speak, only followed him. Was it good to see him?

He'd changed a lot, but just because he'd gotten more muscular, that didn't mean she actually agreed with him, or anything.

"I heard you became a prospect, congratulations."

"Thanks. I'd hoped to be a fully patched in member for a lot longer than I have been, but that didn't happen. I was lucky I wasn't kicked out completely."

She nodded but wasn't about to say anything. They both knew why he didn't make a patched member.

"This is the first time you've been here in five years."

"You've counted."

"Of course I did. I've been hoping you'd come back all this time." Alfie stopped, and she had no choice but to do so as well. She folded her arms across her chest, wanting this conversation out of the way. "I discovered who made the tape."

"Good for you, but it doesn't change anything between us. I mean, it has been so long ago, and I'm sorry that you had to deal with it all too," she said.

"Chloe, I know you hate me right now, but you've got to believe me. I never wanted to hurt you, not ever."

"I really can't do this right now. My mom, I need to see her."

Alfie nodded, and it seemed to make him realize that he didn't have a chance in the hospital.

"I'm glad you made it as a patched member," she

said, walking beside him.

"You are?"

"Yes. I know what happened between us was horrible, but I didn't want it to ruin your life's plans. I know how much you love the club, and well, I did tell my mom to tell your dad no hard feelings."

"Chloe, I'm so sorry."

"Stop it. We don't need to keep on doing this to each other. You can move on. I know I want to."

"You're dating," he said.

This was the most awkward meetings in the history of all of them, Chloe was sure of it.

"Not really. Can we not do this?" she asked.

"You were the one that brought up the club."

"I'm sorry. I just need to focus on getting this together." She tucked some of her hair behind her ear.

It looked like Alfie wanted to say more, but he didn't. He took her to her mother's room, and seeing Lily, lying out, unresponsive, it took every single ounce of control not to break down. Both of Lily's legs were broken, and she looked so pale.

Eagle sat in the corner, watching.

"Do you know who did this?" she asked.

"Not yet but I'm going to get to the bottom of it, Chloe. I promise."

She nodded and moved closer to the bed. Every single part of her mother looked bruised. She knelt on the floor as Eagle had the only chair.

"I'll go and get a couple more chairs," Alfie said, leaving.

Ignoring him and the man in the corner, Chloe kissed her mother's hand. "It's going to be okay. I know it is. We're going to make it through all of this." She pressed her face against Lily's hand, and just took several deep breaths, needing to calm her nerves.

"It's good to have you back, Chloe," Eagle said.

Pulling away from her mother, she turned to Eagle. "How did you find out? You called me before the hospital even did. It's crazy."

"I pulled some strings at the sheriff's office to be alerted on Lily's safety. I didn't like her being alone, and I wanted to be there for her when she needed me."

"It's Satan's Croft."

"I know, but that doesn't mean bad shit won't happen. Someone ran her down, Chloe. They didn't stay behind to make sure she was okay, and as you can see, she's not okay."

Chloe could also see that Eagle was struggling to keep it together. Whoever ran Lily down would pay, and it could even be with their very life.

"I'm sorry. I was only talking to her yesterday, and she was encouraging me to go out on a date." She sniffled, feeling the tears build in her eyes. "I know I'm completely crazy, right?"

"No, not crazy. Your mom only ever wanted the best for you, and I can see her trying to encourage you to date."

Alfie returned with a couple of chairs. He placed one beside her, and she sat down, thanking him. He took a seat in the far corner, watching the door and her mother.

"I'm going to put one of my guys on the door," Eagle said. "I want her protected until we know more about this hit-and-run."

"You think someone could come and hurt her again? You really don't think it's an accident?" she asked.

"I think I want to take care of her, and I'm not willing to take any chances when it comes to her safety."

Chloe nodded. She turned toward her mother, and

for the next hour, she watched her sleep. Lily looked so peaceful in sleep.

One of Eagle's guys showed up, but she couldn't remember his name. Within ten minutes the nurse was there to tell them all they had to leave for the night. She hated the thought of leaving her mother for even a second.

Tucking her hair behind her ear, she grabbed her bag and made her way outside.

"Miss," the receptionist said. "The cab driver left this for you."

Her suitcase was waiting for her, and she nodded. "Thank you." She'd already paid the fare to the hospital, but in her rush to get to her mom, she'd forgotten about her luggage. At least he didn't take off with it, not that there was anything of value there. Just some underwear and clothes, the usual stuff.

"Do you need a ride home?" Eagle asked.

She glanced around, knowing she should take the offered ride. "I can walk."

"No, don't be silly. I can drive you to your place. You have a key, don't you?"

She did.

"If not, you're welcome to stay at my place," Alfie said.

"You have your own place?"

"Yes."

"I've got a key." She reached into her bag, pulling out the keys that included her apartment back in the city.

"I'll drive you, and I won't take no for an answer."

She didn't see any point in arguing with the man. Eagle knew how to get what he wanted.

Following Eagle and Alfie out to their car was

surreal to her. Never could she imagine coming back home and taking a ride, and it was crazy. At one point they were all going to be a family.

Eagle took her suitcase from her and placed it in the back of the car. Alfie opened the passenger door in the back and she climbed in, telling him thank you.

Pulling on the seatbelt, she sat back and stared at the hospital. There was a risk her mother may not wake up from the coma, but the doctor said the risk was low. She didn't know what to think or say. Everything seemed to be working against her when it came to her mother.

Eagle climbed behind the wheel. No music played, and the tension in the car seemed to go up a notch or ten. It wasn't that far from her home, so she didn't have to put up with it for long.

Taking a deep breath when Eagle actually pulled up outside of her home, she was relieved.

"Here we go."

Alfie climbed out of the car before Eagle got a chance.

"That boy is eager," Eagle said.

"He is?"

"It's great to have you back, Chloe."

"It's great to see you, Eagle." She did mean that. "I am sorry for the way everything went down. I didn't want to come between you two. I hope you know that."

"I do. It's just how it happened." Eagle looked out of the window to see Alfie waiting. "You know that boy has never been the same."

"I better go inside." She opened the door without another word and climbed out.

When she reached to take her bag, Alfie wouldn't let her.

"Why?"

"Because I can carry it for you."

She rolled her eyes but walked down the path and put the key in the lock, twisting it. She hadn't done this in such a long time. It seemed so strange to be coming home, and her mother wasn't even here.

Straightening her shoulders, she turned to Alfie, and he placed the bag inside her door but didn't come in.

"Thank you for bringing my bag."

"I want to have coffee with you, or breakfast," he said.

"Alfie, I'm not here for us to get to know each other, or to have dinner, or breakfast, or anything. I'm only here for my mom."

"And while you're here, I'm not taking no for an answer. You're going to have breakfast with me, and we're going to sort out our problem."

"You're ordering me around? You really think that is the smart way to do this?"

"Let's see, I tried to be the nice guy, and what did that get me? Nothing. You left, and I haven't gotten a single chance since then. So now I'm trying something else. I'm not going to let you go this time, Chloe. I don't care who you're dating."

"You heard that."

"Kind of hard not to. Dad had you on speakerphone."

She stared at him and glanced over his shoulder. "I don't know."

"Look, you can try to push me away and I'll even let you try, but I'm not backing down."

"It has been five years."

"Is there someone else? Is that why you won't give me a chance?"

She should lie, tell him there was someone else, but she couldn't do it. "No, there's no one else."

"While you're here, give me a chance, Chloe."

"I'm not going to give you a chance at anything, but I'm not going to push you away or cause a scene. My mom's legs, when she wakes up, she's going to need help, and I'm going to be the one to help her. I'm going to get settled in."

"Okay." He didn't move.

"I need you to leave, Alfie."

"I know. It's good seeing you, Chloe. Even if you can't say the same."

She closed the door after he left, and leaned against it. "It's good seeing you as well, Alfie, really good."

****

Chloe was back.

She was back.

Climbing back into his dad's car, he smiled at the man.

"You do realize it's not going to be that easy winning her back," Eagle said. "She's been gone a long time, and she's changed."

"You don't know that."

"Time changes us all, son."

"Yeah, and you didn't give me the road name Rock for no reason."

"True."

Alfie was about to let anyone ruin his mood. There was a chance here; he saw it, could smell it.

"She left before I got a chance to tell her the truth, to show her I'd changed. I'm not going to let her go now without her hearing me out."

"And if she doesn't want to hear you?" he asked.

"I'll make sure she does."

"Whatever you do, keep in mind your position at the club. You can't compromise that."

"I won't forget it." Alfie ran his hands down his

legs, feeling nervous. "Dad, I never wanted this to happen, you've got to believe me."

"I do believe you. I've handled things like an immature child." Eagle sighed. "I've loved Lily for a long time. I watched her go through hell with Kurt and to keep taking him back. I promised myself I'd be different for her, and when that fucking video played, I was so livid."

"I know."

"I didn't mean to kick you out."

"Dad, I left."

"No, I wasn't much of a father to you. I'm sorry," Eagle said. He muttered the last part underneath his breath, but Alfie heard it.

He smiled to himself, because nothing was going to take away the fact that he was happy.

Chloe was back in town, and he couldn't foresee any problems in winning her back, just so long as he didn't do anything stupid.

Five years was a long time, but it wasn't enough for her to forget about him. He just needed for her to forget the pain.

Eagle dropped him off at his apartment and promised to pick him up the following morning on the way to the hospital. After seeing Lily in the morning with Chloe, he intended to take her out for breakfast.

Arriving at his place, he let himself inside and already heard Riley and Ian watching a movie. His friends had a key, and the moment Chloe arrived in town, he knew they'd be around to be with him.

The moment he entered his sitting room, the movie was stopped, and he couldn't see what it was they were watching.

"You okay, man?" Riley asked.

"Me? Yeah, I'm good."

"You saw her, didn't you?" Ian asked.

"Chloe?" They both nodded. "Yeah, I saw her. It was kind of strange, seeing her after all this time."

"Good strange or bad strange?"

Alfie went to his fridge, and rather than go for a beer, he took out a bottle of water. "It was good. She's … beautiful."

"We're here to make sure you don't go crazy."

"Why would I go crazy?" Alfie asked. He placed the bottle against his lips and took a sip, the water quenching his thirst.

"We know how it was fucked up the last time. You ever wonder why Daniel did what he did?"

"He said he had the tape made, but he had no intention of showing it to anyone but me. He wanted something from me, but he changed his mind at the last minute. Said he didn't want to have to deal with me in the end, as he didn't think I'd take kindly to blackmail. He told me someone took it. Fucking liar," Alfie said. "That guy wanted to hurt me, and he found the way to do it."

The only satisfaction he got from the entire incident was kicking Daniel and all of his family out of town. They didn't have much choice seeing as Eagle was also on the warpath.

It would have been easier for the Satan's Crew to kill all of Daniel's family, but Eagle, he liked to make people suffer, and if they'd stayed, the entire family would have been homeless, begging for scraps.

His father had a vicious streak, and Alfie had barely survived it before.

"He cost you Chloe, and now she's back. You think people around town are going to magically forget what happened?"

"I don't care what they do and don't do. Anyone

who hurts her has to come through me, simple as that."
He was more than willing to take on the entire town.
"You boys got my back, or am I out on my own with this
one?"

"You're never alone, Alfie," Ian said.

"It's an insult to think we'd leave you alone when
it's our fault as well. We should have been more
careful."

Alfie finished his water, and left his friends to go
and take a shower. He wanted to be ready in the event of
Lily waking up and him needing a ride.

Where he'd failed Chloe last time, he wouldn't do
it again. He intended to be everything she needed and
more.

****

Chloe jerked awake to the banging on the front
door. Climbing out of bed, she saw it was only three in
the morning.

Who could be knocking on the door? Her mother
never complained of nighttime visitors.

Going to the door, she saw Alfie on the other
side.

Frowning, she opened the door, a little confused.
"Alfie, what's going on?"

"Your mother's awake. My dad got a call at the
hospital. Do you want us to take you?"

"My mom's awake?"

"Why didn't they call here?"

"My dad handled all the paperwork, and he put us
down as the nearest contact information."

"Oh." Of course he would, but she didn't think
her mother would like the invasion of her privacy. "I may
have to change that." Glancing down at her body, she
groaned. "I've got to get dressed."

She wore a pair of fairy tale pajamas. They'd

been on sale, and were three sizes too big, but she loved how comfortable they were.

Rushing back to her room, which brought up so many memories, she quickly pulled on her jeans, a crop top, and piled her hair in a bun on top of her head. She splashed some water onto her face, and quickly washed her mouth out with mouthwash. She was ready to go. Donning a pair of flipflops, then grabbing her cell phone and keys, she met Alfie, who was still waiting at the door.

"Wow, that took you, like, five minutes to do."

"I'm a girl who knows not to waste time." One too many missed alarms would do that to a person. She hated to be late, and it hadn't taken her long to build up her ability to get ready in a few minutes.

Alfie opened the door for her in the back, and it would take her a short time to get used to the gentlemanly gesture.

In the city, men often tried to steal a cab, or were rude. Not all men, but she'd never been that successful with any.

"Thank you, Eagle, for picking me up."

"It's no problem. How are you settling in?"

"Like I never left."

Her bedroom was spotless. Lily had told her on several occasions she'd go into her room and just remember the time when she was younger. She missed her mom so much, and just the short time of being home, she knew returning to the city would be so hard.

It was strange to her how comforting it was, just going to the fridge and grabbing some food, or sitting on the sofa, not worrying about the couple arguing next door, or the party that shouldn't be happening that was going on down the hall.

Living in the culinary dorms did have a lot of

restrictions in what was allowed. Animals and parties were off limits. Couples could stay together, but the partner that wasn't part of the culinary school had to pay half of the bills, or at least that was what she'd heard.

She had her small apartment to herself, and she'd loved the independence whereas now, well, it was kind of tough to want to go back.

All this in only a few hours. How was she going to handle days or even weeks?

Ignore it all, Chloe. You'll deal with whatever comes your way, like you have everything else.

The silence in the car was almost too much to bear. Father and son didn't speak. She had no idea what to say. The radio wasn't on.

"How is everything with you, Eagle?" she asked.

"I'm good. The club is good. All is good."

She smiled. A man of few words.

Silence once again.

The joy.

Nibbling her lip, she stared out into the dark, wondering what to say.

"I heard you passed your culinary exam and you're looking for a job to be a sous chef."

"I am. Who told you?" she asked.

"Your mother did in passing."

She felt a spark of guilt. If it hadn't been for her and Alfie, Eagle and Lily would have married.

"Have you met someone?" she asked.

"No."

Again, the guilt.

"Don't go there," Alfie said.

"I am sorry," she said, looking toward Eagle. He glanced up in the rearview mirror.

"Yeah, well, nothing ever plays out how it's supposed to."

There was a brand-new tension in the car, and she'd been the one to cause it.

Great, just great.

Finally, after what felt like a millennium, they finally arrived. There was no one at the front desk when they entered, but there was a nurse filling out paperwork.

Eagle took the helm, and the nurse walked them back to Lily's room.

Her mother's lamp was on.

"We don't usually allow nighttime visits, but she was very confused and upset. We told her you'd been by to visit, and she just wanted to see you, Chloe. The only information we have was for Mr. Pace."

"It's fine. Honestly, it's fine. I'll put my contract information down, and there won't be any misunderstanding."

Eagle made a noise, and it sounded like a protest. Ignoring him, she walked into her mother's room. Lily was sitting up in bed, glaring at the door.

"Chloe," she said.

The glare turned to a smile.

"How are you feeling, Ms. Decker?" the nurse asked.

"I'm feeling better, thank you. Can I have a moment with my daughter?"

"Of course." The nurse left.

Eagle and Alfie didn't take the hint.

"I'd like to talk to my daughter please."

"Mom, it's okay. Eagle was the one who called me."

"How is that possible? He doesn't have your phone number." Lily rubbed at her temple and winced.

It would seem every single part of her body was bruised.

"Mom, stop. Don't hurt yourself. You're bruised.

You got hit by a car."

Lily moaned. "I remember, believe me." She smiled. "I can't believe you're here. You're here all in one piece."

"I know. I'm right here."

Lily cupped her face.

"I came as soon as Eagle called me."

"Yes, how did you get her phone number?" Lily asked.

"I used your phone," Eagle said. "How are you feeling?"

"Like a car ran over me and had fun while he did."

"Was it a he driving?" Alfie asked, stepping forward.

"I don't know. I was crossing the road and I was sure I had enough time to get to the other side, but I think the car sped up." Lily groaned. "No, that can't be right. I've never upset anyone in my life to make them want to run me over, have I?"

Eagle smiled. "No, you haven't."

Lily nodded, and Chloe saw pain in her mother's eyes. This was all her fault.

"Mom, you just need to rest and let everyone else figure all of this out."

"You're here," Lily said, changing the subject.

"Yes, I'm here, and I'm not going anywhere else. I promise you." She reached out, stroking some of her mother's hair out of the way. "I missed you."

"Your date. You went on it, right? Please tell me you went on that thing?"

She chuckled. "I did, and it wasn't great. I was telling Eagle about it when I thought he was you."

Lily groaned. "I hate that."

"I'm staying at home, and after I talk to the

doctor, I'll decide what I'm going to do." She touched Lily's legs, and both of them were in casts. *Not good.*

This was going to end with her staying in town, which oddly, didn't upset or surprise her.

"We'll see what happens. The doctor has already done some tests. He said coming out of the coma really fast was a good sign. He mentioned something about shock, and the pain, and he wants to keep me monitored."

"I'm going to stay with you." Chloe sat down in the chair.

Behind her, she heard Alfie and Eagle take a seat.

"You two don't have to stay," Lily said.

"Yeah, I do, Lil," Eagle said.

No one else said another word on them leaving, and Chloe forgot they were there as she caught up with her mother.

Chapter Fourteen

"I've got to get to the clubhouse," Eagle said, later the next morning after they'd spoken to the doctor.

Alfie sat all night watching Chloe and Lily reconnect. He saw how worried both women were, and each one was trying to be strong for the other. It was what he'd gotten used to when he was with them. Neither of them wanted to break or fall apart.

Chloe let out a yawn as her stomach rumbled.

"I can drop you both off in town for breakfast," Eagle said. "The diner is no doubt open."

"And I bet heaving with people."

"Probably. It's the way businesses stay afloat."

Alfie watched Chloe, brow raised. "I could eat breakfast," he said.

"You could always eat something. Yes, I'm starving, and I'm not even in the mood to raid my mom's fridge."

Alfie kept watching her in the mirror. She rested against the door, and he kept expecting her to fall asleep.

Nothing happened.

She stared out the window, and he simply watched her.

Eagle was different since Lily stopped trying to kick them out. His father looked happy for the first time in years, and Alfie knew it was because of Chloe coming back, and her not demanding they were gone.

The drive didn't last long, and it was silent once again.

He wondered how long it would be before they were all able to talk like normal people rather than the awkward silences.

Outside the diner, he thrust his hands into his pockets and waited.

"You sure you want to go in there?" she asked.

"I am. *You* look like you want to take off."

She laughed. "Wow, it has been a long time since I came here."

"When was the last time?"

He watched her do the calculation in her head.

"Six years, give or take a day or two. The last time I came here was with my dad. Just before Mom caught him the last time with the strippers."

"You and your mom share a whole lot."

"We do. She always told me she wanted a close relationship with her daughter. I love my mother. I'd do anything for her."

"Would you be willing to bring your mom and my dad back together again?" He didn't even know why he was asking.

"What?"

"You heard me. I saw the way she looked at Eagle last night. Don't you think five years of torture is enough?"

"I've been home for two minutes and you want us to marry our parents off?"

"I want to do it right from five years ago. I didn't mean for that shit to happen, Chloe. You think I haven't paid for it every single day since then? Believe me, I have. It's all I've ever known. My dad was hurt by what I did, and I don't want to see him hurt again. With you back, we can fix this." Her stomach growled. "How about we eat food first, then save our parents."

He opened the door, letting her walk inside.

There were several people already sitting around eating breakfast. It was still quite early for breakfast. He put a hand on Chloe's back, noticing the people who glanced and pointed. Anyone who looked at him, he made sure with a single glare that they backed the fuck down and got back to their food.

No one was going to spoil his morning with Chloe. He'd already made a vow that he was going to prove to Chloe she was his world.

They took a seat in the corner; Chloe's pick, not his. He had no problem being seen with her.

"It seems a video lasts a lifetime, huh?"

"You don't know if they're remembering it."

"The pointing is really hard to miss."

"Do you want me to kick their asses?" he asked.

"You'd do it?"

"They're upsetting you and in turn, upsetting me. I want to enjoy breakfast with you, and I'm not going to get to do what I want, until you get what you want, which is to be left alone."

"Nah, I don't want to think of blood first thing in the morning."

"What do you want to think about?"

"Pancakes and waffles. Both. I think I want both, drowned in syrup." She licked her lips. "Man, it feels good to be home."

"It does?"

"Yeah. I feel weird saying it, but I do love being home." She pushed some of her blonde hair out of the way.

He'd noticed the length wasn't as long.

Chloe still possessed all of her curves, nice big tits, rounded hips, and legs that had felt incredible as he'd slid inside her.

Their time together had been short, but he'd not wanted to blur the memory with anyone else.

"I'm glad to hear it."

"I could do without the pointing and looks, but we can't have it all, can we?"

"No."

She released a breath. "So, how is everything with you? With the whole prospecting thing. I also want to say I'm sorry. I didn't mean for what happened between my parents to affect your choices with the club. Your standing or whatever it was."

Alfie laughed. "You didn't do anything wrong."

"I didn't? We had a relationship, and I broke down in front of most of the town, if not the entire town. I'd say I was half the blame. I could have stayed with you, and stuck by you. No one else did, but I ran because I'm a coward. I was so hurt and scared, and angry. I … my feelings were all over the place."

Alfie reached across the table and took her hands.

"Well, well, well, if it's not Rock with Chloe. Now, didn't this end badly the last time?"

"Katie, it's so nice to see you," Chloe said.

"Made any porno movies lately?" Katie asked.

Katie had gone to school with them. She'd fucked him a few times before he'd set his sights on Chloe, of course. She had taken it badly when he didn't show her any attention, and after high school, she'd tried to join the MC as a club whore. She'd hoped to bag one of the men so she didn't have to work and for them to take care of her. The problem with Katie, she didn't know when to stop. By becoming a Satan's Crew MC club whore, her pussy belonged to the club. No one else was allowed to have any of the club-owned pussy, and well, Katie didn't like those rules, which was why she stood in the diner, working as a waitress, heavily pregnant with no doubt another married man's bastard.

Not that he was one to talk, seeing as he was one as well.

"Katie, I suggest you change your attitude before I alert Carol to the fact the baby you're carrying is probably her husband's. Not to mention, the other two brats you've got at home." He turned to look at Katie, letting her see the disgust he felt for her shine through. "You may think you've got the upper hand here, but you don't. You're lower than a slut. You couldn't even make club property, and Chloe, before you, is a lady. What you saw five years ago wasn't by her choice. Get the fuck away from my table, now!" He stood up, dragging the chair across the floor, gaining the attention of the other diners. "Chloe's back, and if I hear one of you speak to her or make her feel uncomfortable about the events that happened five years ago, not only will you deal with me, you'll deal with the club."

Alfie sat back down, slamming his chair as he did so.

Looking over at Chloe, he saw her face was red and her mouth open.

"What? Did I upset you?"

"No, I guess I'm in shock. I've never seen you do anything like that. Katie's always been a bitch, but you stood up for me."

He took her hand again, and had completely forgotten what he was going to say to her before they were rudely interrupted.

Another waitress came over. This one was new. She looked young, and took their orders, promising to bring them out as soon as they were ready.

"Alone again."

"Yeah. You don't have to keep holding my hands."

"I want to tell you something, and for the life of me, I can't think of what it was."

She giggled, and he loved the sound.

"Do you have any idea what you do to me?"

"Alfie, this is not a good idea. I don't want you getting the wrong impression."

"Hear me out. I remembered what I was going to say, and it is important."

"Of course it is." She smiled, and he had that at least.

He loved her smile.

"It wasn't your fault. Not at all, and I don't want you taking any of the blame."

"I knew you were back in town, but I had no idea you'd agree to breakfast with this loser," Ian said, once again, spoiling the moment as he and Riley dragged the seats to the table.

Chloe pulled her hands away, and he knew there was no point in trying to continue this conversation. Not at the diner where everyone was sitting.

"Hello, Ian. Riley."

"How is city life treating you, city girl?"

"I'm handling it fine. How's town life?"

"Slow," Ian said. "Do you need a roommate out in the big city? You could take Mr. Miserable off our hands."

"Mr. Miserable?"

"Yep, the one and only. Believe me, I can't handle his sour face anymore. It stings my eyes every time I look at him." Riley covered his face and pretended to cry out in pain.

Alfie slapped the backs of his friends' heads. "They have no manners and don't have a clue what they're talking about half of the time."

"True. You can't rely on anything we say," Ian said.

"I was trying to have a quiet breakfast with my woman."

"So?" Riley asked. "You can't always get what you want."

Their waffles and pancakes arrived.

Alfie slapped his friends' hands away so they didn't try to steal his food or Chloe's. She had gone oddly silent, and he hated it. He'd wanted to talk to her, not have breakfast with his friends there.

They distracted the moment asking her about the city. If she was dating anyone, and she happened to mention the guy called Reginald, who sucked, big time. Of course, anyone she dated would suck.

"This guy here hasn't been on a single date since you left. Not a girl has gotten the chance to sniff around this kid, have they?"

"I can kill you and dispose of your body so no one finds you," Alfie said.

"Damn, you're on fire with the insults today," Riley said.

Chloe finished her food and drank the last of her coffee. "It has been great getting to see you guys again, but I really need to sleep. It has been a long couple of days." She looked toward him. "I enjoyed breakfast."

"I'll walk you home." He got to the counter and paid for her and his food, leaving Riley and Ian to handle their own bill.

His friends would know how important this was to him to make it work with Chloe. He had a deadline. However long it took for Lily to get back on her feet was the only time he had to make this all work.

Following Chloe outside, he took her hand, but she pulled away. During the last year of high school, wherever they went, he'd hold her hand. That wasn't going to happen anymore.

You're not eighteen anymore.

"Sorry, force of habit."

"You hold Ian and Riley's hands as well?"

"No. Just you."

He pressed his lips together, wishing more than

anything he could hold her freaking hand. How lame had he become? He couldn't even form into words what he wanted to say to her.

"There hasn't been any other woman in my life. Not since you," he said. "What Ian and Riley said back there, it's true. All of it."

"You're kidding me, right?" Chloe stopped and turned to him. "You're saying since we were together, it was your last time?"

"Yes."

"You're not lying?"

"No. I've got no reason to lie."

"Alfie, it has been five years."

"As everyone keeps fucking reminding me, don't you think I know that? You think I don't wake up remembering the moment that damn video started to play? It was Daniel who took it."

"My mom told me. She explained what had happened, and he left town. Not long after he went, so did his family."

"I destroyed the tape."

"Good." She sighed. "What do you want from me, Alfie?"

"The chance to make this right. I know I fucked up all those years ago. I know I've got no right to ask for you to give me a chance, but I'm begging you for it. I want to make this work. You've not been with anyone else."

"You don't know that."

"I know you, Chloe. I know what it took for you to give yourself to me, and you don't give easily. Not after what we went through."

"The only reason we went through it was because of you. Why did you do it, Alfie? Why?"

"I was a fucking prick, okay? I didn't know what

I was doing. I thought I knew the kind of woman you were, but I was wrong. I wasn't going to see it through. Not just because of the club but because of *you*. I got to know you, and I realized how wrong I was to have judged you. You're not that person, and I know it now, Chloe. I want to make it up to you. The night you gave yourself to me, I loved it. You made me feel whole, and since you've been gone, I've felt empty inside, like a piece of myself has been torn away from me and there's nothing left."

"Alfie, please, don't do this."

"What you saw at the diner, I'll do it every single day if I have to, to prove it to you." He stepped up to her, staring into her blue eyes. There was so much he'd missed about this woman.

He shook deep inside and knew he couldn't let her go, not now he finally had her back.

Slamming his lips down on hers, he kissed his first woman in over five years, and her lips were everything.

****

Chloe pushed her mother toward the elevator later that same evening.

"He kissed you, and then what?" Lily asked.

"His cell phone rang. The club needed him, kind of reminded me a little of Dad, and he had no choice but to leave. He walked me to my door, kissed me again, and left. I spent the afternoon passed out on the sofa, until my cell woke me up. I've already texted Eagle, I got his number from him in case you were wondering. Let him know I was coming to see you."

"I can't believe he kissed you."

"It was just a kiss, Mom, nothing to think about." She pressed the buttons to the ground floor.

"Nothing to think about? A kiss can be so much

more, if only you'll allow yourself to feel it."

"Just the other day you told me I shouldn't think of coming home. Now you want me to think of the kiss."

"I didn't want you to come home while you still had your dreams and aspirations in the city. You will always come first for me, Chloe, you know that."

"I know you love me and care. You have not one but two broken legs, and city life had stopped agreeing with me."

"Since when?"

Chloe leaned against the wall waiting for the doors to open. "After I graduated culinary school. Reginald demanding I go on a date with him, and not giving me the chance to turn him down. A whole lot of stuff. I don't want to talk about it."

The doors opened, and she pushed her mother out, finding the signs to take them both to the gardens. The nurse mentioned how nice it would be for her mother to get some fresh air, and she agreed. It would be good, for the both of them.

"I want to know what is going on in your head, missy. You can't just push me to one side like this."

"I'm not pushing you anywhere, apart from taking you outside to enjoy the fresh air."

"See, pushing me."

She chuckled. "Mom, you're a hoot."

"I know. So, tell me all about it, come on. I want to hear every single little detail."

She told her mother exactly what had happened. She couldn't remember word for word what Alfie had said, and by the time she made it to the garden and sat down on the bench beside her mother, she was exhausted.

"Now tell me what you want to do about it," Lily said.

"There's nothing to do about it. I don't know if I can come home."

"Why not?"

"I'd be looking for work, and I don't want to work at the diner, not with Katie working there."

Lily wrinkled her nose. "You should see her coming onto all the men. It's kind of gross."

"I don't know what I want anymore. I've loved being away and finding myself. I love cooking and baking. I love being in the kitchen, but the city, it's not home, you know. It always feels different when you're with me, but you won't move to the city because your life is very much here. I'm so confused." She pressed her face against her hands.

"Do you want my advice?"

"Mom, you got hit by a car not long ago. You're in the hospital with a couple of broken legs. I don't know if I should take your advice."

"Move back home. Take some time to find your feet. You mentioned the whole food blogging thing. Try that out."

"I couldn't do that."

"Why not?"

"I'm not very good at the whole computer stuff."

"Then hire someone, or better yet, just take a bunch of pictures and see what happens. It can't be as bad as working in a restaurant with a guy who orders you to date him, and leaves you feeling so uncomfortable. You're my daughter, and I'm not having you treated any way you don't want to."

"Thank you, Mom," she said.

"You're always welcome at home, and I know I'd love to have you around."

"You need someone to take care of you for the next couple of months. I'm not going anywhere. I'll go and pack up my apartment, hand over the keys, and return home feeling like a failure."

Lily lightly tapped her arm. "You are not a failure, far from it, and I won't accept you calling yourself that. You're my daughter. You're a chef. Be proud of who you are."

Chloe rested her head on Lily's shoulder. "Love you, Mom."

"I love you too, honey."

"When I got the call, I was so scared. I thought I'd lost you."

"It's going to take more than a fast car to take me on. Believe me."

She stayed with her head resting against her mother's shoulder for some time. Lily ran her fingers through her hair, and Chloe allowed all the day's stresses to just evaporate into the air.

She forgot all about them, and stayed completely calm.

It wasn't a failure coming home without a job or any career prospects.

"Mom, how do you feel about Eagle?" she asked.

The one part of her guilt when it came to the incident five years ago was Eagle and Lily. They were so good together, and if Alfie wanted her help to fix it, she was more than willing to do whatever it took to bring the two together.

"Chloe, I know what you're trying to do, and it's not going to work."

She lifted her head and looked at her mother. Lily's fingers played with the blanket. "Why isn't it?"

"Eagle and I, it ran its course, and there's no way for us to get back what we lost. I told you, I couldn't be with someone whose son planned to do that."

"If I can forgive Alfie, you'd consider Eagle

again?" Chloe asked, tilting her head to the side.

Lily stared at her, waiting. "Why do I feel like I'm about to be manipulated here?"

"Think about it, Mom, it's what you said. If I can find it in my heart to forgive Alfie for what happened, in theory, you can also forgive Eagle and maybe go out on a date with him, or something. You could at least tell Eagle to start treating his son like a human being and not scum."

"I've got two broken legs, and I … I've always hated the way Eagle is with Alfie. I never felt it was my place to tell him otherwise. I'm not his mother, and well, Eagle is his father. I don't know. I've made so many mistakes."

"Not right now, obviously. I'm talking about in the future. To give you guys another chance, what do you think?"

"I think I'm getting way too old to negotiate this."

"Mom, you're forty-three, and women are still having babies at your age. You're not that old."

"Everything is heading south," Lily said, her face flaming. "You don't think I see the women who hang around the club? I do."

"None of them will ever compare to you, Mom." Chloe put her hand on her mother's. "You've always had Eagle's attention, even when you were a married woman."

Lily shook her head. "I don't know. Maybe if … forget about it."

"Come on, Mom, tell me."

"If you and Alfie were to attempt to give it a shot."

"That's a huge step up from forgiving. Dating is, like, spending a lot more time with each other, and getting used to our spaces, and making it all personal."

"You're home, maybe give it a shot."

"What happened to never coming back to town again?"

"I didn't think you'd want to come back, and besides, you've got the reason you need. You did nothing wrong, and I guess this is something I've been thinking about, Chloe. You ran away, and I let you. I myself didn't fight, and what I've come to realize, we should have. We didn't do anything wrong. Neither of us did. The wrong was done *to* you—and to Alfie. Alfie told me about Daniel and how he got into a fight with him. I watched him destroy the tape as well, Chloe." Lily took hold of her hands. "You shouldn't have to run away. You've done nothing wrong in your entire life."

"Do you think I should forgive him? The video wasn't his fault, I get it, but can I go through all of this again? I'm so confused when it comes to him. What would you do?"

"I can't tell you what I'd do, Chloe. This is all on you, and I won't be responsible for making such a life-changing decision for you."

"Thank you, Mom."

"No, thank *you*." Lily chuckled. "I'm going to be doing a lot of thanking. I can't believe this happened to me."

"I'll take care of you."

"I'm not exactly a lightweight, honey."

"I'll be there to help," Eagle said, joining them. He held a small bouquet of flowers. They looked like wild ones, her mother's favorite.

"Eagle, what a pleasant surprise."

"Alfie is getting us all some food at the café. You care to join us? Hospital food in bed, or in the café."

"Sounds like fun," Lily said.

Chloe saw her mother's blush. The color in her cheeks suited her.

"Are you joining us, Chloe?" Lily asked.

She saw the begging in her eyes without saying a single word. "Sure, why not? It could be fun."

Eagle pushed her mother, and they followed the hospital signs toward the café. It was a rather large room and incredibly loud, but she liked it.

For Chloe she hated places where you could hear a pin drop as it always reminded her of that night at the fair.

Alfie had found a booth, and he'd also gotten plates of food.

"I think I ordered everything," he said.

Chloe bent down and put the locks on her mother's wheelchair. She was about to slide in beside her, but quickly moved, sitting beside Alfie so Eagle could sit with her mother. She would have to get used to being around Alfie if she wanted this to work with her mother.

"You're looking better, Lily," Alfie said.

"Thanks. Apart from the legs, I feel better. Until I look in the mirror and see how bruised I am. The pain meds they're giving me are working wonders."

"You're not taking too many?" Eagle asked.

"Of course not. You know me, I like to keep my wits about me and prove I can handle pain as good as any man."

Chloe laughed. Her mother was a bit of a hard ass when it came to pain. Lily didn't like to take any medication unless it was absolutely essential.

"It's what I adored about you," Eagle said.

Everyone at the table paused, and Chloe knew she had to get this to work for them.

Turning her attention to the vegetable lasagna,

which she'd seen written on the board entering the café, she took a bite. It was a little overcooked, but she wouldn't complain.

"I heard your breakfast date got crashed," Lily said.

"Trust Ian and Riley to invite themselves," Alfie said. "I can't shake them."

"They're okay." She tucked her hair behind her ear. "They're friends, right, and I'm guessing friends can be crazy and drive you insane. All the good stuff people love and hate." She had to shut up as she was just talking for the sake of it.

"Will you be asking her out again?" Lily asked.

"Mom!"

"I'd really like to. I feel we left a lot unresolved this morning," Alfie said.

"Speaking of shit that's unresolved, here you go, son." Eagle threw a set of keys across the table. "The bike's at the clubhouse."

Alfie looked at the keys in wonder and then at his dad. "Is this? This is the key to my bike?"

"Yeah, about that. I overreacted, and I've been working on it with Nick's help. I finally got it finished last month. I've been meaning to, you know, find the right time to tell you."

"This the bike you got back in high school?" Chloe asked.

"Yeah, but Dad trashed it after what happened."

"You trashed his bike after you spent all that money getting it built for him?" Lily asked.

"You knew about my bike?" Alfie asked.

"I saw it when he came riding across my lawn with it before he gave it to you. Told me how he'd been a bit of a mess with you and wanted to make it up. Some father-son, bonding stuff. You really trashed it? Why?

Why would you do that to your son?"

Eagle looked at Lily, the two sharing some kind of moment, and it wasn't comfortable either. Lily glared, and Eagle looked embarrassed.

"I trashed it because he needed to be taught a lesson. We'll talk about it another time."

"Don't worry about it, Lily. Honestly, I deserved it."

"No, you didn't," Lily said. "You were just as much of a victim as Chloe. What happened between the two of you should have remained private, but it didn't. Eagle had no right to trash your bike, and I shouldn't have pushed you away either. For that, I'm sorry."

Silence fell around the table, and Chloe started to feel a little sick. She hated tension or conflict. It was another reason she had run like hell and not looked back.

When she couldn't take another bite, she opened up a bottle of water and took a swig.

"When are you going to ask her out?" Lily asked.

"I'm thinking of doing it right now," Alfie said.

"Don't let me hold you back."

"Alfie, you want to go out tonight, dancing?" Chloe asked, shocking the whole table.

Lily chuckled. "There goes my daughter. She is not one to be told what to do."

"You want to take me dancing?"

"Why not? You can dance, can't you?" she asked.

"Even if I can't, I'm sure you'd teach me."

She'd missed his blue eyes and the smile that always made her think of sex and sin. Being this close to him again after so long apart, she was starting to remember all the good things.

The one bad was slowly canceling out, and she hadn't thought it was possible for her to feel anything but anger toward him, and yet, here they were, organizing a date. A date she'd asked for.

"Of course I'd be happy to teach you."

"Consider it a date then."

Chapter Fifteen

Alfie was nervous as he rode up to Chloe's house. She'd been the one to ask him on this date, and now it was really up to him to show her a good time. A chance to shine for her.

Parking his bike, his brand-new baby, he couldn't help but smile. Eagle had dropped him off at the clubhouse and in his own way apologized. He knew deep down his father didn't mean him any harm. He just didn't know how to deal with his own feelings, and when it came to Lily, it triggered something within Eagle.

With Chloe back, he saw a chance for them to be together without all the bullshit lies. She knew the truth, and now he could work around making her fall for him, the real him. He'd given her a piece of himself five years ago. It wasn't all bullshit, regardless of what she thought.

When he knocked on the door, Chloe opened it a second later with a smile.

"Hey," she said.

"Hey."

She wore a pair of jeans and a long black crop top. "I didn't know where we were going, and I can only remember the bar as a place to dance. Am I good enough?"

"Chloe, even if you were dressed in a sack of potatoes, you'd be good enough."

"You're just saying that."

"I'm not. I want this date to work tonight." He took her hand, and she left her house, locking the door behind her. "Are you ready to see my other beauty?"

"Your bike?" She ran his hand across the back seat. "I still can't believe your dad trashed this."

"He did. He was angry."

"Do you think you give him enough excuses?

You were kicked out of the club, unable to earn prospect until recently. He trashed your bike, and you moved out."

"Every kid needs to move out of their parents' house."

"True, but this all happened because of one night. You'd think he would have taken your side."

"Why would he take my side?"

"You're his son, and we were both victims."

Alfie laughed. "You're cute."

"I'm being serious."

"It's not about being cute. I know this is a little confusing, but Eagle's not just my dad. As a club president he gave me an order, and as the tape showed, falling in love with you wasn't my original plan. That all came after. I did intend to do something similar, Chloe. I did change everything though. At first, because I really didn't want to piss off Eagle with the way he felt about Lily."

"At first? So, what's second?"

"I fell in love with you. There's no way I wanted to hurt you. The night you gave yourself to me, I hated how I hurt you."

"It's supposed to hurt."

"Doesn't mean I didn't want to take the hurt away." He placed a hand on her hip, wanting to draw her in close. "I've never wanted to hurt you."

She rested her hand against his chest. "I don't know if I can talk about this."

"You've got all the time in the world." He pressed a quick kiss to her lips, and then produced the helmet. "This was the one thing he didn't destroy."

"I'm not putting it on."

"Chloe? I'm the one riding."

"Don't care. I want to feel the wind in my hair. You can't make me."

"Can I pay you to wear the helmet?"

"Nope."

"Fine." He tucked the helmet away and climbed on. "You better hold me tight."

"I intend to." She climbed on the back of his bike, arms wrapped around his waist, and he was sure she pressed her lips against his ear, but it could just be him imagining her doing all those things. "Like this."

His cock was paying close attention to how close she was, and he liked it. Damn did it feel good to have her here.

"Yes."

He revved the engine and took off down the street, heading toward the bar. The instant he started to move, Chloe's grip tightened. He wanted to bask in the moment, to close his eyes, and enjoy the feel of her arms around him, but he had to focus on the road.

Not that there were many cars.

His father was still investigating all the security cameras in the guise of helping Ryan. The club wanted to know who would dare run down a Satan's Croft resident without any consequences. So far, none of them could see any cars that weren't accounted for.

Lily had given them a brief description of it looked like a standard five-seater car, brown, and it hurt like hell.

Her words, and it wasn't exactly easy. She didn't see the make or model.

The fact she didn't have time to see those little details, told them exactly how fast they were, which didn't exactly settle his dad's nerves.

Arriving at the bar, he saw several of the club bikes already parked. If they weren't partying at the clubhouse, they were always at the Cove, which was Satan's Croft's only bar.

The small town didn't require much, and rarely did anyone set up a competing business. If it wasn't for the club's investment, this town would have gone bankrupt years ago.

Chloe climbed off the bike and used the seat to help her gain her balance. "That was amazing." She drew out the last word with a laugh.

"You can't ever sit on the back of anyone else's bike."

"I can't."

"No."

"Why the hell not?" she asked.

"You do look so cute when you're angry."

"You think this is angry, you haven't seen nothing." Like old times, she grabbed his waist and pressed a kiss to his lips.

It was so sudden and natural, it made him pause.

She jerked back. "Shit, I'm so sorry."

"We're on a date. You've got nothing to apologize for."

"With how close we were it seemed so natural to just kiss you."

"You don't have to make excuses. I've got really kissable lips." He puckered up.

"Come on, before those lips get you into trouble."

She did another little surprise. She grabbed his hand, and they walked together into the bar.

The place was packed with dancing bodies, the heat already getting to them. Most of them were sweaty, grinding against each other.

"I always imagined this place was empty, you know?"

"Nah, a lot of people love to get their shit on," he said. Gripping her hand a little tighter, he pulled her toward the bar, and once he got enough room, he placed her in front of him, holding her shoulders as she led him to where the bar was. He ordered her a beer, and himself some water.

"Water?"

"You think I'm going to risk you? I don't drink and drive." And especially after just getting his baby back.

"You have become all responsible, haven't you?"

"Can't help it, babe, comes with the territory."

Their drinks were served, and he downed his in one, while Chloe sipped at hers.

With how many people were in the bar, they had no choice but to stand close together. The music was pulsing, almost vibrating the ground.

"You want to dance?" she asked.

"Finish your beer first."

"Are you trying to get me drunk?"

"I don't want to risk it being roofied."

"That's a thing here as well?"

He tensed up. "Someone roofied you?"

"No, not me personally. You know it happens. I've never heard of it in town."

"You'd be surprised how times change a lot of people."

"Not all that surprised actually." She grabbed his arm. "Like this. You work out a lot, don't you?"

She didn't grope his muscle, simply squeezed and let go.

"It's a way to relieve the tension."

"Tension?"

"I don't date, and when I think about all I lost, it stops me from pummeling the first guy I meet to death." He laid a hand on her hip, wanting so badly to be anywhere but here.

Chloe downed her beer, all in one, which he'd

never seen her do before. She took his hand.

"Let's dance."

She once again had his hand, and they were able to push their way between the sweaty, pulsing bodies.

Alfie wasn't looking forward to dancing, but with how close everyone was, he didn't have a problem holding onto Chloe in any way.

Hands on her hips, he pulled her in close, staring into her blue eyes.

"It has been a long time."

"My mom wants me to date you before she will consider being with your dad again."

Alfie frowned. "What?"

"You mentioned about us getting our parents back together. I've seen the way they look at each other, and I don't want to be responsible for tearing them apart. Not anymore."

"What does that have to do with us dating?"

"Mom wants to know I can stand to be around you without it tearing me apart." She nibbled her lip.

"Is the only reason you invited me to this date for them?" Alfie asked.

He'd thought he had a real shot at all of this, and now he was being told differently.

"No," she said.

"No?"

She laughed. "I thought it was, but it's not. I … can we just dance please and talk after?"

"On one condition."

"What?" she asked.

"I get to kiss you."

"You're negotiating for a kiss?"

"You bet your sweet ass I am, baby. I want a kiss. On the lips."

"Do you want to time us as well there, buddy?"

"No, once we start, I know it will last a sufficient amount of time."

"I don't know if you're crazy or not."

"I'm definitely crazy. No doubt about that one." He ran his hand down to her ass. "The kid gloves are coming off." He squeezed her ass and pulled her close to him so she was flush against his body. Fortunately, he had his dick completely under control, but that was about it. "I'm going to fight for you, Chloe."

"You're really not wasting any time."

"I wasted too much of it and ended up watching you go. I'm not doing it again." He stroked a finger down her cheek. "You mean too much to me, and I already lost you once. All of my cards will be out on the table. There will be no one else. Not now, not ever, that will compare to you."

"Alfie?"

He pressed his lips to hers, taking her hands and putting them around his neck, exactly where they should be. With his hands back on her hips, he slowly began to move to the beat of the music.

"You do know how to dance."

"Five years of practice, I kind of got the handle of it. I could swing you around this dance floor, but right now, you're likely to end up with a concussion from smacking into everyone."

She burst out laughing. "Wow."

"What?"

"It's like I've never been gone with you."

"Like the last five years were a sick fucking joke?" he asked.

"Yes."

She rested her head against his chest, and Alfie wanted to fist pump the world. This was more than he could ask for.

Several people would look their way, but he ignored them. Word was already out after what he did in the diner, Chloe was off limits. The memory of the "fair fuck," which was what it had been known as, had to be forgotten.

He wasn't playing around this time.

When it came to Chloe, he was going to win her fair and square.

****

They danced for two hours straight, and rather than go home, Chloe went back to his apartment. He lived about a twenty-minute ride from the clubhouse. The apartment block was a nice one though, a great neighborhood. The block itself only had enough for twenty residents at one time, so it wasn't a huge building, and Alfie lived on the second floor.

"If I'm lucky, Ian and Riley are not here."

"They live with you?"

"No. Ian's got his own place above the clothing store, and Riley still lives with his dad until he can find a place. Out of all of us, Riley likes to spend his money on strippers."

"And you don't."

"There's only one pair of tits I've wanted to see. The only time I'm at the titty place is when I'm ordered to go as part of club duty."

"You really don't want to see anyone else?"

He opened the door, and the light was off.

"Does it mean it your friends are not here?"

"No. They like to crash here." Alfie closed the door and took off. She stepped into his apartment expecting to find beer cans and mess, and instead, she found a really nice place.

She looked around, seeing a small television and a gaming unit. He had a sofa and a chair, both of them matched in color.

There were shelves with a couple of books or figurines and pictures. She stepped up to the one on the far side and picked it up.

It was a picture of her and Alfie, taken on the bleachers, when he convinced her to spend the afternoon dodging teachers.

When Lily found out she skipped a class, her mother had been so mad and told her it had to be the only time she did anything crazy. Her education always came first.

"They're not here," Alfie said.

She put the picture back and saw one that made her frown.

"How did you get this?" Chloe asked, picking one up with her mother. She wore a chef's uniform, and her mother held a plate of food. It had been one of the events at the culinary school.

"I, erm, I stole it."

"How did you even know about it?"

"Your mom dropped it after they got developed."

"Oh."

"I didn't return it. I was so happy for you, and I saw how happy you were. I knew I couldn't come and get you."

She put the photo down. "You wanted to?"

"You think I just wanted to live my life waiting for you to come home?"

"You had an out, Alfie."

"It was an out I didn't want." He shrugged. "You think this has been easy for me? I knew where you were. I wanted to make it up to you, but I knew coming to you at the school, it wouldn't help my cause. You had this plan even before me, and I wasn't going to come between you and your dreams."

"And now?"

"Now you're in town. You've got whatever qualification you've got, and now, I'm not going to stop in my pursuit of you."

"With all the ink, it's kind of hard to take this seriously. Pursuit?"

"Did I tell you since you left, I took up reading?" He stepped up toward her.

"No. You read?"

"Of course I can read." He pulled out his wallet and held up a little card. "I've got my own membership to the library and everything."

"A lot has changed."

"Not my feelings for you," he said.

She didn't know what to say whenever he brought up feelings, a future.

Tonight had been easy. No one had brought up the past, but it still lingered in the air. However, she had to get over it.

She needed closure. "I didn't ask you to go dancing with me just for Mom or Eagle."

He didn't step away or give her space. It was hard to focus with him so close, but she wasn't going to be distracted, or at least she kept on telling herself that.

"Then why?"

"Because I wanted to. I mean, I love to dance. I've never been dancing before. Not on a date, and well, I know Mom wants me to find my peace with you before she would even consider going on a date with Eagle. Don't you think we've come between them enough?"

"Look, what happened between our parents wasn't our fault."

She chuckled. "It was. I can't believe you don't see it."

"I see it. Yes, they didn't make it because of what

happened between us, but you know your mom and I know my dad. If they wanted to make this work, they would have. I don't think they were ready, and they used us as an excuse."

"Your dad was head over heels in love with my mom."

"I know, and it's exactly my point. He'd spent a lifetime watching her and now he had a chance to have her, but also, not too long after her divorce. I'm thinking he was a little worried about being the rebound guy."

"You do realize how crazy that sounds," she said.

"Crazy but true. Dad's not been with anyone serious, not even my mother. Then all of a sudden, your mom is available. The woman he's been in love with for all of his life. There was no way he was going to pass that up."

"What about the last five years?"

"That I can't answer. Club business has pulled him away. You pulled your mom away. I don't know. I want to help get them back together."

"We can do that," she said. "I don't think your dad deserves it though. The way he treats you and has treated you, is wrong."

"Don't do this. It's fine."

"The fact you think it's fine, is wrong."

"You still owe me a kiss."

"Alfie?"

"And you've got to promise me you'll give us a shot."

"You're seriously asking me for this?"

He took her hand and placed it over his chest. She felt the rapidly beating pulse of his heart.

"Do you feel that?" he asked.

"It's your heart."

"And it's beating wildly for you. No one else.

I've been waiting for this chance for five years, and I'm not going to pass it up, not for my dad, not for anyone. You're the one I want, Chloe." He sank his fingers into her hair, tilted her head back, and she didn't have time to fight the rush of heat as he slammed his lips down on hers.

It was an all-consuming kiss.

One that told her he meant business and wasn't going to stop until she felt the spark. For Chloe, the spark had never gone. It hadn't even faded; it just held a horrible memory.

Rather than push him away, she wrapped her hands around his neck and kissed him back.

It had been so long since she'd been with him. There hadn't been anyone else. Reginald had wanted to take her back to his place and show her how a real chef fucked, but she'd turned him down flat. The thought of being with anyone had never appealed to her, until Alfie.

He pressed her up against the wall. The hand on her hip slid up to cup her breast. She let out a moan as he broke the kiss, trailing his lips down to her neck.

"I've only ever wanted you, Chloe. You're not the first woman I've slept with, but you will be my last."

"You've got to stop saying these things," she said.

"Why?"

"Because I'm going to start believing them."

"I want you to believe them." He hovered over her pulse, and as he bit down, she couldn't contain her scream as it consumed them. "They're the truth." He flicked his tongue across her pulse, soothing out the pain.

It felt amazing being in his arms, having his touch.

"Please," she said.

"What are you asking?"

"Don't stop. I need you." Her face heated as she realized what she was asking him.

They had been apart for five years, but it only felt like it was yesterday when she opened her door and there he stood, waiting to take her to the fair.

He pulled up the fabric of her shirt, and she didn't fight him. Instead, she grabbed his shirt and tore at it, dragging it over his head. He let out a chuckle as she fought him to get naked.

He began to move her away from the wall and toward his bedroom. Each of them tackled the other's jeans, until they stood before each other in only their underwear. Alfie wore a pair of black boxers, while she was in her black, lacy underwear.

"I've had so many dreams, imagining you here, like this, and wanting to fuck you so badly."

"I've not been with anyone else."

"Just like me," he said. He stroked a finger around her back, going to the catch of her bra. He flicked it open, and her tits sprang free. She didn't make a single move to cover herself.

Pulling the bra off, she sank to her knees, taking his boxer briefs. The hard ridge of his cock pressing against the front of them had been impressive, but nothing compared to seeing him long, thick, and naked.

Her hand shook as she wrapped her fingers around his length.

He released a cute little growl as she started to touch him. She was gentle at first, getting used to touching him.

"Do you have any idea what you're doing to me?" he asked.

"I know I can make it better."

"Oh, yeah, how?"

She put the tip against her lips and sucked him

into her mouth.

"Fuck!" He yelled the word.

She went as deep as he could go, hitting the back of her throat before she pulled back. She did this several times, sucking on him as if he was a lollipop. When she glanced up at him, he had his hands on his hips, and he looked like he was losing control, which she wanted him to do.

With her other hand, she cupped his balls, playing with them as she sucked him off. Each time he cursed, she knew she'd hit the right spot.

"I'm not going to come in your mouth." He pushed her away, lifting her up, and dropping her onto the bed.

"You were so close."

"Chloe, it has been five years since I've been with anyone. I'm not going to last."

"You've used your hand."

"Believe me, it doesn't compare with your sexy as fuck mouth, or your pussy. There's no way I could ever have that kind of control with you." He slid between her thighs and pushed her up the bed, until his face was directly above her pussy.

She still wore her panties, but in one tear, he had them gone.

"Spread them."

She opened her legs wide and cried out as his face pressed against her pussy. His tongue slid between her slit, stroking over her swollen clit. The pleasure was instant, shocking, painful, and amazing all at once.

He bit down on her clit, drawing the nub between his teeth before soothing it out with his tongue. He glided down to her entrance and fucked her using his fingers and tongue to heighten the sensation.

She couldn't think, couldn't form a single word.

He brought her to a screaming orgasm, and as she came down, he moved between her thighs, sliding in deep. The last ripple of her orgasm was intense as she completed around his cock.

"I forgot how fucking incredible you were," he said. "You never faked it once with me. You always let me see the real you."

He took her hands, placing them above her head as he started to pull out of her. She watched him as he looked down between where they were joined. His cock was already slick with her cum.

Alfie slammed, surprising her with how big he was, and how long. He didn't stop there, he pounded into her, making up for lost time as he claimed her lips.

She was fucking Alfie.

Back in his bed after so long.

This shouldn't be happening, and yet, she didn't want him to stop.

This was real to her.

The past, it needed to be put to bed. She wasn't here for her mother and Eagle. She was here because these feelings for Alfie were not dying. They'd been put on hold, and they both owed it to each other, to make this work. It didn't take Alfie long to find his release. Within a few strokes, he came, yelling out her name, the sound echoing off the walls.

Their orgasms may have come quick, but to Chloe, they were perfect, because they were the start of something amazing.

Chapter Sixteen

The following morning, Alfie pretended to be asleep. He watched Chloe sleep, but when she started to wake up, he lowered his eyes enough to still see her but for her to think he was still asleep.

She turned to look at him, and he saw the smile on her lips.

At least she wasn't angry or regretting last night.

She slowly started to try to leave the bed, but he wasn't going to have that. Quickly reaching for her, he dragged her beneath him.

She let out a little cry. "What are you doing?"

"If you think I'm going to let you leave this bed, you are very much mistaken," he said, claiming her lips.

She moaned, running her hands all over his back, and holding him tightly.

"I could get used to this," he said, pulling away. He smiled down at her.

"I can't believe we did this."

"You're not having any regrets, are you?"

"None. You?"

"None. This is what I've been hoping for. I wanted to come and get you so many times," he said.

"You did?"

"Yeah. A few times I'd think about calling a cab, and coming to visit you, to talk to you, and each time, I'd find a reason that seemed so much bigger." He kissed her again. "I love you, Chloe."

"Alfie, it's too soon."

"I know. I'm not going to hide my feelings for you, baby. I want you. You're back in town, and I'm not going to give you a reason to run. Not again. I'm going to be open, honest, and true with you."

He moved between her thighs.

When he woke, he didn't intend to have sex with her, but pulling the blanket away from her body, and seeing those curves, he just couldn't resist." He kissed down to her tits, sucking on each nipple before moving back up.

He gripped his rock-hard cock and slid it between her wet folds. She gasped and spread her legs wider for him.

Finding her entrance, he pressed forward a couple of inches before slamming to the hilt within her.

She gasped.

He moaned. Pulling out until only the tip of him was inside her, he pushed forward and started to make love to her.

In and out, watching her.

"I want you on top of me," he said.

He spun them so she was straddling him with those beautiful tits in front of his face.

He lifted up and kissed each one before sucking on the nipples. Pushing them together, he pressed his face against the curve of each.

"Alfie." She moaned.

Sliding his hands down to her hips, he guided her over his cock, showing her what he wanted from her.

He drove into her slowly at first, until Chloe gained her confidence. Her hands rested on his shoulders as she worked her pussy over his length.

He watched her take him, and it was such a pretty sight, one he'd been dreaming about for so long. Reaching between her thighs, he began to stroke her clit. "I want you to come all over my cock, Chloe. Let me feel you come."

She cried out as he teased her clit, but he didn't stop.

When she came, it set off his own release. She

was so fucking tight, and as she wrapped around him, every single pulse and clench of her cunt seemed to milk his cock from his cum.

Just as they were coming down from their peak, he heard the unmistakable sound of his door opening and closing.

Chloe looked at him, but they didn't have time.

"Yo, Rock, man, you still here?" Ian said, yelling.

"Get out." He was too late in yelling as the door to his bedroom was pushed open.

Chloe let out a scream and pressed herself against him.

"Shit, man, sorry."

"Get the fuck out."

"Dude, that's Chloe, right?" Ian asked.

"Yes," Chloe said, letting out another little scream.

"I didn't mean to walk in on the two of you," Ian said.

"Get the fuck out," Alfie said.

"Yeah, shit, sorry."

"Close the door," he said, yelling to be heard.

The door was closed, and Chloe had her face pressed against his shoulder.

"Forgive me, I have the most invasive asshole friends," he said.

Her face was bright red. "They were never like this in high school."

"Yeah, well, it would seem they didn't grow up at all."

"I can't believe they just walked in," she said, giggling.

"They're so used to me being on my own." He couldn't get enough of touching her. He ran his hands all over her body, trying to convince himself she was very much real.

"It's all true?"

"Yes. I've been without a woman for so long, and you're the only one I want. I love you more than anything, and I'm willing to do whatever it takes to keep you."

"Alfie."

"I know you don't believe this can work, and you're right, maybe it can't, but what if we *can* make it work? What if you and I are destined to be better, to do better?" he asked.

"I don't know if it's possible," she said.

"You're willing to run away without giving this a shot?"

"I'm not running away."

"Then give us a shot the way your mom is going to give Eagle a shot," he said.

"You know it's weird how you go from calling him Dad to Eagle."

"I'm used to it. I've spent my entire life doing this."

"Come on, guys, I'm hungry," Riley said, banging on the door. "Let's move this morning fuck along."

Chloe's eyes went wide. "Wow."

"Yeah, they've felt guilty about the whole thing and want to make it up to you."

"By shouting stuff like that through the door?"

"No, by making you feel like you belong."

"Have you primed them for this?"

"Nope."

"My clothes are not in here, Alfie. They're outside."

"I'll go and get them for you." He pressed a kiss to her lips and climbed out of bed.

Pulling on a pair of jeans, he opened his door and closed it.

Riley and Ian were both in his kitchen, looking through his cupboards. "What the fuck are you two doing here?"

"Breakfast. You've got nothing. You need to shop."

"You've both got places of your own to eat, so why do you have to invade my space?" He quickly picked up Chloe's clothes. There was no sign of her underwear, so he hoped that was back in the room.

"You love eating breakfast with us," Ian said. "I guess it went really well last night, didn't it?"

"I'm not about to kiss and tell with you guys." He rubbed the back of his head. "Will you all try not to be a dick around her, please? You think you guys can manage that? I want this to work."

"Dude, you think we don't know how important this is for you?" Ian asked. "Five years. I'm surprised you've not rubbed your hand out by now."

"Nice, real nice." He glared at them. "Just, be nice."

"She'll never remember the fucking past," Riley said. "I swear, every time I think of that piece of shit, I believe you let him off lightly."

"Yeah, well, there's nothing we can do about it now." He'd burned the tape and made sure Daniel never stepped foot in town. There was no way the club could bury him as too many people knew what had happened. It would raise questions.

"Go and get her, and we can head to the diner," Riley said. "I'm starved. Hurry up."

Alfie went back into his bedroom, determined to go at his own pace.

Chloe was already out of bed. "They're still out

there?"

"Yep, and I want another kiss." He dropped her clothes to the floor and pulled her in close. "They want to go to the diner."

"Cool."

"Are you coming?"

"I don't know."

"Chloe, you have nothing to be ashamed of. I'm not going to hide it, and anyone who says shit to you, you come to me, got it?" he asked. He kissed her for good measure, and this time, she smiled.

"Fine, got it. I'll give this a chance. All of it. You've got to help me with my mom though."

"Whatever you need me to do, just let me know."

He helped her get changed, which was the complete opposite of what he really wanted to do. He'd been without her for so long, and all he wished to do was spend the day fucking her.

However, he also had jobs to do at the club.

Once they were dressed, Ian and Riley were waiting, and per his request, they didn't speak a word of finding them having sex. So far, so good.

****

"You two had sex?" Lily asked.

"Mom, that wasn't for you to make an announcement," Chloe said, packing her mother's things. The doctor had signed her out as an outpatient. She would need to rest while her legs healed. There were no further signs of concussion, and so long as she had help, he didn't see why she couldn't heal at home.

For Lily, she couldn't get packed fast enough.

Chloe stared at the flowers. "What do you want me to do with them?"

"Keep them. They'll brighten up our sitting room."

"Eagle's going to be here any minute," Chloe said.

"You're avoiding the subject."

"Last time you discovered I was having sex, you were mad."

"No, I wasn't mad, I wanted you to be protected." Chloe paused.

"What is it?" Lily asked.

"Nothing. I'm just remembering the time you yelled at me, telling me I shouldn't be having sex. It's all good." She wasn't remembering that time at all. Nope. Her thoughts had gone back to the previous night and this morning.

No condom.

Protection hadn't been on her mind.

Shit.

This was something she was going to have to deal with.

"I don't like the look on your face."

"Mom, it's my face, and you're going to have to get used to it."

"I don't like it. You're hiding something," Lily said.

"I don't want you to freak out, but I've invited Eagle and Alfie to eat dinner with us tonight. You will be the one entertaining, and I'll be the one cooking."

"You're cooking for all of us?"

"Yes. I pretty much did all the cooking when they were invited years ago. Why not now? We had a deal, remember?"

"I remember the deal. So, have you forgiven Alfie?" Lily asked.

Chloe rubbed one of the soft flower petals as she thought about Alfie. "Yes. I think I have."

"Why are you suddenly so ready to forgive him?"

She pursed her lips. "You're really making me work for this one, aren't you?"

"Why not? Life sucks at times, and I've got no other choice but to force you to use your head."

"Fine. When I'm with him, it's like … magic." She laughed. "Don't get me wrong, I remember the pain from the day at the fair. Knowing what he had planned, but he wasn't going to see it through. He keeps telling me he loves me."

"Do you trust him?"

"I don't know if I trust him. I'm so confused. This would be a lot easier to talk about if you weren't my mother."

"Why?"

"I'd be able to talk about everything and it not be weird."

Lily chuckled. "Fair enough. I take it he took care of you?"

"Yes."

"Good. I'm glad. You've got to learn to take chances in life otherwise you'll live with regrets."

"Do you have any regrets?"

"A couple, yes."

"What are they?"

"I don't want to tell you."

"Why not?"

"I don't want you to be upset by them."

"I'm not going to be upset by anything you do, Mom. Trust me."

"The first regret is putting up with your father for so long. The amount of disappointment we both suffered because of it. I will always regret that," she said.

"You were so heartbroken when you made the choice."

"Because I'd failed, Chloe. I'd failed you and

myself. I wanted it to work so much. I loved him, so deeply, but he killed that love every single day he picked the club over me. They didn't patch him in, and he was so weak as well. He was afraid of the dark, you know?"

"He was?"

"Yes. I had to sleep with the night light on, and whenever there was a noise, I was the one to go and check it out."

"I had no idea," Chloe said.

"Tell me about it."

"What's your other regret?" She saw tears in Lily's eyes.

"It's kind of a joined one."

"Tell me."

"You, Alfie, and Eagle." Her mother pressed her hand to her face.

"Mom, you don't have to do that at all. You don't have to cover your face."

"Yes, I do. I'm so embarrassed."

"Why?"

"I let you run away. I didn't force you to talk to Alfie. I knew it had broken your heart, but I also knew *he* wasn't the one who sent that tape in. Oh, honey, I love you. I love you so much. I missed Eagle. It's why I tried to stay as far away from him as possible. I couldn't stand to be near him and know all of what I'd lost." Lily wiped away the tears, even as they kept on falling. "They're a selfish regret."

"Do you think I should have forgiven Alfie sooner?"

"I think you two should have been able to work this out on your own. I truly believe that." Lily squeezed her hand. "Regardless of how I got in this hospital, I'm so pleased I did because it meant I could see you again, and we could have this chance."

She hugged her mom tightly.

Was it a second chance?

Someone cleared his throat, and she pulled away to see Eagle waiting. She would fix this for her mother.

"I've got the car waiting," he said.

"Will you bring her down? I'll go and load up her bags."

"Sure thing. Alfie is waiting with the car."

Her heart beat a little faster as she made her way to the front of the hospital to find Alfie there. He had the trunk of the car open, and he offered her a smile. "Hello, beautiful."

"Hey, you." She had no clue what to say. "How are you?"

"Exhausted. I've been moving beer for the bar. It's one of the perks of being a prospect. I get all the shitty jobs."

"I've been thinking, it's a rather quick thought. My apartment's lease runs out at the end of the month. I need to head back to the city, grab my things. Would you be willing to take me?"

"I don't have a car, but I could borrow my dad's. If he'll let me," he said.

"He'll let you."

"How do you know?"

"I've got a plan for him and Mom. You'll see."

"You can't use your mom to get what you want," he said.

"Eagle's still as in love with her as he ever was. Believe me, it'll work." She put the bags into the back of the car, and watched as Eagle pushed her mother out of the door. There was no mistaking the love between the two of them. It truly was sweet.

Glancing over at Alfie, she wondered if he did feel as deeply as Eagle did for her mother.

"I can see that look in your eye, and to answer your question, yes. I do."

"I didn't even say anything," she said.

"I can see it. I love you, Chloe, and one day, you will get to see it. I promise." Alfie walked up toward her, wrapped his arms around her waist, and brought his lips to her mouth. The kiss was sweet, and she couldn't deny how much it meant to her. She didn't want to ever stop kissing him.

Pulling away from his lips, she smiled. "You do know how to make an impression."

"I won't let you down this time," he said.

"I know you won't. There's no chance of you ever doing something like that." She patted his chest, and she did feel herself falling.

"That's a good sight to behold," Lily said. "You two always did look good together."

For Chloe, she knew she would always have a piece of her heart that truly belonged to Alfie. No matter what, she would love him for the rest of her life.

****

Three days later

"You really think this is going to work?" Eagle asked, taking a seat beside Lily. He handed her a hot chocolate, and he turned toward her.

"You and I both know our kids needed a push in the right direction. Have you found out who ran me over?"

"No. Did you tell Chloe we'd been working through our problems and were in fact engaged again?"

"We agreed not to say anything," she said. "I'm not lying to my daughter; I'm just withholding a few minute details."

Eagle stroked her hair off her face. They had been dating for nearly two years now. It had started with bumping into her at the supermarket and developed from there. He couldn't get enough of her. He loved her more than anything. The three years they were apart was sheer torture, but with Kurt constantly coming around, he'd kept his distance. After what happened, he had to deal with the club.

When it came to Alfie, he'd fucked up in so many different ways. He had blurred the lines of father and club president. His anger at losing Lily had turned him into a monster to his own son. His men, they had been angry with him for his treatment of Alfie, but when he started something, he hadn't been able to stop.

"You know I've fucked up in every single way with that boy."

"Then stop messing up, and treat him how you'd want your own father to treat you, Eagle. It's not hard. You're pushing that boy away all the time. I'm surprised he's still here."

He rubbed at his eyes. "I'm either the club prez, or I'm the dad, and at times, I don't know which one to be. He loves that girl though. I have no doubt. No other woman has been able to get close to him, you know. He pushes them away and can't stand to be around them. It's surreal, is what it is. I thought she was just some crush."

"Hey, Chloe's special. It takes the right kind of guy to see just how special she is."

"I'm not trying to argue with you."

"Good. It won't do you any good to," Lily said, resting her head on his shoulder.

Before she got run over, they had been making plans on how best to tell their kids, and to also bring them together. It was one of the reasons why Lily had gone into the city rather than invite Chloe home. Neither of them had been ready, and both wanted to make sure Chloe and Alfie were ready for each other.

"Alfie won't fuck this one up."

"What do you think they're doing right now?" she asked.

"Probably having sex."

"Hey."

"What? He's my son, and from what I heard, they have not wasted a single moment and are making up for lost time."

"This is crazy, we're acting like children," Lily said.

"Why? Because we want our kids to be happy and to get over the tape. It wasn't like Chloe was seen."

"It wasn't about the sex part. Seeing that tape, the humiliation, it broke Chloe's heart. She didn't trust him, and little by little, she gave a part of herself to him, and she's never going to get it back."

"I get it, I do." Eagle held her close. "We'll make this right. I promise."

"And you will make sure whoever ran me over, will be brought to justice and not club justice."

"I always knew you'd be a hard ass." He kissed her lips. "I love you, Lil."

"I love you, Eagle."

Chapter Seventeen

"This is pretty much it. It's small, but it has been home for five years."

"And the school lets you stay here?"

"You have to excel in every single class and there's no time for breaks. If you miss too many classes, they can kick you out immediately. It does come with a lot of risks, but the training has been wonderful."

"I'll say. The meal you cooked the other night." He rubbed his stomach. "Your mom is going to be so spoiled because of you."

"I'll try. It's the least I can do." She felt so responsible for her mother's loneliness. She was determined to bring Eagle and her mother together again.

"You've got to stop thinking about all of it. It's in the past, and we need to move on." Alfie pulled her into his arms.

This was why she had to make it work. Whenever he touched her, it was so natural. There was no one else she wanted but him.

Being away from him, she had thought she was over him. Seeing him every single day, he brought back so many old memories and feelings. Not the bad ones either, but the ones that made her feel alive.

"I did tell you it would work asking Eagle to watch her all day."

"He did seem to enjoy that, didn't he?" Alfie said. "Have you ever thought about me here?"

"Are you asking me if I've thought about you and touched myself?"

"Now you're getting all dirty." He pulled her down onto the sofa, so she straddled his waist. "I like it." He ran his hand to cup her ass, squeezing her flesh. She let out a moan.

"There were a couple of times," she said, whimpering. "I would imagine us together. I really wish that tape hadn't come out."

"You and me both." He let go of her ass to open the buttons of her shirt. The bra she wore this time was white, lacy, and it showed off her red nipples to distraction. The clasp for this one was at the front, and he flicked it open. She let out a moan, and he was lost to everything but her. "I wouldn't have seen it through, I promise you."

"We need to stop talking about it."

He stroked his thumb across her pebbled nipple. "I will gladly stop talking about it." He leaned forward and sucked on the bud. She whimpered.

"Yes, fuck, yes," she said, crying out.

He played with her other nipple, pinching the bit with his fingers, getting it nice and hard. Flicking his tongue between the valley of her tits, he bit down hard, and she cried out.

Grasping her ass again, he rubbed her against his cock, and he wanted inside her so badly, he could taste it.

"I want to be inside you."

"Yes."

She pulled back, and they both worked each other's pants down before they butted heads, and ended up taking care of their own. By the time she was back to straddling his waist, they were both laughing.

Alfie stopped her laughing, by finding her core and sliding his cock through her slit. She moaned, arching up, and he lowered her down onto his length.

Inch by inch of wet, hot heat and warmth.

He was on fire.

Running his hands over her hips and ass, he rocked her against him. She held his shoulder and began to work up and down his cock, taking him in deeply.

When he lifted her up in his arms, she wrapped her arms and legs around him.

"What are you doing?"

"Where's the bed?"

"Does it matter?"

"Yes."

She pointed in the direction behind him. "You shouldn't be carrying me."

"There's no law anywhere that says I can't." He kicked open the door and dropped her onto the bed. He didn't leave her soaking wet pussy as he followed her down.

Pushing her hands above her head, locking them together beneath one of his, he slowly worked his cock deep inside her, taking his time as he fucked her. He couldn't resist watching as he slid in and out. His cock was already covered in her arousal, but she'd not come just yet.

Finally, pulling out of her, he held onto her hips and drew her up to him so his mouth was on her pussy.

Eating her, he watched her moan and body arch, pressing toward him.

"Please, Alfie."

"Tell me what it is you want," he said.

"You, just you."

He could gladly give her that. Biting, licking, and sucking at her clit, he brought her to a screaming orgasm. The sound filled the room before he pushed his cock right back inside her.

She was magnificent.

Her cunt still rippled and clenched around his dick as if it was only meant for him, which it was. He didn't want to lose her. Alfie slowed the pace down, taking his sweet time, drawing her to a second orgasm before he finally found his first.

When he did come, he pushed to the hilt and filled her with his cum, wave up wave, as if it went on forever.

They both collapsed together, panting for breath.

"I imagined a lot of things, but I have to say, never like that."

"I blew your mind, didn't I?"

"Yes, you did, and erm, I've got to ask you something?"

"What?"

"Did you use protection?" she asked.

He stopped and turned toward her. "Protection?"

"I know we've been rather lax, or just plain forgot about it. I could get ... pregnant. I'm not on the pill."

He stared down into her eyes. "Pregnant?" He couldn't resist running his hands across her stomach, imagining her swollen. She would look so amazing pregnant. He wanted to see her like that.

"Alfie, focus."

"You know I haven't been using condoms." Protection had been the last thing on his mind, but then, pregnancy wasn't something he needed to be protected from. Especially as, he would really like to get her pregnant. Did that make him an asshole?

"Are you freaking out?" she asked.

"No. Are you?"

"No."

"Then we're agreed. We're not freaking out."

"No."

"Chloe, I need to know what you want to do."

"I don't know. Should I take the morning after pill? Would it be too late? I don't know what is happening right now, and I feel we're putting a lot of pressure on this," she said.

"I'll start using condoms."

"And if I'm pregnant?"

"Then I'll stop using them."

She burst out laughing.

"What is so funny?"

"Alfie, I've been back in your life a week. That's all. One week and now we're talking about pregnancy."

"I want you to move in with me," he said.

"Oh," she said.

"You've got no place to stay, and if we want our parents together, we're going to have to do this."

"You do know this will make us step-siblings, right?"

"We were dating long before our parents were," he said.

"I don't know what is happening right now."

"Simple, I've asked you to move in with me, and that's exactly what you're going to do."

"You're doing that ordering around thing again, aren't you?"

"Yep, and seeing as it has worked for me well before, I'm going to stick with it."

Chloe sat up, and his cock was still inside her and he had no interest in letting her go.

"And if I'm pregnant?"

"Then it's a good thing I got you to move in with me."

"And if not?"

"We'll continue to use the condoms until we're ready," he said.

"I could get on the pill. That would help."

"I don't want you on the pill."

"Why not?"

"So when we're ready to start, you don't have to worry about taking it or not." He teased a strand of her hair between his fingers.

"You don't think this is happening too fast?"

"For me, Chloe, it's not happening fast enough."

She nibbled her lip. "Are you sure?"

He laughed. "Since you left, I've felt like a piece of myself was taken. You took it with you, and now you're back, I finally feel whole."

Tears glistened in her eyes.

"Don't cry, Chloe. Please. I don't want to make you cry."

"Then why do you have to go and say all those nice things that make me cry?"

"Because I'm not going to hide what I feel anymore. I fucked up back then. I'm not going to do it anymore. I wasted five years. Tell me you don't feel the same."

"I do. It's just, sometimes when I thought about you here, Alfie, it didn't always lead to an orgasm. It led to me crying myself to sleep because of how broken I felt."

He cupped her face and kissed her hard. "That guy is gone. I wouldn't have gone through with it. I had no intention of ever hurting you in that way, not when I finally got to know the real you."

"And who is the real me? Do you even know who that is?" she asked.

"I know the real you is loving, kind, sweet, charming, and I know you struggle to connect with everyone. But I get you. I do. I see you, Chloe. It took me a couple of months to see the real you, but as soon as I did, I loved what I saw. I'm not bullshitting you. This is all me. I love you, and I'm going to prove to you that I mean to keep you."

****

Arriving home, Chloe nodded toward Alfie and

entered her home. She found Eagle and Lily sitting together on the sofa.

This was all moving a little too fast, but if she allowed it to slow down, she had no idea what she'd end up doing.

"Hey," she said.

"Hey, sweetheart, where's your stuff?"

She looked over at Eagle. "Can I speak to my mom for a minute?"

"Sure." Eagle got up, and she noticed how familiar they were. The way he touched Lily's knee, and the kiss to her head.

"What is it you want to share with me?" Lily asked. "Where's your stuff?"

Chloe shook her head, knowing she'd ask her mother another time. She moved closer to the sofa and took a seat. "Alfie's got it in the car."

"Why?" Lily asked.

"I … he … he asked me to move in with him."

"He did?"

"Yes, and I'm thinking about it."

"But you're not sure?" Lily asked.

She pressed her hands to her face and groaned. "I don't know what the hell I'm doing. Should I give him a second chance? Ugh, I hate this. I really do. What should I do?"

Her mother smiled. "What do you want to do? The first feeling that pops into your head."

"I want to move in with him." She cringed.

"But?"

"But I'm scared. I don't think this is going to work."

"Do you want it to work? Do you think you can ever forgive him and get past this?"

"I can't answer that."

"Do you want to try?" Lily asked. "Your room is always available here."

"I'm trying not to freak out." She ran fingers through her hair. "Yes, I'm going to do this. I'm in, like, a completely different world." She laughed. "How did I get here?"

"You're doing fine if that's what you're worried about?"

She chuckled and hugged her mother. "I better go. He's waiting outside. I'm going to have to find a job as well. This is crazy."

She said goodbye to her mother and to Eagle before rushing out to Alfie.

He slapped the steering wheel as he listened to some kind of rock band. "All set?"

"Yes."

"You're coming to live with me."

"Yes."

"No hesitation, I like it."

She took a deep breath, running her hand down her thighs, and trying to think of all the right things to say.

No words came.

The only noise in the car came from the radio.

She licked her dry lips.

"You ever lived with anyone apart from your dad?"

"Nope. You?"

"Nope. You nervous?"

"A little."

"Me too." At least they could be nervous together, so there was that.

"You're overthinking everything over there."

"I'm not." She snorted.

"I can hear you thinking. Tell me what's on your

mind."

"I'm just trying to organize an entire list of stuff I've got to go. You know, find a job, and that's pretty much the top of my list."

"For five years away, you didn't exactly make much of a life for yourself."

"I wasn't trying to win any social awards. Are you sure we're doing the right thing?"

"Yes."

"This is serious, Alfie."

"Look, Chloe, I know you've moved away, but I've had a long time to deal with my feelings. You're my biggest mistake and the best decision I've ever made."

"Okay, you do realize that makes no sense."

"Being with you, was the best decision. Letting you go without a fight, that was the mistake." He reached over, taking her hand. "We're going to make this work."

"I think our parents are already together," she said.

"What? Nah, it's not possible. I'd have noticed it."

"You would? How?"

"I know my dad, and if he and Lily were dating, he wouldn't hide it."

"Unless he was giving her time. It's the way they were together. He touched her knee and kissed her head."

"Memories of their time together. Force of habit. When I'm with you I do the same thing."

"I don't know, it was just different." Chloe sat back, frowning. "Huh."

"You've got your thinking head on again. Let's hear it."

"It's not much. Forgot about it. Honestly, it's not worth it."

"Now I need to know," Alfie said.

"Do you think our parents are trying to move us together?"

"Why do you think that?"

"Mom never wanted me to come home for any of the major holidays. She always came to me, and I swear there were a couple of times she had a guy at home when she was talking to me," Chloe said.

"You're making it up."

"Not completely," she said. "Ugh, this is so frustrating. I wish you could have seen them."

"Well, if their intention is to bring us together, we'll find out about it soon." Alfie pulled the car into the parking lot. "Time for you to move in."

They climbed out of the car, and she helped him unload her bags. As she walked into the apartment building, her stomach started to tighten as her nerves hit her.

"There is a huge chance Ian or Riley, or both of them are here, waiting."

"Oh, do they know you invited me?" she asked.

"I wasn't planning on offering you a place. It just kind of slipped out."

"A good slip or a bad one?" She really needed to get her confusion in check.

Alfie opened his door, and there was no noise inside the apartment. "Shock of a lifetime, no one else is here." He put her bags on the floor and closed the door behind her.

In the next second, she was pinned to the door, both of her hands pressed up against the hard wood.

"What are you doing?"

"I'm going to be making up for some lost time. Keep your hands right there."

"And I'm supposed to stand here?"

"You will enjoy it. I promise."

Chloe waited as he slowly removed her clothes. She had no choice but to move her hands, but each time he was done, she'd place them above his head.

"I've missed you so much," he said.

"Alfie, you had me not long ago."

"No, I've missed being able to keep you. To have you as mine. Right now, I feel like someone should punch me or something so I know I'm not dreaming."

There he went with saying those words that were just so dreamy to her.

"Now you've got me, what do you want to do with me?"

He skimmed his fingers up her body, gripping the back of her neck and drawing her toward him. His lips brushed against hers, lightly at first but by no means gentle. His tongue slid across her mouth until she opened up, and when she did, he plundered inside.

Letting her hands fall around him, she held on, not wanting to let him go for fear of falling.

The kiss was everything, and during it, Alfie picked her up, carrying her across their apartment, toward his room. He kicked the door open before pressing her to the bed. He followed her down onto the covers, and she stroked down his arms, toward his chest.

Suddenly, he stood up, and Chloe watched as he removed his clothes. He wasn't in a rush. Each item seemed to take him time to get naked.

"You want to drive me crazy here?"

"You got it, baby." He pulled his shirt off last, and there he stood. Over six foot of tall, muscular, man.

"Why do they call you Rock?" she asked.

"My dad gave me it."

"Why?"

"Because I'm stubborn. I just won't budge. I'm a pain in the ass, and there's no stopping me. I'm a rock."

"It suits you."

She watched as he began to kiss from her ankles, moving up each thigh, getting closer to her pussy. When he was there, she opened her thighs as he spread the lips of her pussy. His tongue stroked between her slit. She cried out as he circled her nub before using his teeth to bite down.

The pain was instant, but the moment he licked across with his tongue, the pain lessened and the pleasure drove her wild.

Back and forth he stroked until she was so close to the edge, but he kept her poised at the peak, waiting for her to fall.

She couldn't stand it.

"Please, Alfie," she said.

"You want to come all over my face?"

"Yes."

"Then come, baby. Let me have it."

He flickered back and forth across her clit, and the heat built until she was thrown across the peak into bliss. She screamed his name as she found her release.

Before her orgasm had even finished, Alfie moved up between her thighs, his cock bumping her clit, and her pussy, even without any touch, was still pulsing to life.

He pressed against her entrance and slammed to the hilt, making her cry out.

With him so deep inside her, he grabbed the headboard and used it as leverage to start fucking her.

He began slow, taking his time, driving in deep, until he changed and suddenly began to thrust harder and deeper within her.

She gripped his ass, thrusting up to meet each one of his, craving his touch, needing his cock.

Alfie didn't give up or stop. He let go of the

headboard, wrapping his arms around her and kissing her as he continued to thrust within her.

This wasn't fucking. This was making love.

He held her so close, and his thrusts began to slow, taking his time.

"You feel so amazing wrapped around my dick."

"You're not too bad yourself."

He smiled that sweet, wicked smile.

"Do you trust me?" he asked.

"Yes." There was no hesitation as she spoke.

He pulled out of her, spun her around so she was on her knees. "What are you doing?" she asked.

"Have a little trust, remember? I'm not going to do anything you don't like." He stroked across her back, and as he cupped her pussy, she jumped, not expecting the touch.

His fingers teased between her sodden folds, and she gritted her teeth as the pleasure was almost too much for her to bear. He didn't stop though, nor did she want him to.

He pressed his finger against her clit, as two fingers filled her.

In and out, he pressed inside, fucking her.

She wanted his cock, not his fingers, but as his thumb started to work her clit, she couldn't deny the instant hit of need that swept through her.

"I feel a change inside your pussy, baby. You want my cock, don't you?"

"Yes."

His fingers were gone, and she gasped as he pressed his cock against her entrance from behind.

He'd never taken her from behind before. Moving her hair out of her way, she glanced back at him, and he was already working his cock inside.

"You feel that?" he asked.

"Yes."

With a couple of inches of his dick inside her, he grabbed her hips and thrust in deep. This angle, he seemed deeper than ever before, and she didn't think it was possible for him to be able to fuck her any harder.

He pulled out until only the tip of him was inside, before sliding in. The hard slap of their bodies filled the room with the noise.

Over and over, he pounded inside her pussy. The need for another orgasm began to build, and she sank her teeth into her lip in a way to try to contain her own need, but it was next to impossible.

Alfie was in charge, and as he filled her to the hilt, she had no choice but to reach between her thighs and stroke her clit.

"Oh, fuck, yes, that's what I'm talking about. You take care of your own pleasure, baby. That's it. I can feel your cunt wrapped around me." He didn't let up, fucking her hard and deeper with every passing second.

There was no end or beginning.

He had the control, and she loved it.

She wanted to give every single part of herself to him, and him alone.

Alfie didn't stop, and she came hard.

With his cock deep inside her, it felt different, more powerful somehow, and this time, Alfie wasn't too far behind her.

As he came, he did so with a cry.

His cock pulsed inside her, and she felt wave upon wave of his cum as he filled her.

He'd not worn a condom again, and she told him so as they collapsed.

"I'm sorry," he said.

"I'm starting to wonder if you're trying to get me pregnant." She let out a little laugh.

"Would it be so bad for us to start a family?" he asked.

Chloe paused and glanced back at him. "I've only just moved back to town and you want to start a family?"

"No time like the present."

"I don't know if I'm ready to start a family." She pulled off his cock, feeling his cum trickle down her leg. She wanted to stay and talk to him, but she really needed to take a shower.

Walking away from the bed, she went to their bathroom. Turning on the hot water, she put her hand beneath the spray, waiting for it to heat up.

"I've scared you," Alfie said, stepping into the room just as she climbed into the shower.

"You haven't scared me. Not really. It's just a lot to take in, you know. Kids? I mean, it's a huge step."

"I know. One I think we can both take together." He stepped into the shower with her. "What are you afraid of?"

"This not working out would be top of the list."

"We're not living in the past anymore. We're here because we want to be here. I'm not going to give you up, Chloe."

"Please don't tell me you love me again. It seems cruel because I don't know if I can handle it." She put a hand on his chest. "I haven't said it to you."

"I know, but it doesn't mean you don't love me."

"Alfie, please, stop." She tilted her head back.

He cupped her face. "I'm not going to stop. Not when it comes to you." He kissed her again, harder, leaving her breathless. "If we have kids, I know it will make me the happiest man in the world, and you'd make a fantastic mom."

"How do you know?"

"You've always been this pessimistic person.

Even as kids. I'm putting it down to your dad."

"Now you're a therapist?"

"Nope. I'm simply a guy that understands his girlfriend when it comes to the matters of the heart. I get it. You don't trust me."

"I didn't say that at all. In fact, I recall telling you I did trust you."

"With your body. I'm not going to hurt you. I've never hurt you. But here is another question for you, do you trust me with your heart?"

"It's still the same thing, it's my body," she said, knowing deep down, she was lying.

"It's not, and I'm not dumb enough anymore to fall for it. I know you trust me with your body, but when it comes to your heart, it's a whole different thing." He spun her around so she was facing the shower, and he grabbed the sponge.

"What are you doing?"

"I'm going to wash you. You think I haven't stroked my cock thinking about you here?"

"You have?"

"Chloe, the guys weren't wrong when they said I could have rubbed my hand out with how often I touched my cock thinking about you. I intend to live out every single fantasy I had. I promised myself if you ever came back to Satan's Croft, I would make it up to you, and give you so many reasons to stay rather than push you away."

"You're doing a pretty good job right now," she said, meaning it.

"Good." He soaked the sponge with the soap and pressed it to her body. "I aim to please when it comes to you. Now, back to the problem at hand. Yes, I remember. You don't trust me with your heart, and the truth is, I don't have a single clue what to do or say to make you realize I love you, and I'm not the asshole bully of the past. That guy is fucking gone and dead. All that remains is me, and I want you more than anything. I'm willing to do whatever it takes to keep you."

She spun in his arms, and he started to soap her tits.

"What if a few years down the line, a couple of kids, you change your mind? What then? What if the club becomes your main priority?"

"What if I turn into your dad?" he asked.

"I didn't say that."

"You think I don't see the damage he did, fucking asshole?" Alfie sighed. "I'm not going to be him. When my daughter is sitting on a park bench waiting for me, it'll be because my car won't start. If I know or ever find out some little biker brats are bullying her, I'll take care of them, and make sure they know they treat my girl like a princess, just as her mother should have been treated. I won't miss an anniversary. We will have to decide on a date for ours." She chuckled. "And unless I'm away with the club, I will be in your bed, and only your bed. When I am away, I expect you to send me naked pictures and with how amazing technology is, I want you to give me a show."

"A show?"

"Oh, yes, we're talking naked, and I'm going to have to buy you some sex toys and you're going to have to do everything I say."

"You're in charge?"

"You got it." He held her face, kissing her lips. "Chloe, I waited five years for you. I didn't look at another woman. I wasn't even tempted by another woman. What does that say about how I feel about you? I love you. I want to be with you, and I'm willing to fight for this, for you. Every single day. I'm not your dad. I'm

Alfie, the love of your fucking life."

Chapter Eighteen

One week later

Alfie sat on the open trailer of his father's car, sipping at a bottle of water. He'd stopped drinking beer through the day since he made prospect; he never knew when he'd get a call demanding his presence. He'd seen some of the prospects get kicked out for being too intoxicated before the club was done with them for the day. It had stood him in good stead as his father liked to call him up at all hours of the day and night.

Thinking about Chloe's assumptions the other day, he stared over at his father, who was finishing up a deal with the mechanic. Alfie had unloaded everything from the back of the truck, and he wasn't part of the whole organizing shit.

Eagle had been different the past couple of months.

He hadn't really noticed it, seeing as he didn't spend every waking moment with his dad. There wasn't a darkness to him, but could that have something to do with spending time with Lily?

Each morning he dropped Chloe off at her mom's, and she spent the day. So far, there hadn't been a sign of her period, and deep down, he was really hoping she was pregnant with his kid.

He needed an extra reason to keep her with him.

In the back of his mind, he was counting the days since the fuck fair incident had been mentioned.

One week so far.

Chloe never brought it up, or even hinted at it. In fact, most of the guys at the club asked him about it and how Chloe was.

They needed a fresh start, and he knew Eagle had told the guys to nip that sharing shit in the bud.

If Chloe stayed in town, her mother would be a lot happier. The times he'd seen Lily after the incident, she'd always been so sad and miserable.

Her daughter was gone, and he'd known it was all his fault.

Eagle shook hands with the guy and moved on toward Alfie.

"Another deal?"

"Yep. We can start distributing parts and repairs."

"That shit sounds legit, Dad," he said.

"It is. Not all our money can come from drug and gun runs."

"I bet Lily's not happy with you going on those runs either."

Eagle tensed up.

"Are you seeing her?" Alfie asked.

"You know I can still whoop your ass."

"Yeah, here's the thing, Pop, you could have been doing it for months, if not years. I know we don't have the best relationship and all that, but you've got no problems raising your fist to me."

He watched Eagle flinch. It was the first real kind of emotion he'd seen in Eagle.

"How are things going with you and Chloe?"

"Good. She's moved in. She wants to help and get a job. I've told her to do one of those food blog things. I don't see her working at the diner, do you?"

Eagle laughed. "The food she cooks would be wasted on those guys. If she needs help with a camera and a setup, the club has a base out back, we can set up for her. It would be at the back of the clubhouse. We can convert it into a kitchen. It's fucking hot in the summer. It'll burn her ass off, but we'll install some AC units and whatnot. It'll be good."

"Are you fucking serious?" Alfie asked.

"Yeah, I'm serious. You think I don't see the way you look at her? I do. I see it, and I know she means a lot to you."

"Is this about Lily? I've noticed you haven't answered my question."

"What's going on with Lily and myself is for Lily and myself to know."

"Chloe thinks you guys are already together."

"We're getting off subject here."

"I never meant for it to happen, you know. I was an asshole kid," Alfie said.

Eagle sighed. "I've never been a good dad to you. The club, it has always come first, and I didn't know what to do with you. I made so many mistakes. I don't want to keep making any more. I know this doesn't make up for the years I've been horrible to you, but I want to start making it right. It'll take time, I know that."

"We won't keep making mistakes."

"What do you think Chloe would say to the back of the club? It will mean she gets to keep an eye on you," he said.

"She has nothing to worry about."

"Not even any of those club whores?"

"You think Lily worries about them?" Alfie asked.

"She has nothing to worry about when it comes to another woman. I know what I've got, and I intend to keep it."

"Same for me, Pop."

"When did you start calling me Pop?"

"I don't know. I guess I'm testing it out. What do you think of Granddad or Grandpop?" Alfie looked toward his father, who seemed to have gone pale.

"She's pregnant?"

"What?"

"You're asking me what my grandkids will call me and you're telling me she's not pregnant?"

"No, I mean, we don't know," Alfie said.

"You're going to be a dad?"

"No. I don't know. We haven't found out yet. It's a possibility."

"One you want?"

"Hell, yeah, why wouldn't I want it? Chloe's amazing. She's fucking incredible. I want her to have a reason to stay."

"And you think getting her pregnant is the best idea?"

"Yeah, of course."

"Son, I hate to break it to you, but no woman has to stick around to raise her kid. If you want Chloe to stay, it's going to have to be for you, otherwise you're going to spend your entire life wondering if she stayed for the kids or for you."

"Why did you have to go and suck all of my happiness out?" he asked.

"I'm keeping it real for you, son."

"This isn't real. It's not fucking fair." Alfie ran a hand down her face. "We … when I'm around her, I can't imagine being anywhere else. This started in high school, when I stopped trying to hurt her, and find something against her. I gave myself a chance to get to know her."

"And you liked what you saw?"

"Yeah. She was … fire and sweet, and she had this amazing laugh. It was almost a giggle, but it wasn't an annoying fake giggle, you know the kind I mean?"

"Yeah, I do."

"When she first made it, I'd been the one to make her laugh. I listened, and I realized no one had taken the time to make her laugh. No one cared, you know? No one gave a fuck about making her happy, and I wanted to be the one to do all of those things."

"You fell in love with her."

"Her smile. Her eyes. She has the most expressive eyes. I can't even begin to describe them. When she's down or something is bothering her, they seem to go a dull blue. There's no happiness within them. But the moment she's happy, they sparkle, and it makes me think there's no place else I can find that high she creates, you know?"

"I think this is the most we've spoken in over five years."

"In our entire life, Dad. You're not the easiest guy to talk to. The club, it always comes first. I know she's worried about it as well."

"The club?"

"Me turning into her dad."

"It's not possible."

"I'm not a patched in member. Kurt only ever made prospect."

"Alfie, Kurt never made it because he wasn't good enough. Everyone knows that. We told him no matter how much he hung around the club, he'd never make prospect again. The patch was stripped from him. He ran when the club needed him most. Nearly killed a couple of guys in the process. He ran over them with his bike. I promised them for as long as I lived, I would never see him a member, and my father was the same before he passed. Kurt being allowed to hang around the club was the club's decision, not mine. I didn't want him there."

"You didn't?"

"No."

"Trust and loyalty. It's why it always annoyed me to see him with Lily. He didn't deserve her, and the club should have killed him for what he did."

"Why didn't you?"

"Your grandfather liked Lily."

"He did?"

"You were born, and he'd seen how she took care of you, and I think he knew how I felt as well. How I loved her. Killing Kurt, it would have caused her heartache."

"But it was a club decision. Didn't any of the guys he nearly killed speak up?"

Eagle chuckled. "That's the thing, they wanted to hurt him, kill him in fact, but Lily, she inspired a great deal of love in people. She's loyal, sweet, and whenever she came around, people would shine in her company. She never made waves. Never judged anyone. If someone was upset, she'd bake them a freaking cake, and the guys who, funnily enough, got broken legs, got a visit from her in the hospital, each with food and ways to make them more comfortable."

"You and her are dating, aren't you?" he asked.

"Alfie."

"You can tell me you're not, but the look in your eye, that says a man who has fallen in love all over again. You and Lily are dating."

Eagle sighed. "You were going to find out eventually," he said.

"From who?"

"Lily and I want you and Chloe to have your second chance."

"If you wanted us to have a second chance why did it take Lily getting run over to bring her back? Why didn't she ask for Chloe to come back? Did you run her over?"

"What? Hell, no, I didn't fucking run her over." Eagle ran a hand down his face. "Fine, look, Lily and I, we wanted to make it work with no one knowing we were actually together. It was a secret."

"What about Chloe?"

"Fine. Fine. We had thought about Chloe coming back home, and bringing the two of you together, but Lily had special demands first."

"Such as?"

"She wanted her daughter to finish out her culinary school thing. Chloe was excelling, and all of her drive and focus was on that. Not on men. We figured it would give us time to see if you two were really serious about each other."

"You waited?"

"Yes. Chloe was hurt by what happened. Lily told me until she left, she spent every single night crying herself to sleep, and she was torn apart."

Alfie felt a pain strike him hard. "I never wanted to hurt her."

"I know, son. We had to make this happen for all of us."

"If you didn't run her over to bring Chloe here, who did?"

"I'm still looking into that one."

Alfie sighed. "Do you think it could be Kurt?"

"Why would he run Lily over?"

"I don't know. She's his ex-wife, and if he caught you two together, you don't think he's got the vindictive bone that would make him do some stupid shit?" Alfie asked.

"Nah, there's no way Kurt would run Lily over. It's not like him to do that."

"It's also not like him to take off the way he did. I've seen him around town a couple of times, but I never really thought about it. I think we should check him out. There's no one else in town who would want to hurt her.

Not even any of your ex-club whores as they're still all in the club," Alfie said. "He's the only one I can think of who would be stupid enough to do it and cowardly enough to drive away as well."

****

Two days later

Chloe stepped out of the car. She glanced across at Lily and Eagle as he helped her out of the back of the car and into the waiting wheelchair. She'd still not asked her mom, but Alfie had told her about his conversation with his dad.

She wanted her mother to be the one to tell her, but each day that passed, she figured her mother was waiting for the right moment, only, she didn't know which time it would be.

"You've brought us to the clubhouse," Chloe said.

At breakfast this morning—with Ian and Riley as they were permanent breakfast guests—Alfie had taken the application form for the diner and torn it up. She had no desire to work there, nor to open up a restaurant in an attempt to compete for business. The diner was part of Satan's Croft, almost an institution in itself.

"This is for a real special occasion," Alfie said.

He'd been so happy the past couple of days. She couldn't exactly put her finger on the why of it, but she followed him as he flung his arm across her shoulders. There were several club whores hanging outside, smoking.

Chloe noticed the looks they threw Alfie's way, but not once did he look in their direction.

"Those women want you," she said, whispering against his ear.

Alfie laughed. "Babe, they want every single man. Their mission is to have the title of banging every single clubman they can. Some of them want to get the whole set."

"Ew."

"They're going to be sadly upset. I'm not banging anyone."

"That's good to know."

"Have you got your period yet?" Alfie asked.

She had warned him she was a couple days late. With the stress of her mother and coming home, she figured it was late because of that.

"No."

"We need to get you a test."

"Tests can lie."

"We'll take one test and then get it confirmed by the doctor."

"You really think I'm pregnant?" she asked.

"I'm hoping for it." He smiled. His lips brushing across her neck. "Aren't you?"

"I don't know."

She allowed herself to possibly daydream of a small baby.

Alfie let her go, and she went to stand beside her mother. She gripped the wheelchair as Alfie and Eagle both opened a lock on the old warehouse. She'd never been here as a kid as it was always locked up. They pulled the stiff doors open, and she couldn't help but admire the sheer bulge of Alfie's muscles. The man worked out constantly. He had weights in the apartment, and she spent so much time simply drooling as he pumped them.

"What do you think?" Eagle asked, dusting his hands off.

He moved her out of the way, pushing her mother toward the door.

"What do I think of what?"

"The space?" Eagle entered the warehouse and flicked on a light.

She moved up to Alfie's side.

"I don't know. What am I supposed to think? Are you guys planning on renovating it?"

The scent of mold was heavy in the air.

"You shouldn't work at the diner. It's not why you trained at a culinary school. Your mom was showing me all these food blogs, and the kind you can create your own show and stuff."

"Yeah," she said. "I know about them."

"This is your chance to set one up. The guys will stay out of the way, and we'll help you film and get set up. You've got complete design control."

"You're saying this place is mine?" Chloe asked, pointing at it.

"It's not a lot, but it's a start. We can get some cupboards installed, a pantry, stove, sink. Get everything hooked up, and you can go live within a month, I reckon. I've got several favors owed to me, and well, you can have this place."

Chloe's mouth was open. Shock filled her.

"You're serious."

"Yes."

"I think it's amazing, sweetie," Lily said. "I can see you right now doing your thing. Singing and dancing as you cook." Lily clapped her hands. "It will be wonderful."

"I think it's crazy," Chloe said. "What do you want for it?"

Alfie tensed beside her, and even Lily looked uncomfortable.

"I don't want anything, Chloe."

"I wasn't raised stupid, Eagle. You don't just give this stuff to people for free."

"Chloe!"

"No, it's okay. I'm impressed you asked." Eagle smiled. "Your delivery needs some work, but you're right. I don't give shit like this for free. There's always a price."

"What do you want for it?" Chloe asked.

"You to stay in town. To give Alfie a chance, the club a chance, and me and your mom a chance."

"Eagle?"

"I told you Alfie already knew, and I know he got that little nugget of information from you," Eagle said, nodding at her. "There are no terms and conditions with this, Chloe. I'm hoping we can all be a family and learn to get along without all the bullshit lies or sneaking around. I love your mom more than anything in the world, and I know my son loves you. I don't know what you think or feel, but I'm willing to bet it's pretty strong to move in with him. This is a second chance. That's all."

Chloe nodded. "I'm sorry. I'm … nervous. My dad always said the club didn't do anything without payment."

"You're not just anyone, Chloe. You're family, and from what I've tasted, you're talented. I know we've all got a lot of history to work through, but I'm willing to do it, if you are," Eagle said.

The space was amazing, and she could really put her touch to it.

"What do you think?" Alfie asked, coming toward her.

"I think … it's everything I could ever want." She let out a giggle and threw her arms around Alfie's neck. "Thank you."

"It was all Dad's idea," he said.

"Thank you both, and the club."

"Technically, I've done this for selfish reasons,"

Eagle said.

"How come?"

"You'll be feeding us. Nothing will ever go to waste, unless it tastes like shit."

She chuckled. "You and Mom, are you two going to be making this official?"

"If your mom will have me," Eagle said, taking hold of Lily's hand.

"Yeah, I'll have you. We've wasted enough time as it is."

Chloe rested her head against Alfie's shoulder as she watched Eagle and Lily. They'd been apart for too long, and now it was just good to see them together.

Chapter Nineteen

One month later

Alfie was very much aware of how long it had passed since he and Chloe had been together. He also knew she hadn't gotten her period. The test he'd bought was in his jacket pocket, but as she was getting hugs and words of encouragement from the club, he didn't want to spoil her day.

They needed to know if she was pregnant or not.

The old warehouse had been converted into a cooking studio, one she could be more than proud of. He'd helped with the decorating and installing. They'd gotten electricians, gas men, and builders to make sure the structure was sound, and now, after four weeks of hard labor, she was finally able to get started cooking.

Eagle had even given her a thousand bucks to start her pantry, and Alfie saw the tears in her eyes as he moved past the guys and pulled her into his arms.

"Hello, beautiful," he said.

"Hey, you. I can't believe all of this has been done for me."

"Why? You're worth it."

"I can't believe it, in all honesty. This, coming back to town, you, us, it's all a little surreal."

He knew it hadn't been easy. Several guys in town had tried to bring up the fair fuck, but he'd dealt with them, and seeing as his dad was currently her number one fan, he had a whole club at his back.

Ian and Riley, well, they were her fans as well. Her food did that to people. It made them want to protect her, not that he saw a problem with that. She was worth protecting and loving.

Wrapping his arms around her waist, he placed his palm flat on her stomach.

"Don't think I don't know what you've got in your pocket," she said, whispering against his ear.

"I don't have anything."

"You've got a pregnancy test."

"How do you know?"

"Someone told my mom they saw you buying one and asked if I was knocked up yet."

He chuckled. "Okay, so maybe I bought one because we can't keep putting this off."

"But I feel fine."

"I know you want to wait until you start throwing up in the morning, but not all of us are like that. We want answers, real answers."

"I know you're right."

"Good," he kissed her cheek. "There's a bathroom in the clubhouse. Let's go."

Alfie didn't give her time to argue. Without another word, he marched her out of the warehouse and to the clubhouse.

A couple of the club women quickly jumped out of his way, clearly not wanting to anger him. He couldn't blame them. None of the club women held a patch to his girl. The bathroom was all clear, and the moment they were inside, he pushed the bolt home.

"You're going to watch me pee?"

"No. I'll give you the privacy, but you will be peeing and I'm going to stay in the room." He pulled the test out of his pocket. "Here you go."

"What if it says no?" Chloe asked.

"Then we carry on as we were." He'd try to not remember condoms. He wanted her knocked up, and he knew it made him a really bad person. But he didn't give at shit what others thought of him, only that, he really, really wanted to be with her, and only her.

"And if it says yes?"

"You marry me." He'd been waiting for this opportunity, and he wasn't going to squander it.

"You're crazy," she said.

"Am I, or am I just madly in love?" he said.

"You keep saying those words."

"They're the truth. You're everything to me, and I'm going to keep on saying them until you realize I mean business."

"I know you mean them."

"Good because I regretted not saying it to you before you left. I'm not going do that to you again. I've changed."

"I can see that." She started to tear up, and he pulled her into his arms. "I'll marry you," she said.

"You don't have to sound so sad about it."

"I'm not sad. I'm really happy."

"You have a weird way of showing it."

"Alfie, I've been really scared to say this to you in case it doesn't ever work out, but I do … I do love you. I know I don't say it as much as you, but please, don't break my heart."

"I won't. I promise." He stroked a finger down her cheek. "I've learned my lesson. This what you're giving me now, being part of my life, it's more than I could have ever hoped for." He kissed her again. "Please, take the test."

She chuckled. "This is crazy."

"I know it's crazy, but this is our life and I want to live it to the fullest with you. Kids, no kids, lots of kids. All I want is you."

"Okay. Let's do this. No baby, we carry on. A baby, we get married." She let out a breath, and gave him the signal to turn around.

"You know I've licked and sucked at your pussy more times than I can count," he said.

"And you think this is going to make me feel better when I've got to pee on a stick. I want you to have some sexual desire intact."

"I was reading women sometimes shit while in labor."

"Ew, gross, what are you reading?" she asked.

Alfie laughed. He had given her his back so she could pee, but he liked to tease her, even if it did make her uncomfortable.

"Just a few things on pregnancy. I figure I better start getting all the information now when we're ready."

"This is insane."

"We'll make it work."

"I know we will." Seconds passed. "I'm ready."

He turned around as she put the test down and washed her hands.

"Now we wait," he said, staring at the stick.

"It's not going to go any faster with you glaring at it."

"I'm making sure it knows what to do."

"By glaring?"

"Yes." He wanted to know if he'd finally made her his.

He knelt down, arms, crossed, chin resting on his hands.

Chloe stood beside him after drying her hands. She stroked her fingers through his hair, humming.

"This reminds me of high school," she said.

"How does it?"

"You were always impatient for me to finish. I know this isn't the same thing because hello, it's a test, but it kind of is."

"I don't know how much I can handle," he said. His nerves were only increasing the longer they waited.

"Just give it a couple of minutes. It'll surprise

you."

"I'm not ready to be surprised yet." He stood up, running fingers through his hair, banding his arms around her, squeezing her ass. He loved her curvy shape more than anything. "What time is it?" he asked, giving up with his patience level.

She checked her watch and smiled. "It's time."

He picked up the test and saw the answer.

"Well, what is it?" she asked.

Alfie smiled. "You better get used to being called Mrs. Alfie Pace. Your ass is mine."

"We're pregnant?" She let out a squeal as he picked her up and twirled her around.

"We're pregnant," he said, yelling.

He didn't know if he was ready, but he'd make it work. The two of them together could face anything, and that's how he knew they were both ready.

Just as he was about to kiss her, he heard gunshots ring out in the clubhouse.

Acting on instinct, he pushed Chloe down to the floor.

She let out a scream, but he wasn't having anything happening to her.

"What is that?" she asked.

"I don't know. Don't move," he said.

Several more gunshots went off, and then there was silence.

Chloe was panting.

"Please tell me you're fine," he said.

"I'm fine."

Alfie heard screaming. A man was shouting.

"Who is that?" Chloe asked.

"You don't leave this room. You understand me?"

"You can't leave me here."

"I'm not having you go out there," she said, grabbing his arm. "You can't leave me, Alfie."

"No, I won't leave you, but I've got to go and see who it is."

"Please."

"Chloe, I'm no coward. I will be back, and I will protect you. I'm not about to have a madman charge this fucking room and hurt you." He grabbed her face, kissing her hard. "I love you, Chloe, but stay here."

Alfie opened the bathroom door and came to a stop as he saw Eagle on his knees, Lily on the floor, blood pooling beneath her hand that covered her chest. She looked pale.

"You think I'm a coward. I'm looking you in the face right now, Eagle, and I don't see a coward. You're on your knees before me."

"You've just shot Lily," Eagle said.

"The slut had it coming. I figure she had learned her lesson in getting fucked by this club, but after seeing the two of you together, I had to put a stop to it. She was just walking on by as if she didn't have a single care in the world, and you know what? I want her dead."

"No!" Eagle yelled the word trying to draw Kurt's attention back to him. "You let her go."

"You think I gave up everything and I'd be happy for you to take my place? Do you think I'm that fucking stupid?" Kurt spat at Eagle and then landed a blow. All the time, the gun in his hand was pointed at Lily.

She was pale, shaking, and Alfie couldn't have anything happen to them.

Kurt hadn't seen him. Keeping to the shadows, he tried to get as close as possible.

"We can talk about this," Eagle said. "You don't have to kill her."

"You don't think I know what killing you means?

I will kill every single motherfucker here. Anyone who comes through that door will end up dead, just like Stallion." Kurt sneered. "You always did think you were better than me. You never were. You're evil fuckers. Why would I stick around to get my ass shot at while you guys were more than willing to take the bullet?" Kurt shook his head. "Lily's mine. She was always mine. You don't think I didn't see how much you wanted her? Every single time she'd come to the clubhouse I'd see you panting after her like a little puppy dog. But I had her first. I gave her a daughter, not that it did me any good. Until Chloe was too fucking stupid to keep her legs closed."

Alfie frowned.

"Then she proved to be very valuable indeed. The tape that little fucker made, Danny, Duke, something or other. It had my daughter on it, and he tried to blackmail me with the tape, threatened to expose my daughter to the town. I figured I could use it for myself. I don't know, I found it, and made sure you didn't get what you wanted, Eagle. You got everything. You got the club, the respect, but I got the one thing you always wanted. I got the woman, and I knew it killed you inside to know you'd failed and I had won."

"You didn't win," Eagle said.

"I won. You're the loser, not me. I'm the winner. I won."

"*You're* the reason the tape was played," Alfie said. "You're the one responsible for showing the entire town everything."

Kurt jerked, and Alfie had caught him by surprise. He'd lost the shock element though, and now there was no way of sneaking up on him.

He didn't care.

"That little fucker came to me. He thought I

should see my daughter and this little asshole punk screwing. He thought I was a cowardly fuck and would go to your father, and deal with it. The tape scared him, the little pussy. Well, as soon as I saw it, I had another idea, so I used him, but he didn't like it. Wouldn't think of playing it, not even at your graduation. So, I took it and whatever better way of separating Lily and Eagle, and pushing my daughter out of the equation than learning the truth."

"You did that?" Chloe asked, coming up beside him.

Kurt sneered. "You women, you're all the same. Fucking sluts. I've had enough of all of you."

Kurt lifted the gun and took aim. "Now it's time to say goodbye."

****

Wrapped in a blanket, holding a hot mug of chocolate, Chloe stared ahead, feeling a little sick.

Kurt had been going to shoot her, and if it hadn't been for Alfie taking the bullet, he would have. The bullet had grazed Alfie's arm, and even as she shook from shock, he was already patched up by the medic, and looking more relaxed than she would ever feel again.

The doors to the clubhouse flew open, and Ryan the Sheriff took Kurt down before he could shoot again. He was wanted in the case of a murdered eighteen-year-old woman and her son. Kurt had last been seen leaving the woman's apartment, covered in blood. Her father had started telling them she deserved it.

All women were whores.

"You okay?" Alfie asked, coming toward her.

He held her legs, and she nodded.

"I will be, I think. I can't believe he's the one that showed everyone the tape, you know. My own dad." She pushed some hair off her face.

"Yeah, well, Daniel shouldn't have filmed it. I'm glad it got shown," Alfie said.

Chloe frowned. "Why are you glad?"

"So I didn't have to lie to you anymore. I don't want there to be any secrets between us. Me and secrets are done. I will only ever tell the truth from now on."

"This is your vow?"

"This is my whole fucking life. Honestly, I want nothing to do with lies or what it entails. I only want to handle the truth."

"And the truth is I'm pregnant."

"And we're getting married," he said.

"You're still going with the whole marriage thing?"

"Hell, yeah, of course I am. You think you're going to get rid of me that easily you've got another think coming."

She started to laugh and then cry.

"Is everything okay out here?" Eagle asked, coming toward them. He was on crutches, and his leg had been bandaged up.

Kurt had injured several club whores, and Stallion had also taken a bullet, but no one was going to die from their injuries.

"Yeah," Chloe said.

"I'm getting married."

"You are?"

"Yes, and you're going to be a granddad," Alfie said.

"I'm getting a daughter-in-law and a grandkid all in one day," Eagle said. "Your mom may freak out. She wants grandkids."

"I'm still trying to process all of this myself."

"It sounds like you don't have a lot of time to process. If I know my son at all, he's probably already picked out the place he wants to get married, and where it has to be."

"I've got a couple of ideas."

Chloe didn't have to worry about any more wedding conversation as the nurse called for her. Alfie and Eagle followed as they entered her mother's room.

"I'm starting to feel like this is my new home."

"I'll bring some pictures," Eagle said, moving past her to go and kiss Lily.

One look at them, and Chloe knew they were perfectly matched with each other. Their love shone through, especially as Eagle stroked Lily's cheek.

"We've got some news, and you need to brace yourself for this," Eagle said.

"What?"

"Chloe and I are getting married, and we're pregnant."

Chloe's cheeks were on fire as her mother turned to look at her. "And you're happy about this?"

"I don't have much of a choice. We agreed, and I'm pregnant."

"How are you feeling?" Lily asked.

"Great, before Dad did what he did."

"Well, at least we now know who ran me over," Lily said.

"Don't joke about it, Mom." She moved toward the bed, taking a seat. "Are you okay?"

"Honey, your father and I, we were having troubles, you know that. I'd always take him back, regardless of what I thought to his endless promises. The man didn't know how to keep a promise to save his life." Lily stroked some of her hair. "I really wish you didn't have to see or hear that today."

"It's okay, Mom."

"Chloe, all I want for you is to be happy. If Alfie

makes you happy, it's all I need."

She looked back at him and smiled. "Yes, he makes me happy."

"Then don't do what I did. Don't wait around expecting life to happen, and hoping the decision will be taken out of your hands. Embrace it, love it, and allow yourself to love again. I know he was an asshole, but he's proven to you more than once, he's not that person anymore."

"I'm standing right here," Alfie said.

"If I get my daughter to marry you, you've got to stop moaning about all the same old stuff. I mean it," Lily said. "You both have to move on from the past, and in doing so, you will allow me and Eagle to do the same."

Chloe took Alfie's hand with a smile. "It looks like we're getting married."

Chapter Twenty

Four months later

"I hate my stomach," Chloe said.

"It's fine. I love it." Alfie knelt in front of his very pregnant wife and pressed kisses all across her stomach before finally taking possession of her mouth. He'd much rather have her naked and showing her in so many different ways how he could fuck her, but he had to settle for what he could get, and a kiss on the lips was all he had. When they were home, he'd make love to her, and show her their baby wouldn't get in the way of any fun time.

Their wedding had taken place a month ago when Lily finally got the casts removed from her legs. She'd been using crutches but was able to walk down the aisle as Chloe's maid of honor. She didn't have any other bridesmaids, and she refused to have any of the club whores.

She'd also asked Eagle to give her away, and his father had been so touched. Alfie smiled recalling how he had to go to the bathroom because he had something in his eye.

Ian and Riley had been his best men.

His bachelor party consisted of him texting Chloe while playing video games and drinking beer.

Of course, his bachelor party wouldn't have been complete without earning his patch. He father had surprised him with his own leather cut, his road name, and his place within the club. Ian and Riley had also earned theirs, and it was a chance to put the past to bed, once and for all.

For Kurt, there had been video and fingerprint evidence to put him at the scene of the crime, and he went down for the murder of a young mother and child.

Chloe had been heartbroken at seeing the news but pleased he'd been brought to justice.

"I can't believe I let you talk me into coming here," she said.

Six years exactly after the last fair, he'd brought her to this one. He hadn't done it to be cruel, but he didn't want her to be afraid of the fair.

With his leather cut on in pride of place, he put his arm across her shoulders, daring anyone to say anything.

If they wanted a fight, he'd gladly give them one, and he'd have the whole club at his back as well.

Unlike before, he wasn't on his own now.

Neither was Chloe.

The club had both of their backs.

"You have got nothing to be ashamed of. This is our place just as much as it is theirs, and I'm not going to have you hiding."

"Looking good," Ian said, striding toward them. His own leather cut seemed to stand out. "You have got the sexy young couple thing, and Chloe, you do not look like a tank."

"Wow, thank you, Ian. That's what every single pregnant woman wants to hear, just how big they look."

"What? I told you, you didn't look that big. Hormones are assholes, aren't they?" Ian winked at her. "Everything is in place."

"What's in place?" Chloe asked.

"Nothing." They both spoke at the same time, and Alfie wanted to curse. Chloe wasn't stupid. She could sense lies a mile away, and now, her suspicions would be right on point.

"If nothing's going on, what is in place?"

"It's a little something."

He didn't have to answer because Riley returned.

"About five minutes."

"What is going on?" Chloe asked.

"It's nothing," Riley said. "You look beautiful. Not like an elephant at all."

Chloe's hands went to her hips, and she turned toward him. "Do I need to kick your ass?"

"No. Well, it depends."

"I don't understand what is going on, and I'm kind of scared right now."

"You've got no reason to be scared," Alfie said. "You may like what I've got planned or you might hate it."

As if on cue, the television screen went dark.

"No, this isn't happening again, is it?" Chloe said.

She went to walk away, but he wasn't about to allow her to do that.

The screen changed, and it showed him. He was frowning at the camera.

"Will you guys freaking stop?"

"Freaking?" Ian asked. "When did you start to say that?"

"This is going to be shown in front of a bunch of kids. I don't want them to pick up bad language. I'm going to be a father in a matter of months. I've got to learn some respect."

Alfie wanted to cringe at how he sounded.

"I don't know if this fucking thing is recording," Riley said.

"This was a totally lame ass idea if ever there was one," Ian said.

"Will you two shut up?"

The editing went off again for a few seconds.

Chloe tried to pull out of his arms, but he wouldn't let her go. There was more, and she needed to see it. He couldn't just let her walk away.

Finally, the camera came on again, and he breathed a sigh of relief.

"If this is going the way I hope it is, we're all at the fair. Riley and Ian are thinking how lame this is. My dad may want to kill me, and even Lily. Love you both. But the person who matters the most is Chloe. I'm hoping she doesn't hate me after this, and well, she's pregnant with my kid and has a ring on her finger, so I'm hoping this will help me keep her." He took a breath. "Nearly six years ago now I think it was. Most of you were at the fair when another kind of video was played. A video that showed what a complete and total bastard I was. You see, I thought I knew Chloe. I thought she was a stuck-up little bitch that believed she was better than me, the club, than us. Taking those assumptions, I was going to hurt her in every single way imaginable. I intended to get close to her, and well, you all know the rest. For any newbies, the story has traveled, and I know it still gets talked about. Here's the thing, Chloe wasn't anything like I imagined." He smiled. "She was … everything I didn't even realize I'd been searching for. Being around her was like heaven. I know some of you are probably laughing, but the moment she laughed, or smiled, or even teased. The time she tried to flirt, I realized she didn't have a clue what she was doing. Little by little, my plan, my revenge, it changed. I started to fall in love with this amazing woman, and I couldn't let her go. Only, I didn't know we were being filmed. To everyone watching this today, I want to tell you to leave my woman alone. Chloe is one of the most amazing, beautiful, kind women I've ever known. You all didn't get the chance to see it, but I did, and what I saw, it was a wonderful thing." He lifted up his hand. "I married her. I'm doing this because I know she feels what was seen was an embarrassment to her, but I can tell you, Chloe, you have nothing to be embarrassed over. I bullied you. Made your life hell, and in return, you gave me nothing but happiness. I've known hell, I've lived it, and it was when you left. I will spend the rest of my life loving you, taking care of you, and showing you what it means to be my woman. To Chloe Pace, you are my heart, my old lady, and my reason for living. Thank you for giving this asshole a chance."

The screen didn't go off.

There were pictures and videos. Some from high school, others taken just recently. They were a montage of their love, and he made sure each frame showed his love for her.

When it was over, the screen went black and returned with the movie.

He released Chloe, and she turned toward him.

He waited, nervous, not exactly sure what was going to happen next.

Tears were in her eyes, and she nibbled on her lip.

"Surprise," he said.

"That was the most amazing thing I've ever seen. You really, truly feel that way for me?"

"Every single day."

"I'm the luckiest woman in the world." She threw her arms around him. Her body flush against his, he felt the rounded curves of her tits, as well as her stomach. Their child was growing inside her, an extension of his love and need for her.

"I love you," Chloe said. "And it's gone. The doubt, all of it. I don't care anymore. The only person I want, is you. All of you." She cupped his face. "I'm not wasting another moment."

"I will make you happy."

"You already do. Now shut up and kiss me."

In front of the entire town, he cupped her face and claimed her as his. Doing the video was a spur of the moment kind of thing, but he wanted to do something for Chloe, to let her see what he saw, and he hoped, as the years went by, he could wipe away the pain he'd caused her. His love for her would never fade.

Each day, it got stronger, and he was like a man possessed.

Epilogue

Ten years later

"Don't you think it's weird your brother and sister are playing with your son and daughter," Ian asked.

With his arms folded, Alfie "Rock" turned toward one of his best friends.

"No."

Lily and Eagle had gotten married a month after his video love confession. At the time, his father had thought it was a little extreme what he did, but Alfie didn't regret it. Every day he woke up and saw Chloe, he was a happy man.

"Come on, it's, like, weird as fuck!"

"That's my son and daughter you're talking about. Not to mention my brother and sister."

So, he and Chloe had a son, Luther, and five years after that, they had their daughter, Drew. Chloe was pregnant with their third child, but neither of them wanted to know the sex until the actual day she gave birth.

It was always a challenge on how to decorate the nursery, but until he got it perfect, they had the baby in their room.

He had no choice but to move out of his small apartment, and with the help of the club, he'd been able to get a small three-bedroom house.

Lily and Eagle didn't waste any time, and it wasn't long before Tulip and Rome were born. His brother and sister.

Eagle was so happy, as was Lily.

Speaking of happiness, he glanced over toward Chloe's warehouse. Her food blog had taken a while to take off. She spent hours getting used to the camera and of course becoming more natural in front of the camera.

Not that they needed the money. As a fully patched in member of the club, he was able to support them all.

"Keep an eye on the kids," he said, slapping Ian on the back. Riley was probably off somewhere fucking a club whore. He didn't believe in settling down.

Entering the warehouse, he watched as Chloe stepped back, camera in front of her, and snapped a shot of the birthday cake she'd made for him.

"Hello, beautiful," he said.

She let out a gasp, putting a hand to her chest. "This is supposed to be a surprise." She stood in front of the cake, trying to hide it from him.

"It can stay a surprise. It's my birthday, and there's only one person I want to spend my time with and she's trapped in her kitchen. I'm starting to get a little jealous."

"You've got no reason to be jealous."

"No?" He walked toward her, grabbed her hand, and pulled her close. "Then kiss me."

He didn't give her a chance to argue with him as he slammed his lips down on hers. She let out a moan, banding her hands around his neck.

"How about you and I put the cake to good use? The only way I can think of to eat it is to smear it on your very naked body and lick it all off."

"I like the sound of that."

Flicking the catch on the door, Alfie closed the blinds, moving his wife to the table and lifting her up.

"You once said you were the luckiest woman in the world, but I can tell you, I'm the luckiest man, because I've got you."

The End

www.samcrescent.com

BIKER BULLY

EVERNIGHT PUBLISHING ®

www.evernightpublishing.com

www.ingramcontent.com/pod-product-compliance
Lightning Source LLC
Chambersburg PA
CBHW050712180626
46814CB00002B/403